PENGU

AN ORDINARY LUNACY

Jessica Anderson was born in Queensland, Australia, but has spent most of her life in Sydney, where she still lives. *An Ordinary Lunacy*, her first novel, was published in Australia in 1963. She is the author of a number of novels, including *Tirra Lirra by the River* and *The Only Daughter*, winners of the Miles Franklin Award in 1978 and 1980, respectively (available from Penguin Books); short stories, including *Stories From the Warm Zone and Sydney Stories* (1987, Viking); plays; and television adaptations. She is at work on another novel.

AN ORDINARY LUNACY

by
JESSICA ANDERSON

PENGUIN BOOKS

PENGUIN BOOKS
Viking Penguin Inc., 40 West 23rd Street,
New York, New York 10010, U.S.A.
Penguin Books Ltd, 27 Wrights Lane, London W8 5TZ
(Publishing & Editorial) and Harmondsworth,
Middlesex, England (Distribution & Warehouse)
Penguin Books Australia Ltd, Ringwood,
Victoria, Australia
Penguin Books Canada Limited, 2801 John Street,
Markham, Ontario, Canada L3R 1B4
Penguin Books (N.Z.) Ltd, 182–190 Wairau Road,
Auckland 10, New Zealand

First published in Australia by
Macmillan and Company Limited 1963
First published in the United States of America by
Charles Scribner's Sons 1963
Published in Penguin Books 1987

Copyright © Jessica Anderson, 1963
All rights reserved

LIBRARY OF CONGRESS CATALOGING IN PUBLICATION DATA
Anderson, Jessica.
An ordinary lunacy.
I. Title.
PR9619.3.A57074   1987   823   87-10544
ISBN 0 14 00.9707 4

Printed in the United States of America by
R. R. Donnelley & Sons Company, Harrisonburg, Virginia
Set in Baskerville

Except in the United States of America,
this book is sold subject to the condition
that it shall not, by way of trade or otherwise,
be lent, re-sold, hired out, or otherwise circulated
without the publisher's prior consent in any form of
binding or cover other than that in which it is
published and without a similar condition
including this condition being imposed
on the subsequent purchaser

Chapter One

'ONE seldom sees hair like that nowadays,' said David Byfield.

Myra Magaskill, whose party this was, peered in the direction he had so discreetly indicated. 'Hair like what?' she asked.

'On that woman behind the stand of potplants. Odd, she could almost be hiding. Look again, a little less obviously if you can manage it.'

Provoked by this remark into open staring, Myra this time saw a woman standing between the potted plants and the balustrade of the terrace. Her back was towards them, but through the barrier of leaves Myra discerned a hand holding a glass, a sleeve of black and tarnished gold, and, more clearly visible through the thinner spread of top leaves, the woman's hair. Myra recognised magnificence in its frosty ashen-gold, in its weight, and in its glittering nimbus of escaped curl. But to her modern sense its very sumptuousness condemned it; it was dated. Moreover, she thought it was dressed in a style suitable only for taking a bath—hoisted up in that great lax knot, so indolently jabbed with pins. She laughed a little and said, 'Oh, that's Isobel Purdy. Do you want to meet her?'

'No. I've spoken to her already. I offered to get her a drink.'

At the resentment in his voice, Myra shot him a glance that was both sharp and amused. Fifteen years ago she and David had been lovers, and their intimacy had left behind it a residue from which they now drew their comfortable familiarity. 'She must have snubbed you,' she said.

'No, not exactly. But I might have been one of the waiters. She showed me her glass, half-full, then turned her back on me. She seems to be watching someone in the garden.'

'Her husband's down there, frightfully drunk. I didn't ask either of them, by the way. Liz Trotter brought them. Everyone does that to me. Hughie wanted to ask them to leave, but I said, no, don't. He's a vile man, but I feel rather sorry for her. It's not a very good party, is it? Too hot, and I do hate people being goatish in my garden. It was clever of Daisy not to come.'

'Mother wanted to come,' said David.

'I don't believe it. If she had wanted to, she would have. I know Daisy. Is it true that she's going to do the Swinnerton house for Max and Helen Dobie?'

'What? Are the Dobies buying the old Swinnerton place?'

'They're trying to, though I can't imagine why. Leaking roof, great fissures in the walls, rheumatic miasmas floating all around it. Max has gone overboard on that convict-built stuff and has dragged poor Helen after him. That house is a wreck.'

'Then Max will have it restored, you may depend on that.'

'Ah, but it will still be damp. Hughie says those old stone houses have no damp courses.' For in matters of that kind, and in no others, Myra blindly accepted her husband's word.

'Then Hughie is probably right,' said David. 'I know nothing about damp courses.'

'Oh, neither do I,' Myra said happily.

'But what has Mother to do with all this? Are the Dobies hiring her to decorate it?'

'Helen says so. Heavens, David, does Daisy tell you nothing?'

But she saw that his look of sudden comprehension had nothing to do with Daisy or the Dobies. His eyes were distantly focused again, and Myra sent an irritated glance over her shoulder to where Isobel Purdy stood.

He said, 'Not Richard Purdy's wife, surely?'

'Yes, David,' Myra said resignedly. 'Richard Purdy's wife.'

'Good Lord!' He gave an incredulous laugh and drew his upper lip taut over his teeth. It was a new habit of his, and was becoming characteristic. Myra thought it gave him an almost prim look.

'It's a darned shame,' he said.

'Quite so,' said Myra.

'She's so beautiful.'

'Yes, she's very beautiful.' Myra spoke in the carefully detached tone women use when they wish to make it clear that they are not envious. 'But she exasperates me, rather. Why doesn't she dress?'

'Money?' suggested David.

'Oh, no doubt, but she doesn't even try. After all, plenty of us are poor,' said Myra, who was rich.

'Purdy is flat broke, they say. I did some work for his father once. The Purdys were very decent, reputable people.'

'Lovely to be reputable,' said Myra.

'Very hard on them,' David went on, 'having a no-hoper like Purdy. An only son, too. He got all their money. A flying start.'

Myra gave an artificial yawn. 'Well, he didn't fly far.'

'Look, she's moved,' said David.

'I refuse to look,' Myra rapped out.

In her new position Isobel Purdy was so clearly visible that David could see how the light, striking through monstera leaves, laid grotesque and shifting shadows on one cheek, and a band of shadow, like a domino, across her luminous eyes. And the total, odd effect of her, of slovenliness and beauty, of poverty and insolence, an effect that placed her outside all known categories, so tantalized him that though he knew Myra to be irritated by his questions, he could not help asking, 'Why does she put up with him? A woman like that!'

'A woman like what?'

'Well, surely she rates something better?'

'One would think so, certainly. I expect she loves him, God help her. It's the only answer. She must love being married to that . . . that lecherous clown.'

'How could she love it?' David said doggedly.

'In that department all things are possible,' Myra sternly replied. Here she could speak with authority; she was on her own ground. Two years ago her first husband had divorced her. She had lost her marriage and her sons, and all for Hughie. 'She must love him,' she went on. 'They have no children. She could leave him. But she doesn't. She stays. She's stayed ten years.'

'Ten years. Then he must have married her when he was in England.'

'Oh yes, she's English. Can't you tell? We don't grow skins like that here.'

'No,' said David, 'we don't. How long have they been back in Sydney?'

'Oh, David, I hardly know them. And must we talk about him? He's a dreadful man, a shocking man. He's the worst man I know. Nobody else makes a *cult* out of being outrageous.' She considered this for a moment, then said with real curiosity, 'And the odd thing is that he so often gets away with it. I wonder why?'

'Because he doesn't give a damn for anyone's opinion,' said David. 'People respect that.'

'Do they?' Myra sounded interested. 'Perhaps I ought to try it.'

'Very hard on her,' David said lightly.

Pleased by the dismissive sound of this, Myra agreed at once. 'Oh, I know. I'm sorry for her. All the same, it's too bad of her to lurk behind those potplants and refuse to talk to anyone. If she feels like that, she ought to stay home.'

But David thought he knew why she had come. He had met women like her before. Nursemaids and watchdogs to wild and drunken husbands, they hid humiliation behind poker faces and were stiff, pitiable, and unapproachable. In spite of her extraordinary beauty, he now felt her to be of reduced value. He decided not to go near her again.

Myra was claimed by someone who wished to leave, and a little later a southerly wind sprang up, forcing its shafts of coolness through the torpid air and sending those on the terrace indoors. Here Myra, though busy with people, managed to keep David under her pensive surveillance. Because she felt alienated from him, each glimpse she caught of him across the room seemed to flash a new facet of his character at her. She had never noticed before, with the engaged vision of a familiar, how stiff was his back, how condescending the inclination of his head, and she reflected sadly that he had changed, that he was becoming pompous.

David was tall, would in later years be imposing, and bore himself as if he already were. His eyes were guarded, his lower lip Hapsburg, and his chin long, jutting, and undented. It was his mother's opinion that he resembled the Velazquez portrait of Philip IV at Fraga, but Myra, who had no such standards of comparison, had once told him that if he cut off his nose he would have a face like a coal-scuttle.

He was a barrister and at thirty-five his reputation was beginning to be brilliant. People who claimed to know about these things said he had a great future in politics. He was being groomed, they somewhat mysteriously claimed, and there were very few like Myra, who would dissipate the mystery by cutting in on such conversations with: 'Tell me, who *does* all this grooming one hears about?'

So people believed in him, and he had begun to attract sycophants. Hugh Magaskill was one of these, and when he encountered David that night he suppressed his glittering grin, spoke in a lowered voice, and made his voice as grave as David's own.

But when Myra saw this, feeling shame for her husband, she hurried to interpose her strained but smiling face between them, and begged Hughie to go and do something about all those people in the garden.

'I would do it myself,' she said, 'but you're so much better at being rude to people than I am.'

Hughie looked as if he doubted this, but went, all the same, leaving Myra to turn to David with a yawn that brought tears to her eyes.

'Heavens, how tired I am.'

David said obediently, 'I must go home.'

'Yes, do that. Then I shall go and yawn at all these other people.'

But at the door she detained him, a hand on his arm, while she said in her abrupt way, 'You really liked her.'

'Who?' David's eyes flickered quickly over the room behind her, but Isobel Purdy was nowhere in sight.

'She left ten minutes ago,' said Myra.

'Who did?'

'David, don't be crafty. I dislike you when you're crafty.'

'This is beyond me,' David said mildly.

'Oh, you liar.' And Myra laughed, but suddenly crossed her arms, hugging herself, while for a moment her face became blank and her eyes sightless with longing. But she knew that the object of this longing was not David. 'You are simply too cautious to live,' she said. 'But never mind, never mind. Goodbye, David, and give my best love to Daisy.'

Outside, the wind was now in full force. In the floodlit garden palm leaves crashed and camphor-laurel branches tossed and strained like surf. And David, walking towards the double gates where he had parked his car, involuntarily raised his eyes to the sky, where clouds were racing and flowing over the moon and the stars, then looked down at his watch to calculate his hours of sleep. He liked to get eight, but was satisfied with seven.

Near the gates Isobel Purdy stood, her back turned to him and a loosened strand of hair blowing out from her head like a pennant. She was talking to a man, whom she half-obscured from David's view with her body. It seemed to David that she crouched slightly.

David, who guessed that the man was Richard Purdy, suddenly found himself unwilling to pass them. He had a moment of panic, a desire to turn back, to find some other way to his car.

He had time to wonder at this illogical impulse, but none

to examine it. All his energies were bent on the effort he must make to walk on.

Straining for casualness, his walk became stiff and self-conscious, and as he drew nearer he knew that Richard Purdy had observed his moment of indecision, his briefly broken step, for though he stood passively against his wife's murmur, and though his mouth hung slackly open, his eyes rested on David's face with a look contemptuous, knowing, and amused.

As David passed them, Isobel's loose strand of hair leapt out at him, whipping him lightly on the cheek, and he angrily jerked his head to one side. A lazy laugh broke from Richard Purdy, but Isobel did not turn her head; nor did her voice falter.

Fury welled up in David, breaking into curses as he wrenched open the door of his car and flung himself into the driver's seat.

'A madman . . . a bloody madman . . .'

He felt—he did not know why—that he had made a fool of himself. He had experienced, as he passed them, the shock in chest and throat of a missed heartbeat.

. . . . .

Though David determined each year to move to quarters of his own, he still lived with his mother in a small but much-admired harbourside house to which his car descended through curving, quiet, tree-hung streets.

Daisy's house had been built by an Englishman who at first had meant to reproduce the Georgian home of his boyhood, but who in mid-building had made a concession to the climate by running a shaded, cast-iron filigree balcony along its top story, and a paved verandah beneath. This addition was entirely successful; the house was beautiful, and with its grace and calculated proportions served as a reproach to the houses among which it stood. These, built in the twenties and thirties, were mostly of Spanish or Tudor intention, though there were also a number of massive, dark, thick-set bungalows. These last were loathed by Daisy. A house, she said, ought to nestle or soar. These skulked.

Her own house she loved, and sometimes wished she had owned it before high rates and taxes had forced its former owners, one by one, to subdivide and sell the acres of wooded foreshore on which it had once stood. It was the only one of her houses she had vowed never to sell. She had been badgered into selling all the others, she said, at irresistibly high prices, but although she sometimes sold pieces of furniture out of this one, so that her rooms tended to have strange gaps in them, she had so far rejected all offers to buy it.

There was a light in her bedroom when David reached home, and when she heard him she came to her open door.

'Was it a good party?'

'Very pleasant,' said David. Guarding the friends of his early youth from his mother's comments was a habit he had not outgrown.

'Was anyone there?'

'No,' admitted David, who knew exactly what she meant.

'None of Myra's lame dogs?'

'I noticed none.'

'I wish she would stop feeling sorry for people. Last week she sent me a little girl with dirty fingernails. Her housekeeper's niece, who wanted a job.'

'Did you give her one?'

'Goodness, no. I sent her to Marion. Last time I saw Myra she was trying to put on weight, of all things. She looked quite dessicated, which I suspect makes her Hughie cross. He does so like his women pretty.'

'They're very happy, Mother. Hughie's a pleasant fellow.'

'And so he may be. But oh, those clothes,' sang Daisy. 'Oh, those hacking jackets and leather patches and loosely knotted scarves. On him they look like fancy dress. And of course they're happy. Myra can't afford not to be happy, not after all that fuss. All the same, she's a dear girl, and I'm fond of her.'

'Goodnight, Mother,' David said dryly.

She put a hand on his shoulder. She was five feet tall, stiff and slim as a baton.

'Goodnight, dear boy.'

David kissed her, and she retreated to her bedroom and began her nightly maintenance work on her face, on which she worked in the same affectionate but business-like spirit that she brought to the preservation of fine furniture. She knew, of course, that it was a losing battle (Time must win), but she could at least console herself with the reflection that it was the only lost cause in which she had ever engaged.

Daisy at sixty was zestful and gay. Her beautiful, melodious, ringing voice always carried beneath it a hint of barely suppressed laughter. She was one of those charming bullies whom it seems rather churlish to resist.

She had been born to a poverty that she now neither disowned nor discussed. As a child, she had lived in a melancholy outer suburb of Sydney, where the houses, ramshackle even when new, had then just began to encroach on the dairy farms. She had been offended by these surroundings even before she had been able to compare them with others, and had left home as soon as she had earned enough money to keep herself.

Some years later she had married a man many years her senior. He was a musician or a remittance man, no one quite knew which, but he had borne, like a faint halo, the reflected glow of a title somewhere in his family. Daisy had left him when David was a baby. Drunkenness was her excuse, but it was really his lack of success that she could not bear. She had developed a savage contempt, painful even to herself, for his increasing seediness, his sad razor-notched face, his frayed cuffs, and above all, for the submission with which he bore these marks of failure.

After that, she and a woman named Hattie Green had opened a gift shop. Hattie had the money, and Daisy the talent, but it was not long before Daisy had both. 'Daisy has diddled me,' publicly cried Hattie, half-laughing and half-angry. But although she was diddled, she was by no means ruined, so in the end her amusement had prevailed, and she and Daisy remained friends.

Many years later, on one of her visits to England in search of furniture, Daisy had seen her husband in a street in Bath, and had concealed herself in the porch of a famous building. Daisy was by this time prepared to pit her opinion against anybody's, and as she waited for her husband to pass, she decided that the columns flanking the porch were too broad at the base, their curvature too emphatic. 'So much for Georgian perfection,' she said to herself as she emerged, trembling slightly, from her hiding place.

The thought of her husband, though never painful, had slightly fretted her until he had freed her by dying. This event had coincided with the boom years after the war, and Daisy, the last of her ropes cut, had soared and expanded into real success. She was now engrossed in her work, of which she considered David a part, and she loved her possessions. She was as pleased with her life as she was with her face.

After she had finished with her face she took two sleeping pills and got briskly into bed. She was pleased that she had not gone to Myra's party, and was rather sorry that David had done so. She did not dislike Myra, but she sensed about her, in spite of her money, an aura of failure, and Daisy hated and feared failure.

She was soon asleep, but David, who mistrusted sedatives, lay awake for a long time. He thought of Isobel Purdy, crouched so ignominiously on the Magaskills' garden path, and wondered what she had been saying to her husband, for though the supplicating murmur of her voice was clear to him he could not remember a word she had said.

At last he got out of bed, turned on the shaded lamp on his desk, and opened the telephone directory. He was thus able to add one meagre, lifeless touch to his image of her: She lived in Double Bay.

He stood staring at the line of print for a long time, as if by concentration he could make it yield something of importance, but in the end it was his own memory on which he was forced to draw, and as she rose up before him in her several remembered attitudes he found himself attacked not only by desire, but by a melancholy quite new to him.

Almost stealthily, he closed the directory.

. . . . .

'I don't think she's beautiful at all,' said Hughie. 'At least, not in those clothes.' Hughie sounded cross. He was one of those men who considers an ill-dressed woman a personal affront.

'The clothes are nothing,' said Myra. She was weaving her way among the ruins of her party, carrying an enamel basin into which she swept the depressing leftovers of food. 'Forget the clothes,' she said.

'One can't forget them. But I assure you, there's no need to worry about old David.'

Myra laughed. 'Worry is hardly the word. He was only being inquisitive, I know that. Even as a boy he was a dreadful sticky-beak, always asking, "What's his name?" and, "What does his father do?" David keeps dossiers.'

'Old David's as safe as houses,' Hughie said complacently.

'As houses,' drawled Myra. 'How nice for old David.'

But these words were no sooner out than she sought to make amends for them by skimming across the floor and throwing one long arm about his neck. Her other hand, outflung, still held the enamel basin.

She shut her eyes when they kissed, but Hughie's eyes, open, roved the room until they returned to rest at last on the basin of food. As they probed among the broken crackers, pasties, and cubes of cheese, he began to frown, and as soon as Myra released him he said, 'Let's face it, sweetie, the food was awful. Let's get a decent caterer next time. Craddock or Fearn. The best.'

Myra's money had opened up a new world to Hughie, and nothing fretted him more than Myra's apparent repudiation of it, her refusal to act rich. This seemed like treason to Hughie.

Chapter Two

EACH morning and evening of those last summer days, as David drove through Double Bay to and from the city, he looked for Isobel Purdy.

In spite of having no fresh knowledge to feed on, his idea of her was undergoing a change. He no longer saw her as insolent, but as gentle, amorous, and smiling. Her husband he had transformed into a purely farcical character, then had pushed him into the background, where his propensity to scandal and disruption could do no more than faintly threaten.

One evening he made a detour and drove slowly past the block of flats in which she lived. It was a four-storied building of dark brick, utilitarian and characterless, a box set squarely on the ground. Its windows looked uniformly dead; at none of them did a face appear or a hand adjust a blind. Near the front door stood a plane tree, now beginning to lose its leaves.

Autumn set in with a succession of beautiful, warm, and windless days. David still looked for Isobel, but when several weeks had passed, and he had not seen her, his watchfulness became automatic, and it began to seem to him like a game he was playing. He felt that he would never see her there. He could not imagine her carrying a basket, buying fruit and meat. He thought of her now as always indoors, dreamy and listless, marking the passing of the days and seasons only by the stripping and burgeoning and bearing of the plane tree. And he saw her as always alone; Richard Purdy was never there.

His idea of her was entering that phase of unreality that precedes extinction.

Then one morning he did see her. She stepped suddenly from the footpath into the flow of city-bound traffic, and passed blindly in front of the cars forced to brake so perilously close to her. They included David's, but before he could recover from his shock of disbelief, her head and shoulders had passed out of the frame of his windscreen. Ducking his head, he saw her disappear into a shop, and had time to notice that her dress was loose and sleeveless and that she was carrying an empty milk bottle.

As he drove up the hill and over its brow, he wondered at the poverty of his own response. All he thought, with some amusement, was that she had such an imperious, go-to-blazes air about her.

And when he thought of the incident during the day, it was only to speculate on the empty milk bottle. (The milkman had not called; they had not paid their bill.)

'What's the joke, Mr. Byfield?' asked Tom Hood, the clerk.

'What joke?'

'You were kind of snorting, as if something amused you.'

David snorted again. 'Yes, I probably was.'

But that night, working late in his chambers by the light of a shaded lamp, tired, and more than usually aware of the big building expanding in loneliness about him, he suddenly recalled the heroic, foreshortened lines of her head, caught for a moment in his windscreen, and her paleness that was not a pallor but that gave the effect of vivid colour held in check. And what he had seen as imperiousness that morning now presented itself to him, with great conviction, as the indifference of misery. He saw her place one sandalled foot on the step of the shop and pull herself tiredly up after it, and the gesture appeared to him now as careless, beautiful, and desperate.

He said aloud, 'Isobel.'

After that, it no longer seemed like a game, and his resistance began in earnest.

• • • • •

'You are scowling, dear boy,' said Daisy, 'and pulling your upper lip down in the oddest way.'

She pulled her own lip down in imitation, but her eyes were speculative. He had a new look about him, a parched and prim look that she found disturbing.

'You're not eating,' she said, 'and I suspect you're not sleeping. You won't take sleeping pills, I know, but do take some of my vitamins. See how pretty they are. Onyx and cornelian.'

Looking at the red and black capsules in the palm of his hand, David smiled, amused that he should be exhibiting so plainly the classic symptoms of his malady.

'You must take two every day,' said Daisy.

And to her friends she said with pride, 'Poor dear. It's this wretched Dangerfield brief.'

When she said this to Myra, Myra replied, 'Well, I hope he loses it.'

'I don't,' said Daisy.

'Then you're anti-social. Horace Dangerfield has no right to wall in the harbour with his great slabs of home units. This one will be right in front of us. If he's allowed to build it, we'll have to move.'

But to David the Dangerfield brief was very important indeed. 'If I can bring this off...' he thought. He regarded it almost with superstition.

He worked on it most nights, but as he was unwilling to submit himself to the silence of his chambers, he now worked at home, where he could count on being irritated by Daisy's blithe intrusions or by her housekeeper's offer of Ovaltine. With both women he was curt and distant. He was aware that his work was going badly, that his enthusiasm was diminished and his impetus checked. Like a dancer who loses his affinity with the music and thinks too consciously of the mechanics of movement, he had begun to balk and fumble. He had the sense of plodding.

But David had much faith in plodding. He was not as brilliant as people believed. He himself knew that at least half his success was owing to his thoroughness, his capacity for work, and his ability to plod tenaciously on when the going was hard.

His eyes suffered. He was constantly rubbing them or kneading them with the ball of his thumb.

'You must do eye exercises,' cried Daisy, and showed him how.

David watched her in silence, then said, 'Perhaps it would be simpler if I got glasses.'

'What a preposterous idea! *I* don't wear spectacles.'

But David, as was his way, ignored her, and got his spectacles.

'Library frames, sir,' said the optometrist, tenderly adjusting them on David's nose. 'Most gentlemen are wearing them now.' (He was wearing them himself.)

'They seem rather heavy.'

'Oh no, sir. We believe that frames of this kind underline the character of a face. It's not uncommon for gentlemen to have them fitted with plain lenses.'

David pulled off the spectacles, snorted at them, then put them on again and looked thoughtfully into the mirror, straightening his shoulders and pulling his upper lip over his teeth.

Daisy broke into laughter when she saw them. 'But how *heavy* they must be. You will have to walk with your chin on your chest.'

All the same, she thought he looked very impressive, and she prodded him lightly and mockingly in the stomach. He was her best creation, and she regarded him with pride and condescension.

'David is wearing glasses,' said Hughie.

'Only for reading,' said Myra. 'Daisy told me. I saw her

at Helen's. All the men are wearing them now. All looking like owls, and all blinking so solemnly behind them.'

She looked briefly across the table at Hughie, who nervously slid his spectacles up his nose with a forefinger. He was one of the gentlemen who had had them fitted with plain lenses.

  .   .   .   .   .

The autumn ended at last, and was followed by a dry and windy June.

Horace Dangerfield, with a building programme blocked by ordinances he considered archaic, chafed at the law's delay. 'If that's the way we did things in business,' he said, glaring at David, 'I'd be bloody well broke.'

But David met these outbursts with a staid smile and brought him back each time to the matter in hand. Horace soon found that David's voice, resonant, quiet, and a little tired, was setting the pitch for his own. He resented this. A street urchin boyhood had left him with a secret hostility for all forms of authority.

Irritated by details, he waved a hand. 'Don't bother me with all that stuff. That's why I'm hiring you. Just tell me what kind of chance we've got.'

But all David would say was: 'Fair.'

'Half these legal blokes,' Horace said round the town, 'are bloody frauds. They wouldn't last two minutes in business.'

The case was heard at the end of June. 'A test case,' people called it, and for David, too, it was a test case. It lasted for three days, and in the late afternoon of the third day a verdict was given for Horace Dangerfield. David left the court in a group of men. The wind had dropped and the low western sun struck deep into his eyes. He was smiling.

Someone grasped his arm. 'Horace gets back tonight. He'll want to see you. Where'll you be?'

'I don't know,' said David.

Horace caught up with him that night at the Federation Club, where he was dining with Sir Gordon Haggett.

A little drunk, backed by his retinue, Horace took the chance offered by the lofty dining-room, with its columned doorway, to make one of his entrances. Walking very slowly, his hands clasped behind his back, he moved each leg stiffly from the hip and swung his compact paunch from right to left, left to right, as if he had a headlamp strapped to it.

'Here is Dangerfield,' said Gordon Haggett, taking mustard, 'to present the prizes.'

Before Gordon Haggett had taken silk, David had read with him, and their relationship still carried undertones of master and pupil.

Horace halted at their table, looked lovingly at David, said, 'Ah-h', then turned to Gordon Haggett and inclined his head. 'Haggett,' he ventured.

Gordon Haggett also inclined his head. 'Dangerfield.' He closed his eyes for a moment, then went on eating.

Horace turned to David and gripped his shoulder. 'Beautiful work, Byfield, beautiful work.'

'You're happier now?' asked David.

'I never doubted the outcome, not for one moment.'

'*I* did.'

Horace flung his shoulders back and roared with laughter, while Gordon Haggett, chewing, raised his head to give him a glance of mild curiosity.

When Horace stopped laughing he gave David a long look, nodded, and said, 'You'll do, boy, you'll do.'

'Do for what?' David wondered aloud, when Horace had gone.

'For him, presumably. He'll keep you busy, but take care you earn his money, and take care he knows you've earned it. Don't let him do you any favours. They'll cost too much. But he's a good enough contact, as they say these days, and from now on he'll think you're some kind of medicine man.'

David nodded. 'Remarkably naïve, isn't he, in many ways? One wonders how he made all that money.'

'That's very simple. He made it because he has a real passion for making money. Given enough passion for one's objective, it's not hard to succeed. In fact, it's hard to fail. The important thing is to sustain the passion. Tiredness,' said Gordon Haggett, with the lightest of sighs, 'sometimes sets in. And there are other diversions.'

'I suppose so.' David sounded as if he himself knew of none.

'Dangerfield is impressed only by the verdict. He has no idea of how good you really were. You were very good indeed.'

'Thank you,' said David. 'Thank you.'

After that, David turned with renewed interest to the backlog of work awaiting him. When a fortnight had passed he was pleased to discover that his longing for Isobel Purdy, or for what she represented, had grown faint. He seldom thought of her now, and when he did, the curious melancholy she could still evoke was mingled with the complacent feeling that follows an escape from danger.

Daisy often found him now, at night, leaning back in his chair, a knee propped against his desk, his spectacles hanging from his dropped hand. Since he no longer cut off her conversation by bending to his work and presenting her with the top of his head, she often lingered to talk to him.

'David,' she said to him one night, 'you must marry.'

'Yes,' he said, 'I must.'

She looked startled and pleased. She had made the suggestion so often that it had become perfunctory, even a joke.

'Ah,' she cried. 'Then we must think of someone you can woo.'

David cocked his head and looked at her, smiling but critical. He was one of the few people who could resist her, who did not allow her verve and self-confidence to hypnotise them into taking her at her own valuation. 'Perhaps you had better leave that to me, Mother,' he said. 'Do you mind?'

Daisy laughed. 'Not at all, dear boy.'

She could not help trying to dominate him, but would have despised him if he had allowed her to succeed. But he could not control her thoughts, and she was already outlining in her mind the characteristics of his future wife, who would be capable, but not officious; pretty, but not conspicuous; intelligent, but not intellectual. And she would, of course, have money.

'What a pity,' thought Daisy, 'that Brenda Elliot is still in America.'

To David, too, the name of Brenda Elliot occurred. He had heard that she was homesick, and would soon give up her job with U.N.O. He remembered now how much he had always liked her, and her name lingered in his mind, comforting in its very lack of insistence, until the day he heard of Richard Purdy's death.

It was in one of the morning newspapers, a very small paragraph. David missed it, and Daisy, if she read it, made no comment; the Purdys were nothing to her.

But Myra, who had another reason for ringing David that morning, rushed in as soon as their greetings were over. 'Now you can marry her,' she said.

'Who?'

'Isobel Purdy.' And into the blank silence that followed she cried impatiently, 'He's dead. Didn't you see it in this morning's paper?'

'Richard Purdy?' he asked stupidly.

'Yes, he put his head in a gas oven.' Then, as David was still silent: 'Say something,' she demanded.

'What am I supposed to say?'

'Hughie said "Poor fellow".'

'Poor fellow,' said David.

There was a pause, then Myra said abruptly, 'I hardly knew him, I never liked him, but it frightens me that I can't care.'

'Yes, Myra. And did you ring to tell me that I may marry his widow?'

'How snubbing you sound. I never used to have to tell you when I was joking. No, I'm really ringing about that rather sweet young cousin of Hughie's. He's not happy with Whoosit and Whoosit. We thought you may be able to suggest something for him.'

As she talked on, David made notes on his pad, observing with a curious detachment that his hand was trembling. When Miss Mundy came in with a letter, he silently took it and read it while Myra went on speaking.

At last he said, 'I'll do all I can for him, Myra.'

'Thank you, David. We knew you would.'

But before she rang off she had to say, 'I think she'll do you very nicely, David, if you could tidy her up a bit, but how do you think she'll get on with Daisy?'

Their conversation ended with David's strained laugh. While he was signing the letter, he said to Miss Mundy, 'Get me both the morning papers, will you?'

Chapter Three

'Neck chops,' said Daisy firmly.

'I thought some nice thick steak,' ventured Possie, 'and a few mushrooms . . .'

'Mushrooms!' Daisy's little scream of horror was not wholly simulated; she was mean about food. 'That's what I call infantile squandering,' she said.

They stood in the airy chequered hall, waiting for David, who now appeared at the head of the stairs, running lightly, putting on his overcoat as he came, his whole attitude so exultant that Daisy's voice rose to a cry of curiosity.

'Dear boy, how gay you look!'

He halted before her, tucking the ends of his scarf beneath his coat, his smile young and secretive. 'I feel fine,' he said.

'Apparently. But why?'

Since he could not say, 'Because Richard Purdy is dead,' he intensified his smile and turned to Possie. 'Lovely day, Poss.'

Gratified, Possie put a hand on his arm. She was Daisy's cousin, and David had been her sole charge for five years of his childhood, while Daisy was working in England. But she was seldom encouraged, nowadays, to make such gestures of affection. 'It's cold enough out,' she said. 'You'd do well to wrap up.'

'He *is* wrapped up,' Daisy said impatiently. 'Come along, David. I can't dawdle like you professional people. I have a shop to open.'

'So you have, so you have.'

Clowning a little, he propelled her before him to the rear of the hall, while Possie followed, an indulgent spectator of this domestic horseplay. But at the kitchen door he remembered to stand aside to let her pass through before him. His lovely manners, she always said, were a credit to him. She slithered through the doorway with folded hands and a queenly smile.

Standing in the gentle winter sunlight, her parting wave ready, she watched them disappear into the garage. And when presently the car nosed its way out of the automatic doors, there they both were, both sitting very erect, their heads held high in the curiously stiff manner that was their only striking similarity. But even at the distance at which Possie stood she could see that they were engrossed in talk, and she knew that they had already forgotten her, that they would not wave, nor even turn their heads.

Her half-raised hand dropped to her side. She turned back to the kitchen and shut the door behind her.

So greedy was Possie for even the most perfunctory gestures of affection that if they had waved she would have been fortified against this, the worst moment of her day, when the silence of the house rushed to engulf her, and when she was most defenceless against the rancorous thoughts that would creep into her mind.

'I'm getting old. Neither of them give tuppence for me. If I died tomorrow . . .'

But if they had waved she could have kept at bay for that day at least the bitter realisation that she was in Daisy's orbit, but not of it, that she had been picked up in a moment of distress, used for thirty years, and was now used up.

It was on silent mornings such as these that the memory of past humiliations would swell into her mind. Long silted over, believed forgotten, it was as if in their dormancy they had gathered fresh strength and power to hurt.

So while washing up on this particular morning, when she suddenly heard the Daisy of twenty-five years ago saying firmly, 'This dinner party will bore you, Poss,' she gave a cry of rage and shame. 'So it would bore me, eh?'

'Bore me, would it?' she was still muttering an hour later, as she ran a finger down the Situations Vacant column of the *Herald*.

'The money they get these days!' she mourned. 'And me still on pocket-money. If only they didn't all want them young.'

'Possie is getting more mulish every day,' said Daisy in the car.

David had heard this so often that he did not think it required an answer, so they drove in silence, each preoccupied. Daisy was churning over her one insoluble problem, the employment of a housekeeper who was also a relation. She had all but forgotten what a good idea it had seemed at the beginning. In those days she had not known that it is not enough to charm someone into your service, but that the same charm must constantly be exercised to keep them there. Such are the disadvantages of cheap labour. She now thought of Possie as her Old Man of the Sea, and she herself a flagging Sinbad.

To David she said, rather tentatively, 'Possie will soon be eligible for the old-age pension.'

'Possie is our responsibility,' he absently replied.

'You mustn't think I'm not aware of that,' said Daisy, who was content for the moment to plant the seed, and to postpone the inevitable argument.

They were driving through Double Bay, but David looked neither to right nor left. For weeks he had forced himself not to look for Isobel, but this effort of will was no longer needed. He was like a man who stops writing letters to a friend he is soon to meet in the flesh.

Of a meeting with Isobel he was certain, though when and where it would take place he did not know. His emotions were of a dual nature, compounded of earth and air. Predominant was a sense of suddenly expanded horizons and of almost violent joy, but underlying this transcendent mood was the plotting of the practical man, the executive, seeking means to his end. He had half-decided to enlist Myra, but shrank from her teasing.

'Have you ever heard of some people named Purdy?' asked Daisy.

'Purdy?' David repeated it to gain time. The fusion of his thoughts with his mother's words had startled him, though it was a common happening with them, and Daisy had once explained it by waving a hand and saying, 'The umbilical cord, dear boy.'

'What about them?' he asked.

'Nothing, except that Richard Purdy has committed suicide, and that they say he had a very beautiful and rather peculiar wife. But then, she would have to be peculiar. He himself was quite dotty.'

Not interested enough to pursue the subject in the face of David's silence, she sang softly to herself for a few minutes, waiting for the ascent of the car to bring into view the expected fragment of city skyline — the new, bold, immediately intelligible skyline that was so rapidly imposing itself upon the haphazard scrawl of the old. She had fallen into the habit of waiting for it, for although she often publicly deplored its monotony, she could not help responding to the energy implied in those thrusts of scaffolding and towered blocks. This morning it gave fresh vibrancy to her voice as she struck her knee and cried, 'Max Dobie has run into every kind of trouble with the title to the Swinnerton place. It's not Torrens. I'm beginning to think he'll never buy it, blast him!'

She did not sense the strain beneath David's continued silence. She was reputed to have great powers of observation, but for many years these powers had served only the interests of her business and the pleasures of her eye.

As for David, his withdrawal from her was an instinctive attempt to preserve his mood. When they reached the city he let her out of the car as near as possible to her shop, heard her last laughing admonishments with testy patience, then drove in a greatly relieved mood to the parking lot.

Free again, he walked from the parking lot to his chambers, mentally dressing Isobel in the clothes of some of the women he passed. He was moved by her in soft swinging coats and hats mysteriously brimmed; in smoke and food colours: greys, blues, the browns of crust and the cream of milk.

There was no negligence about these clothes, nor about her hair, which he dressed in a smooth and shining knot. He was engaged, Myra would have said, in tidying her up a bit.

In spite of his resistance to reality, it did occur to him once or twice that he was taking a great deal for granted — for example, that Isobel would like him well enough to allow him to tidy her up. But his calm self-esteem did not allow him to consider this possibility for long. Beneath all his musings lay the mean (though unacknowledged) thought that Isobel, poor, broken, and adrift, would be very lucky to get him.

He did not yet know in what capacity he was to offer himself. His natural caution counselled him to wait and see. But because he had for some years felt the lack of a wife, he hoped that he would want to marry her.

His mother's word for Isobel, 'peculiar', recurred to him several times, and as he turned into Phillip Street he recalled that he himself had once held the same opinion of her.

But he now believed that her only peculiarity lay in her alliance with Richard Purdy, who was safely dead. David calculated that she had married when very young, and had stuck to her husband out of loyalty or pity, both admirable attributes.

While standing in the crowded lift, dispensing his smiles and guarded greetings, David decided that Myra must help him, though it would be difficult to ask her to say nothing at first to Hughie.

At that moment Isobel Purdy, at her breakfast table, was looking with uncomprehending eyes at one of the two men who stood opposite her. He was warning her that anything she said might be used in evidence.

When at last she seemed about to speak, she was prevented from doing so by the violent trembling of her lips. She stubbed her cigarette in the saucer of her teacup, then rose clumsily from her chair, which fell to the floor behind her. The younger detective at once picked it up and placed it neatly against a wall. She watched him doing this, then said in a thin, childish voice, 'But I didn't do it.'

The door was pushed open and a fat, elderly woman, wearing a too-long coat, took one step into the room, then stopped abruptly. Even when standing still, she had a bustling air about her. She eyed the three of them in turn, then breathed, 'Good God!'

'Hello, Sheila,' Isobel said in the same high voice. 'These men are arresting me for killing Richard. For *killing* him,' she repeated incredulously.

'Killing him!' echoed Sheila Jack. 'Good God!'

She advanced into the room and threw her pile of magazines on the table. 'Well, I've seen a lot of things . . .!' she exclaimed, then put her hands on her hips and looked at the two men as if they were some strange and hitherto unsuspected species of mankind. But the older man returned her stare alertly and warningly, and at last she took a deep breath, expelled it, and said, 'Well, Isobel, you'll need a lawyer. I'll get Theo Cass.'

'Theo Cass?' asked Isobel, but before Sheila could answer she turned to the two men and cried, as if this were her only concern, 'But I must get dressed. And what does one take?'

The older man pointed a pencil at her. 'Look, Mrs. Purdy. About dressing. Just take off your dressing-gown and slip a warm coat over what you've got on. Pack anything you need, but leave the bedroom door open.'

Isobel nodded, then walked awkwardly to the bedroom, her right hand raised and wavering as if she were guiding herself by an invisible wall. Behind her trailed the soiled cord of her dressing-gown, which was of grey flannel, and which had belonged to Richard Purdy.

To the detectives, Sheila Jack said in a low, excited voice, 'This is monstrous. Richard Purdy was my cousin. *I* knew him, if anyone did. He committed suicide.'

Sheila spoke the truth, but an unverified truth was not capable of stopping the machinery that had been set in motion and to which these two men were themselves subordinate. So the younger detective went on watching Isobel pin up her hair, and the older one, making notes, nodded politely but did not answer.

On his way out to lunch David stopped on the broad steps to receive the sun on his face. Below him two girls were passing, their heads together, sharing a newspaper.

'Funny way to kill anyone,' said one of them.

'Yeah, gas. It's a new one on me.'

There were no newsboys in the street, and David had to walk halfway round the block before he could confirm his suspicion. He forced himself to walk at his usual pace, but failed to greet several acquaintances he passed.

Chapter Four

THE Magaskills were dressing to go out. Hughie was almost ready, but Myra, still in her petticoat, sat at her dressing-table with the evening newspaper spread over the bottles, brushes, and jars.

'But the police may have made a mistake,' she was saying. 'They *do* make mistakes.'

'Practically never. They can't afford to,' said Hughie.

'But there's always that possibility.'

'Oh, you'll find she did it, all right.'

With the tips of two fingers Myra touched the blurred picture of Isobel's profile. 'So you've hanged her already?'

'They don't hang people in New South Wales,' Hughie pointed out.

'Life imprisonment, then,' said Myra, impatiently disposing of this negligible difference.

'No chance of that, either. Good-looking women always get off.'

'But, Hughie, you have missed my point. Supposing she is innocent, who will believe it, once she is tried?'

'Everyone, if she is acquitted.'

'You know that's not true. No one will *quite* believe it. You said yourself that good-looking women always get off. That's what everyone will say.'

'Well, never mind,' said Hughie soothingly, 'it's odds on she's guilty.'

Myra did not look up from the newspaper. 'Darling,' she said bleakly, 'sometimes you are very, very strange.'

'Strange? Strange?' murmured Hughie to his rack of ties. He selected one. 'This tie?' he musingly asked himself.

'And Theo Cass to appear for her!' cried Myra. 'Theo, of all people!'

'Old Theo gives it a bit of a whack,' said Hughie to his reflection.

'Oh, not all the time. But he *is* a dipsomaniac.'

'Ha! One of those Sydney-or-the-bush boys. Well,' said Hughie cheerfully, 'she could have a better lawyer than *that*.'

Myra smoothed the newspaper. 'I feel so desperately sorry for her.'

But Hughie only said, 'A fine old family, all the same, the Casses.'

. . . . .

'I can't imagine why people are so fascinated by it,' said Daisy. 'A gas stove! What a weapon to choose.'

'What would you have chosen?' asked David. He felt obliged to say something.

'Poison, probably,' she said carelessly.

'Women usually do,' he said, and raised his newspaper again.

'Yes, dear boy. Everyone knows that.'

They were spending one of their rare evenings together, in Daisy's white-panelled sitting-room at the back of the house, for the night was cold and this was a small room, easy to heat. David sat reading the newspaper at a gabbling pace, without comprehension, wishing he were in bed, but too listless to move. But Daisy, alert and straight-backed as ever, had before her on her desk a sheaf of drawings, which she was slowly examining and putting aside.

'Tina has become very casual,' she said. 'She's getting too much advertising work. I'll need something better than these to show Max Dobie if he buys the Swinnerton place. What a lot of problems it would solve if I could draw myself. And how very strange that I can't,' she added, flexing and unflexing her hands and looking at them with wonder. 'I *feel* that I can,' she went on, 'yet when I pick up a pen or brush it simply won't obey me. It's strange, very strange.'

Looking at her hands, her head on one side and her eyes half-closed, she said in the same preoccupied way, 'Willy has a friend who is exactly what I want to do my sketches. Stylish little scribbles he does, yet he manages to suggest *texture*. It's like magic. I wish I could get him, but he's a very difficult boy, so evasive. I could help him so much, too. I could introduce him to people who would buy his work.'

From behind his newspaper, David said, 'An ambiguous arrangement. Perhaps he would prefer cash on the knocker.'

As if she could see through his newspaper, Daisy cocked her head and smiled at him. She herself was quite at home in that world where promises and favours were accepted currency. Negotiation in such currency is tortuous and full of suspense. Daisy had the good nerves, guile, and audacity necessary to it. She took pleasure in it, but was pleased that David did not, for though men inhabited this world, its prevailing character was feminine. She saw him taking straighter, grander, and less cluttered paths than hers.

His newspaper did not move. Turned towards Daisy was the front-page photograph of Isobel Purdy, her head bent, one hand clutching closed the lapels of a dark coat.

'Mrs. Purdy must photograph badly,' Daisy remarked, and turned her smile to the doorway, where Possie had just appeared with a tea tray. 'Come in, Poss. But only one cup. David is drinking whiskey.'

'And I made a full pot.' Possie put the tray on Daisy's desk and lingeringly touched the extra cup.

Pouring her tea, Daisy said decisively, 'And of course you have had yours.'

But Possie, determined to linger, pointed at random to a drawing. 'That's nice.'

'Is it?' Daisy was leaning back with her eyes almost closed, gratefully drinking the hot tea. She was very tired. 'I shan't take sedatives tonight,' she thought. 'I shall have to start weaning myself sometime.'

Possie, her first overture rejected, was trying another. 'That poor thing,' she was saying.

'What poor thing?' asked Daisy.

'That Mrs. Purdy who killed her husband. She looks so droopy there on the paper.'

'Don't let us be too sorry for her,' said Daisy. 'There are less barbarous ways of getting rid of a husband.'

David lowered the newspaper, removed his spectacles, and said with deliberation, 'It never seems to occur to anyone that a murder suspect may be innocent — a fact that never fails to amuse me.'

He did not look amused, and Daisy glanced at him with some surprise. 'We're treading on his legal corns, Poss.'

'Ah, we meant no harm,' said Possie. 'It was just a manner of speaking.'

But David had already dismissed the subject by retreating once again behind his newspaper, though he showed his irritation by a restlessly jigging foot.

Daisy set her empty cup on the tray. 'Thank you, Poss. If you're going now, you might take the tray with you.'

'If you've quite finished with it,' said Possie with sudden belligerence, 'I'll pour myself a cup in the kitchen.'

But Daisy appeared not to notice her tone, nor the indignant bustle with which she bore off the tray. Her puzzled gaze was on David's jigging foot, and as soon as the door closed she said, 'So you believe that woman may be innocent?'

David's newspaper crashed to his knees. 'Did I say so? I believe nothing. She's charged with murder, and that's all I know. Nor can I imagine why you should ask me such a question. *I* am not appearing for the woman.'

'If you were, I *would* not ask it. Nor do I care. It was an idle question.'

'Idle! Exactly. There is perhaps some excuse for Possie, but I am surprised that you should give way to this cheap sensationalism.'

'David! You make me sound like a gossipy old woman.'

'You spoke like one.'

'And you are speaking like a rude and peevish child,' cried Daisy in a high ringing voice. But she never lost her temper, and was determined not to do so now. 'I'm sorry if I wounded you,' she added coldly.

With dying but still stubborn indignation, he settled his shoulders and shook his newspaper; and Daisy, who had expected some conciliatory response, could not help saying sharply, 'All the same, you're much too touchy. I think you are becoming very, very queer.'

Warned by the real anger in her voice and by the pettiness of the scene, David said with a show of lightness, 'Then I shall soon qualify for a job in your shop.'

Relieved, she matched his tone. 'Ah, don't be unkind to my poor Willy.'

After a moment he said, 'I'm tired.'

'I can never see tiredness as an excuse for bad manners,' she said pleasantly.

'No, you're right. I'm sorry.'

'Don't be, though I admit you alarmed me. On top of the world this morning, and down in the depths tonight. I hope you're not becoming what they call . . . what I *think* they call . . . a manic-depressive type,' said Daisy, who knew perfectly well what they called it, but who liked to show her disapproval of such jargon.

After that, they had a short, cautious conversation about trivial matters. They were not intimate enough to quarrel without embarrassment, and David found himself avoiding his mother's eyes. Soon he sighed, set his feet heavily and heaved himself from his chair.

'Like an old man,' thought Daisy. 'You haven't finished your whiskey,' she said.

'No,' he said vaguely. 'No.'

'My dear boy, my dear boy . . .' Daisy paused helplessly, then rapped out, 'David, why not take a week off?'

He hesitated in the doorway. 'I might do that.'

'Do. I can never see any sense in these legal vacations when you people work harder than ever during them.

Unless they're to air the courtrooms, which certainly need it.'

'I could go up to Forster.'

'Yes, go and fish,' said Daisy, who thought fishing an idiotic occupation, suitable for men.

Upstairs in his bedroom, David stood looking out over the harbour, where ghostly little pleasure boats were rocking this way and that, turning their painted flanks to the light of the moon.

Now that he was alone, Isobel's plight rose to confront him. On all his former images of her was now imposed the newspaper photograph, where he saw her as drooping and exposed, her loneliness magnified, and the light beating cruelly down upon her head.

In spite of his admonishment of his mother and Possie, he himself took Isobel's guilt for granted. He made, however, no special point of it. What mattered was that she had got herself *charged* with murder, and by that circumstance, so irregular, so bizarre, had put herself quite beyond his reach.

'Very pleasant at Forster at this time of the year,' he thought.

But he wondered why he should feel encumbered by guilt, which urged him to stay, turning him towards Isobel as if he were committed to her.

'I'll leave tomorrow night,' he decided.

Downstairs, Daisy carefully poured his unfinished whiskey back into the bottle. Nobody, she assured herself, would notice a little extra water.

Chapter Five

David said, 'There's nothing that can't wait for a week except the consultation with Mr. Collingwood. See if you can fix that for today.'

He did not look at Tom Hood while he spoke, but sat with his chair swivelled sideways, staring out of the window. The early morning sunlight had been forced back by cloud. It was an ochre and grey day, cold, still, and oppressive.

The clerk's glance followed his. 'I know you can do with the break,' he said dubiously.

'Then see to it, will you?' said David patiently to the window.

When Tom Hood had gone he jerked his chair upright and drew his papers towards him. He felt dulled, not unpleasantly, and yawned frequently. When his telephone rang, and Miss Mundy announced a personal call from Mrs. Jack, he had to grope for a while before he could fit the name to its owner.

'Oh, Mrs. Sheila Jack? Well, tell her I'm busy.'

'She says it's very important. Of the gravest importance was how she put it.'

David gave a crabbed smile. All Sheila Jack's business was of the gravest importance. 'Put her on,' he said.

Without preamble, Sheila Jack's loud and excited voice said she was ringing from a public telephone, from the Post Office, actually, and David, bored, watched a violet pigeon come to rest on the scaffolding opposite his window. It was with an effort that he brought his mind back to Sheila Jack's conversation, some of which he suspected he had missed.

She was saying that she had just come from Theo Cass's office, and that she had rushed to the Post Office to ring David before Theo could do so.

'Am I in time?' she demanded.

David, to whom the name of Theo Cass had sounded like a warning bell, assured her that she was. She expressed relief, and explained that she had advised poor Isobel, who had no friends, to retain Theo Cass because he was *good*. Did David agree that he was good?

David hesitated, then said coldly, 'Of course.' He discovered that his grip on the receiver was tense, and deliberately relaxed it.

'I think so, too,' shouted Sheila. 'I have the utmost belief in him. Now here's the point, Mr. Byfield. Apparently Isobel has no particular barrister in mind — she's quite, quite stunned — so I suggested you. I want her to have the best. But Theo doesn't think you'll take it.'

David was silent. 'Are you there?' she asked sharply.

David said carefully, 'By Isobel I take it you mean Mrs. Purdy?'

'Didn't I say so?'

'No. And Mrs. Jack, I haven't had a criminal brief for years, not since the Paine case.'

'Ah!' cried Sheila triumphantly. 'But we all know what you did with *that*!'

'And you do know, don't you, that I can't take it unless it's offered to me by Mrs. Purdy's solicitor?'

'Oh, is that ethics?' She sounded impatient. 'Well, never mind that. Theo will ring you. My reason for ringing first was to prepare you, to beg you not to turn it down without thinking it over. She's innocent, of course, as innocent as I am. Let's face it, the police in this state are shocking bunglers. It's quite monstrous. It's the kind of gross injustice that makes me see red. That's why I want you to take it. That's why I know you *will* take it. I consider you one of the few legal men I know who is dedicated.'

David did not like this. It was too much a parody of

the effect he hoped to give. He said coldly, 'I'm very busy.'

'So am I. I have my political work, you know that. But I'm never too busy to step out of my way to help a fellow-creature, Mr. Byfield. We all owe that much to society, don't you think? I find that I just can't be cynical about these things.'

'Quite so,' said David. 'Well, thank you for ringing, Mrs. Jack.'

'And you will help her?'

'I shall expect Theo's call.'

'Tell me I haven't done wrong in ringing you.'

'That's quite all right, Mrs. Jack.'

In the Post Office, Sheila Jack cradled the receiver, jerked out an arm to look at her watch, and rushed home to feed her six Alsatian dogs, feeling more alive than she had done since the last elections. But David sat hunched in his chair, trying to combat his rising excitement. He told himself that the situation had not changed, and that he was sick of Isobel Purdy and her dubious affairs; but even as he thought this, the process of adapting himself to this new circumstance was taking place, and he was soon able to marvel that he, instead of one of the many likelier men, should be offered this brief. He even fleetingly suspected that something less capricious than coincidence was responsible; he suspected the workings of his own hidden will.

It was the absurdity of this thought that checked and warned him. If Theo Cass had rung him then, he would have refused to involve himself. But no call came, and at the end of an hour David, restless and hopelessly distracted, realised how tensely he was braced to meet it.

When another hour had passed, he began to fear some change of plan. Perhaps Isobel herself had intervened, demanding another barrister.

He went out to the corridor, where Tom Hood sat in his glass case. 'Look, Tom, I shan't be going away after all.'

Tom's face was expressionless. 'I've just cancelled all your appointments.'

'Then un-cancel them, un-cancel them. And turn down that Wragge brief. You'll be getting a call from Mr. Cass's office. He'll want to retain me in a matter he has at the moment. Accept.'

'In a matter . . .?' murmured Tom. It was not like David to be vague.

'This Purdy thing,' David said impatiently.

Tom ducked his head and gave him a sharp look from beneath his eyebrows. 'And I'm to accept that?'

'Yes, accept,' said David.

To Miss Mundy he said, 'There may be a personal call from Mr. Cass. Theo, not Phillip. Don't put any more calls through till it comes. Say I'm out.'

But at that moment the telephone rang.

'Theo,' he said to himself.

And so it was.

. . . . .

'I'm going round to see Byfield,' said Theo Cass to his nephew. 'I'll be an hour or so.'

But instead of going, he put his hands in his pockets and said in a confidential voice, 'I wonder if he's making as much money as they say he is.'

Phillip Cass, a painstaking, sour, and sarcastic young man, eyed Theo in critical silence for a while, then said, 'Why?'

'He's taking the Purdy brief. You'd think he'd be able to do better than that. You know, I've never thought him as smart as people say he is.'

'No, he's not smart,' said Phillip. 'That's why Horace Dangerfield uses him. Dangerfield's not smart, either. He made those millions by accident.'

'Then why is he taking it, if he's getting plenty of the other stuff? There won't be much in it. And he's not the man I should have chosen, anyway. He hasn't had a criminal brief for years. He said so himself. It struck me that he lacked confidence in himself.'

'Never mind,' said Phillip. 'He'll have you.'

Theo gave him a look of suspicion, then went out, slamming the door behind him, not because he was angry with Phillip, but because he always slammed doors. It was merely another expression of the misdirected physical energy that made him throw himself into chairs, blunder across rooms, knock things over, and trip.

It was only during his outbreaks of drunkenness that this clumsy energy was quelled. As if alcohol gave his body some needed ballast, his movements at these times, though ponderous, were defter. During these bouts Phillip Cass, who was poor, did Theo's work as well as his own, while Theo, his eyes glaring and unblinking, drove about the city with amazing dexterity, or took up a watching position in some bar, his mouth set in a rigid smile and his feet anchored as much as possible to one spot, for he was cunning when drunk, and calculated every movement.

Transporting his fifteen stone of tightly packed flesh towards David's chambers, he seemed to take up the whole width of the pavement with his widely swung arms and flinging feet. To his many acquaintances he raised his hat high in salutation, with a grin so intense that it looked as if he were barely suppressing a shout.

Theo was tolerated almost everywhere, not only because he was a son of an old-established grazing family and had expectations of riches, but because his bouts of drinking were short, and his sober intervals long enough to allow his family and friends to rebuild their confidence in him. Only by his dealings with women had he made some enemies. He was frequently unfaithful to his wife, but because he despised the women in these affairs for submitting to him, and let them see it, none of them lasted for long. As for his wife, she publicly played the game of I-know-nothing, and played it with great poise. She was a domesticated, prettily-harassed woman, who drove around in a station-wagon full of Theo's handsome children, all of whom were young enough to tell people, when Theo was drunk, that Daddy was sick again.

Sheila Jack had come upon him at the end of one of his bouts, when his wife and children were at the beach, and had at once made him the object of a crusade. Chaperoned by her age, she had carried him home to cure him. He did not resist her. At a certain stage in his bouts he made a sudden descent from king to dog, and at the moment of their meeting this transition had just taken place, leaving him too sad, lumpish, and supine to resist anybody.

For a week she had talked into his expressionless, swollen face, and had served him with his meals (which tended to be of something raw or wholemeal), a sour claret or a sourer hock. 'Civilized drinking,' she had pointed out.

When at last she had delivered him to his wife (who received him warmly, and Sheila very coldly indeed) she was convinced that she had cured him. After that, reasoning that since she had saved him he must be worth saving, she had begun to talk of him as a legal genius, causing many eyes to widen when she did so.

David, on the other hand, had few illusions about him. He had been forced to agree with Sheila Jack when she had asked him if Theo was good, but he privately thought him slovenly and imprudent. He had known him to miss the most obvious points in the preparation of a case, and had once heard an intelligent lay client put him right on a point of law.

But they had been at school together and had graduated in the same year, and because this common past still provided them with points of contact, David could be tolerant of Theo's bungling ways, and Theo was sometimes able to forget that he thought David a prig. Without warmth, they accepted each other as friends, and when Theo arrived that day at David's chambers, they greeted each other with raised voices, facetiously, before Theo spun his hat across David's desk, scattering papers, and sat down.

'What's the hurry about this thing?' he demanded.

'I should think in fairness to Mrs. Purdy . . .' murmured David.

'Ever seen her?' Theo shot out.

'No,' said David, and at once regretted the instinctive lie. 'Not to my knowledge,' he added.

'Oh, you'd remember her,' said Theo, watching with irony as David gathered into a neat pile the papers displaced by his hat. 'Tidy bastard, aren't you?' he remarked.

'Yes,' said David. He leaned back in his swivel chair, one knee at the edge of his desk. 'Let's have the story.'

Theo slowly slapped his thigh, while his eyes took on a glazed, memorizing look. 'Purdy was found dead at nine o'clock that night. He'd been drinking that day, and she'd been out. She came home about five that afternoon and found him passed out on the kitchen floor. She says there was a pot of coffee on the stove. It had boiled over and extinguished the gas jet. Says she turned off that gas tap, then tried all the others. Old stove. Loose taps. Says they were liable to leak unless they were turned off hard.'

'One moment,' said David. 'Did she say she turned them off because she feared the effect of that trickle of gas on her husband?'

'No. Habit, she says. Just habit.'

'Very well. It's five o'clock. She finds him drunk and turns off the gas taps. What does she do then?'

'Goes out again. Intended to stay out for a few hours to give him time to come to and haul himself off to bed. They had these violent scenes when he was drunk. Says she'd reached the stage where she couldn't bear another one. Easier to go out.'

'Any proof that she went out at five?'

Theo gave a sudden bray of laughter. 'Proof? Plenty. Too much. I picked up some odds and ends from Charlie Hannaford. Not sure of all this, but here it is, for what it's worth. There's an old duck in the opposite flat says she heard Mrs. Purdy leaving at five. Running, she says. Says she had a feeling something was wrong. Wise after the event, of course.'

'What kind of woman is she?'

'Don't know, but I was told that she was awfully keen to talk. Nice people,' said Theo, 'aren't.'

'No, they're not.'

'Anyhow, she was going out about nine, and got a whiff of gas as she passed the Purdys' door. Got the janitor to open up.' Theo pointed to the floor. 'Found him dead, and every gas jet on full blast.'

'And what made the police reject the obvious explanation, suicide?'

Theo said morosely, 'Her prints were on every tap.'

'I see. And who turned off the gas?'

'The janitor.' Theo checked David's interruption with a raised hand. 'Ah no, boy. He didn't touch the taps. Smart lad, this. Reads detective stories. Oh, and *he* says La Purdy was running, too. Passed his flat on the ground floor, he says, running. And another thing. This woman opposite claims she heard Mrs. Purdy threaten her husband. "I'll have to kill you, Richard." That's what she's supposed to have said. Only a few days before he died.'

'Obliging of her. She threatens him at the top of her voice, leaves her prints all over those taps, then makes herself conspicuous by running out.'

'Most murders are sloppy jobs, you know that,' said Theo with indifference.

'Yes.' David swivelled his chair to face the window, looking without attention at the faded sky chequered by red scaffolding. He saw a man, not Richard Purdy, sprawled dead on a kitchen floor, and a woman, not Isobel, running down flights of steps. They were puppets, posing an impersonal problem. 'I must see that flat,' he thought.

He brought his chair back to face Theo. 'And what time did Mrs. Purdy get home again?'

'Just after the janitor had opened up. Nine. She tried to revive him, then rang a doctor. The doc rang the police.'

'And she protests her innocence.'

'She says she's innocent.' Theo ran a hand hard over his cheek and chin, contorting his face. 'I wouldn't say protests. Seems not to give a damn. Quiet about it. Damn queer woman altogether.' And Theo added reflectively, 'Still waters.'

'But she must have some story.'

'Oh, according to her, she took suicide for granted right from the start. She says he must have come to, feeling sick and depressed, and smelled the gas. She says it must have given him the idea of suicide.'

'Sounds reasonable, except for the prints.'

Theo said, 'If he'd turned on the gas, his prints would have obliterated hers.'

'Yes yes,' said David testily. 'I see that.'

There was a long pause, then Theo said warningly, 'Oh, they have a case, make no mistake about that.'

'Of course they have.' David looked at his hands, spread before him on the desk. 'Was the oven gas on?' he asked suddenly.

'Yes, and the door wide open.'

'If her prints are on the handle of that oven door, it seems to me they can prove their case. But in most of those old stoves the ovens have ridged handles. No, milled. They wouldn't take a print. If that's the case, we've only the prints on the taps to worry about.'

And into Theo's laughter he cut with a cold, raised voice. 'Look at it this way.' He waited with a strained courtesy for Theo's laughter to subside. 'I am a drunkard,' he said, 'a known, habitual drunkard, waking up after a bout, miserable. I smell the gas. It triggers off my decision to suicide. I'm lying on the floor, and I do the whole thing without getting up. All I have to do is reach up one hand, open the oven door, and flick each tap on with a finger on the edge of it. Those taps are loose, remember that.'

There was a silence, then Theo said, 'Feeble.'

'Feeble, petty, and contrived,' David agreed. 'The kind

of explanation I hate to present. All the same, it may be a possibility. And a possibility is all we need.'

'Oh, it may be possible,' Theo conceded, 'but I wouldn't say it was too damn probable.'

'No, but if she persists in her plea, it may be enough to establish a reasonable doubt. It depends on that handle. I'd like to see it before we see her.'

'Suits me.' Theo yawned, stretched, then said easily, 'But she'll get off, you know. She's a bloody beauty. Sloppy dresser, though,' he added.

'If you think she'll be acquitted because she's good-looking . . . ' David began.

'Well, won't she? Juries always let 'em off. Never mind about the poor bastards they shoot or stab or gas. They acquit them, and off they go, free as birds. Look at that Abel girl. And that other one. Dutton. No, Denton.'

'It's precisely because of them that she may *not* be acquitted,' said David. 'Very soon there'll be a jury that will lean over backwards. They'll remember those cases — both recent, mind you — and consciously *not* allow themselves to be influenced.'

Theo shrugged. 'Oh, if she cops one of those . . .' And his voice trailed resignedly away.

'In fairness to her, let's leave that right out of our calculations.'

But Theo suddenly clamoured, 'A bloody stunner!' He looked awed, and indicated feminine curves with his hands. 'She's got it. She's full of it. What beats me is how she ever came to marry him.'

'The question of motive is interesting,' mused David. 'Granted that the Crown don't have to prove motive, it's still helpful if we can imply a lack of it. Now let's suppose that she hated her husband . . .'

'Her hair,' Theo dreamily broke in. 'Long heavy stuff, always falling down.'

'Stop leching, Cass.' For this cry of their student days, David used the old tone, rallying and mock-severe. He even smiled, and waited for Theo's laugh of recognition before he went on. 'If she hated him, she didn't have to kill him to free herself. She could have left him.'

'Then why didn't she?' a voice inside him asked. For though he had not forgotten the answer he had once provided to this question, it no longer carried the same conviction. Once again his idea of Isobel was blurring, wavering, assuming new shapes.

'Then why didn't she?' Theo asked. Then he said, 'Oh, I see what you mean. If she didn't hate him enough to leave him, she didn't hate him enough to kill him. But that doesn't hold water. Love-hate, you know, and all that. Purdy and she——'

'Purdy was half mad,' David curtly interrupted. 'Mad enough to kill himself. And we ought to have no trouble proving it.'

Theo's limited concentration had expended itself; he was becoming restless with confinement. He yawned, then gasped on the outgoing breath. 'There's old Sheila.'

'Sheila Jack? She rang me this morning about this thing. Did you know that?'

'Not surprised. Did she tell you that Purdy said he was going to do himself in?'

'She did not. Did he say it in her presence?'

'She reckons he did. Only a week ago.'

David slapped both hands flat on his desk. He looked alert and pleased. 'Oh, that's splendid. It's hearsay, of course, and may not be allowed. But it will be. I'm certain it will, in a matter as serious as this. There are plenty of precedents. Did he threaten suicide on only one occasion?'

'She mentioned only one.'

'Couldn't there have been others?' And when Theo did not reply, David said persuasively, 'She's a woman who likes to prove her point.'

'Dirty work,' thought Theo. 'He'll leave that to me.' His smile was triumphant. 'Leave that to me,' he said.

'Very well,' David said carelessly. 'Now when can we see her flat? Tomorrow?'

'Will you have time? I thought you were the busy boy.'

'I'll make time.'

'Well, if you can, I can.' Theo reached over and swept his hat from David's desk. 'I'll fix it,' he said.

As Theo rose to his feet, David leaned back in his chair and clasped his hands at the back of his head, marking with his smile and his attitude of relaxation the end of business and the resumption of intimacy. 'You've seen her, Theo,' he said. 'You've talked to her. What's your personal opinion? Is there a possibility that she's innocent?'

Theo stood very straight, and with both hands held his hat ceremoniously against his chest. 'My dear fellow,' he said in a deep voice, 'all my clients are innocent.'

It was not until the echo of his laughter had died away down the corridor that David unclasped his hands and let his chair drop back into place. Theo's little joke had seemed like a rebuke of his naïveté, and it was with some defiance that he told himself, 'All the same, it's happened before.'

Chapter Six

'Why shouldn't he defend her?' asked Myra. 'I see nothing odd about that. He's a lawyer, isn't he?'

But Hughie shook his head. 'He specialises in company and constitutional stuff, everyone knows that. It's not his line.'

'As if everyone must have a line, and never step off it!' Myra amiably scoffed, flinging herself from their bed and grasping her gown from a chair. But she returned at once to the bed, trailing her gown behind her, and stood looking down at her husband. 'And what about the Paine case?'

'That was years ago.'

'Before they began *grooming* him, I suppose!'

'Exactly,' Hughie flashed defiantly back.

'Hughie, what are you implying?'

'Nothing. Only that his interest in her may be personal. You thought so once yourself.'

'Heavens! Because of a casual remark I made years ago . . .'

'Months ago.'

'Months ago, then. Oh darling, please darling, don't say this to anyone but me.'

'I shouldn't dream of it,' Hughie stoutly declared.

But Myra, turning away, looked both miserable and unconvinced. Hughie's love of showing himself privy to secrets pained her the more because she herself was scrupulous in such matters. She stood at the window, wrapping her gown tightly about her. Like David from his chambers, the Magaskills now looked out at scaffolding. Horace Dangerfield's home units were rising implacably between the harbour and their windows. 'I think you would make rather a fool of yourself if you went round talking like that to anyone but me. Other people,' Myra said carefully, 'may not understand.'

'What do you take me for?' cried Hughie from the bed.

'Besides, he can't afford a personal interest in her, not if he's going to be all these wonderful things people are always hinting at. Attorney-General or Prime Minister or what-have-you.'

'Everyone is not always wise,' Hughie said soberly.

'Ah, but David is, always,' said Myra with a touch of contempt.

. . . . .

'For you,' said Daisy, 'it seems rather out of line, a detour.'

David did not answer, but continued to eat his breakfast, very rapidly. Sunlight flooded the room, casting the silky shadows of bamboo on one white wall, and Daisy, admiring this Oriental tracery, presently said, 'Of course, I don't pretend to understand these things,' meaning that, in her opinion, she understood them very well.

David said, 'Mother, I am not Gordon Haggett. I'm not able to pick and choose my work to that extent.'

'No? I rather thought you could. But in that case, don't you think it better to *pretend* that you can? You'll find that in no time at all people will believe you.'

David responded to this with one of his putting-off smiles, remote and slightly sour.

'I wonder why that foolish Theo offered it to you,' Daisy persisted.

'I believe someone suggested me.'

'But isn't only Mrs. Purdy herself entitled . . .?'

'I was suggested to her,' David explained, too patiently, 'by a woman named Sheila Jack.'

'Sheila *Jack*! Can you mean that fat woman with bloodshot eyes, whose coats always look like military overcoats?'

'Then you know her,' said David with finality.

'Yes indeed. She rants.'

And Daisy, considering the shadow of the bamboo,

decided that if it were *painted* on the wall, it would be very tiresome indeed. 'Beautiful, variable, unreliable shadow,' she lovingly thought. 'Rather a sordid case,' she said aloud.

'Very sordid,' David promptly agreed.

Daisy looked at him with sudden vigilance, wondering if he needed the money. She set her empty cup delicately on its saucer. It was Limoges, and used daily. Keeping such china for rare occasions was another thing she thought sordid.

'Dear boy,' she said, 'you do still tell me things, don't you?'

'Don't be silly, Mother. Of course I don't.'

Daisy laughed, reassured. 'Max Dobie is all set to buy the Swinnerton place, after all,' she said. 'He's taking me out there today. Helen, too, of course. And Hal Bonniface. That's Willy's friend. He has agreed to do the sketches.'

'So you got him?'

Daisy's smile warmed and spread. 'Oh yes, I got him.'

Possie came in, and began to stack the breakfast things on her tray. 'Clouds in the south,' she reported. 'It's going to rain.'

'It can't rain,' said Daisy, 'not when I'm going to an empty house. Nothing could be more miserable.'

'I wouldn't go all that way today if you paid me,' Possie said triumphantly.

'No one is likely to,' Daisy said in a bored voice.

'And I'm going to an empty flat,' David quickly cut in. 'The Purdys'.'

'Snooping,' Daisy detachedly remarked, but Possie cried, 'What? Are you defending her, David?'

'Something like that,' said David.

'Oh, I think that's wonderful.'

Daisy gave her a look of cool interest. 'And what is wonderful about it, Poss?'

'Think of the publicity,' said Possie.

'I have,' said Daisy. 'And Possie, there's quite enough on that tray. Do come back for the cups.'

'It's not having a traymobile.'

'What is not having a traymobile? David, I'm ready.'

'What I mean is, if I had a traymobile . . .'

But Daisy was already at the door, and would not answer. It was only when David and she were walking to the garage that she burst out with: 'Publicity, indeed! And a tray-mo-beele!'

'Useful things,' commented David.

'First, those ugly Venetian blinds for her room, and now a tray-mo-beele. Soon she will demand one of those devices for washing dishes.'

'You mean those recent inventions?' asked David, who was sometimes irritated by his mother's affectations. 'I hope the off-side grey is not lame this morning,' he added.

But Daisy's laugh was unwilling. She wished to remain annoyed. 'No, I'm serious. She would fill my house with things that click and clack and whirr and trundle.'

David's instinct was to stay out of these disputes. He remembered the battle of the Venetian blinds too well. The harbour waters soughed; the sun shone quietly down; and it seemed as if Possie and his mother would go on bickering for ever, and that he would go on for ever laughing, placating, and taking his mother's arm as they walked to the garage. Nothing could be duller, nothing more desirable.

. . . . .

At two o'clock that afternoon, the low mass of purple clouds on the southern horizon, which might have been mistaken for a distant mountain range, suddenly became mobile, heaving and rising and flowing rapidly over the sky until only a small aperture at the west was left, and that a limpid green. A hush descended. Lighted trains sped through the suburbs, and women deep in cushioned houses drew their curtains against this strange daytime dusk. And Possie, hearing the first reverberation of thunder, thrust a hand from the window to receive on her palm a heavy drop of rain.

'Ha!' cried Possie.

'I tried to warn her,' she said with satisfaction, when a little later she was forced to shut the window against a wall of rain.

But Daisy did not get wet. Max Dobie had issued his whole party with plastic raincoats, taken from the boot of his car, and at that moment she was standing, dry, in the hall of the Swinnerton house. 'But the staircase is disappointing,' she was saying.

'Yes, too mean, too narrow.' Max Dobie ran the tip of his wet umbrella over the nearer balusters. 'Nothing can be done about it, unfortunately. Structural reasons.'

'There's always illusion. I'm sure we'll be able to make it look quite grand.'

'I don't want a museum, Daisy. None of that Life in Colonial Days stuff. We intend to live here.'

'Max dear, I know. You have told me that one hundred times.'

He pointed his umbrella at her, jabbing the air as if he did not quite dare to poke her in the chest. Under his moustache his smiling mouth was thin, soft, and cold. 'And no whimsy,' he said.

She laughed. 'What are you afraid of? Rocking chairs and bobble braid? If you hire me, Max, you must trust me.'

She moved away from him, happily spinning and skimming over the floor of the great grimy lofty hall. Drops of water flew off her raincoat. She seemed about to break into a dance, perhaps a waltz. 'The pediments are lovely,' she sang. 'Better than mine.'

'Hipple and Bartley start the restoring next week,' he called across to her.

Behind him, Helen Dobie was slowly descending the disappointing staircase, looking about her fearfully as she came. 'Upstairs is even worse,' she said mournfully.

'Upstairs is wonderful,' Daisy laughingly returned, while Max cried angrily, 'Project, Helen, project! Have you no imagination?'

'None.' Helen opened and flung back her coat, revealing a cumbrous dress of pink wool. It was by Givenchy, and did not suit her, but she wore it with as much aplomb as if it did. Pale and plain, she had that tenderly nurtured look that cannot be imitated, and which is more convincing evidence of riches than any number of possessions. She said sadly, 'There will always be dead leaves in the bath.'

'Helen,' laughed Daisy, 'we shall give you a bathroom of crystal and velvet. You'll grow in the bath like a white rose.'

Helen's beaky little face took on a look of pleasure, and Daisy, not wishing to labour the compliment, said in the same laughing voice, 'And Helen, where have you hidden that boy?'

'Hal?' Helen looked vaguely up the staircase. 'Oh, he took his shoes off and climbed out of one of the upstairs windows, down that big magnolia tree. He said he was going to look at that little summer house.'

'In this rain? And with no coat?'

They all looked at the heap of wet plastic on the floor, Hal's coat, then out through the open door, where, beyond the columned veranda, the rain was crashing unrelentingly down on broken paving and rankly growing roses.

'I fear that boy is being *original*,' Daisy dryly remarked.

And as if he had been standing concealed there, awaiting this cue, Hal Bonniface appeared at that moment in the wide doorway. A small and spectacular young man, he stood dashing rainwater from his eyes and flicking its silver cascades from his fingertips.

'There's something Oriental about that boy,' murmured Max.

Helen nodded. 'That wonderful compactness.'

Daisy, who had once heard them talk in exactly the same tone of an Italian table they had bought from her, flung at Hal a glance of the liveliest calculation. He was advancing at his leisure, looking beautifully unconcerned with his sodden clothes. Water streamed off him. He was so wet that as soon as he stopped before them a pool formed at his bare feet.

'I've been for a walk,' he said. He spoke childishly, without emphasis or affectation, unless the very simplicity of his speech was an affectation, which Daisy suspected it was.

'You remind me of a Japanese wrestler,' smiled Max.

'No, a magician,' cried Helen.

Hal ran his hands over his head, and his hair, released of its weight of water, sprang up in vigorous and glistening spikes. It was cut very short. 'And I found a gazebo,' he said.

Daisy laughed. 'Then you *are* a magician. There's no gazebo here.'

But Max was saying, 'What's this? A what-a? A what-a?' And Helen was crying at the same time, 'But what *is* a gazebo? It sounds *heavenly*.'

'He means that little pavilion at the back,' Daisy explained, as if interpreting for an idiot.

Hal ignored this failure of tact. He spoke directly to Max. 'Come and see it.'

Max, looking out at the rain, made a sound of indecision, but it was then that the rain stopped, suddenly, and Helen flung both arms wide, declaring that she had *told* them he was a magician.

Soon Helen and Daisy stood in the doorway, watching Hal and Max making their way to the back of the house; Hal plunging straight and unconcernedly through the sludgy vegetation, while Max, careful of his clothes, hopped and leaped beside or behind him.

'His drawings are not as good as *that*,' said Daisy tartly.

But Helen was looking amused, almost fond. 'I'll run upstairs and get his shoes,' she said.

Left alone, Daisy walked out on to the veranda. Over the rampant garden flowed a strange and beautiful light, which defined each leaf and blade of grass darkly and exactly, which set reds vibrating and gave to greens the liquid lustre of deepest water. Walking along the veranda, her high heels sounding tentative and lonely in the silence, Daisy smiled, stretching out a hand to all this as if blessing it for its beauty, while at the same time she wondered if the cost of restoring the house would make Max mean about his decorating bill.

At the end of the veranda the light was subdued by a great magnolia tree, and beyond that by masses of Indian hawthorn spilling over from what had once been a hedge. Here Daisy halted to run a hand over the cornerstones, then to place it flat, appreciating the texture of the rough grey stone, its wonderful solidity, a solidity she loved the more because she carried always within her the hateful memory of the gimcrack house of her childhood, which on windy nights had creaked like a dead tree.

The crash of footsteps through undergrowth reached her from behind the hawthorn, and Hal's voice. 'I love those old-fashioned jokes of hers,' it said.

'Old-fashioned?' Max sounded a little unsure of himself.

'All jokes are old-fashioned, aren't they? But especially *that* kind.'

'Her taste is infallible; it's uncanny,' said Max.

'Taste,' said Hal, and Daisy wondered how with such complete tonelessness he could convey such complete condemnation.

They pressed through a gap in the hawthorn, neither of them looking in the least disconcerted to find Daisy standing there. 'Hello, Daisy,' said Hal, with his customary simplicity, while Max patted the wall and said, 'Convict-built. No labour problems in those days. I wonder what poor wretch cut that stone,' he added sententiously.

'Whoever it was, he was transported for stealing one loaf of bread,' said Daisy. 'It was always a loaf of bread.'

Silence greeted this. 'One of my old-fashioned jokes, I expect,' thought Daisy.

Helen Dobie came slithering along the veranda, holding before her a pair of rope-soled espadrilles, each containing a dirty white sock. 'Your shoes, Hal.'

'Thank you, Helen.'

He sat on the edge of the veranda to put them on, everyone watching him. Helen, hovering behind him, lightly touched his damp hair. 'Vous êtes comme le roi d'un pays pluvieux,' she haltingly misquoted, laughing to show that she herself had no illusions about her accent.

'Nothing could be less apt,' her husband crossly snapped.

Hal said, 'I don't understand French, Helen. Was that poetry?'

'Baudelaire,' murmured Helen, a little abashed.

'Oh, was it, Helen? I've heard of him. He was the one who thought he was being so madly wicked.'

'But wickedness has been old-fashioned for a *long* time,' said Daisy.

Hal stood up, looking bored. 'We're not going to talk about lit-er-a-chewer, are we? And dead people?'

Daisy was preparing to step off the veranda. 'It is difficult to find a place to set one's feet,' she said.

Max had left the car in the road, for purple lantana had long ago pressed into and narrowed the driveway. So they took the footpath, where weak-stemmed primulas sprang between the broken slabs of stone. Helen walked ahead with Hal, and Max said to Daisy, 'I've given him the gazebo . . . the little pavilion to do, Daisy. You don't mind?'

'Mind? My dear Max, I'm delighted.'

'Good.' Max did not look at her; he was prodding at garden statuary with his umbrella. 'It will keep him amused.'

Daisy was looking thoughtfully at Hal's back. 'Though if you dislike whimsy . . .' she began.

'Oh, it won't matter there. My God, look at that!' Max, lashing out with his umbrella, knocked the little finger from the extended hand of a flower-girl. 'All these will have to go. And those urns. And that rotten little balustrade.' He stabbed viciously with his umbrella. 'And that. And that . . .'

. . . . .

'Dirty bitch, wasn't she?' said Theo Cass in a conversational tone.

David, squatting on his heels before the stove, gave a backward glance over his shoulder, and found himself looking into the interior of the refrigerator, the door of which Theo Cass was holding open. It was empty, but evidence of food remained in the smears of butter, the flecks of mould, the coagulated driblets of red jam.

He said, 'When a place has been closed up . . .'

'No. That's old dirt.' Theo sounded primly censorious. He shut the door of the refrigerator and wiped his hands on his handkerchief. 'It's the one thing I hate — muck where food's concerned.'

David got to his feet. 'As I thought, that handle's milled. Look, it wouldn't take a print. Nothing there to refute a theory of suicide.'

'Nothing to prove it, either.'

'We don't have to prove it.'

The kitchen was so narrow that he and Theo stood only inches apart. Rain ran thickly and incessantly down the curtainless windows and raged and spumed in a nearby pipe, its presence so manifest that the dryness of their bodies seemed miraculous, as it does to children who stand among rocks and bracken behind a waterfall.

'The whole place stinks,' said Theo.

'Does it? I hadn't noticed.'

Both men stood with their hands in their pockets; both frowned as they looked about them. David was nervously aware of Theo's snuffling, glaring disapproval, and on guard against his own instinct to defend Isobel from Theo's remarks.

'Funny the way women litter the tops of refrigerators,' said Theo.

'Yes.' There was a dusty fruit bowl on top of the refrigerator, and David picked from it a broken ear-ring. He held it in the palm of his hand for a moment, a cheap pearl, then tossed it back among the other things that Isobel had dropped into the bowl and forgotten: the rubber bands, the headache powders, the receipts — the debris that day-to-day living leaves in its wake, as extraneous, as mute and meaningless, as the bottles and tins that the tide dumps on the beach.

Theo was looking at the window, the battering rain. 'Marooned,' he grumbled. 'Couldn't even get as far as the car in this. Get wet through.'

'I wanted to come here before I saw her.'

'Damn place gives me the hump.' Theo reached past David's shoulder and pushed the door violently open. 'Come on,' he said.

In the living-room, Charlie Hannaford sat on a low divan, his elbows on his spread knees, his hands clasped, his red tie plummeting down. He looked up as they came in. 'You fellers right now?' he asked.

'Yes,' said David. 'Better hang on though, Charlie, till she eases a bit.'

'Suits me.' Charlie hoisted his legs on to the divan, lay back, and tilted his hat over his eyes.

David went to the bedroom and walked about like a man assessing the value of the furniture. In the damp air everything seemed slightly sticky. The bed was covered with a pink cotton counterpane and on this lay a man's dressing-gown, the sleeves turned back to the length of a woman's arms. David looked at this for a moment, his hands clasped behind his back, then turned his attention to the dressing table, observing on its varnished top the shallow troughs burnt by abandoned cigarettes, the bleached crescents left by wet glasses.

The window overlooked the plane tree.

Half a year had passed since he had imagined her sitting there, like another Rapunzel, watching the lapse of the days and seasons, a half year in which he had seen her for only a few seconds and had spoken to her not at all. Yet his conception of her had so changed that he recalled that early fancy almost with disbelief, as if its author had been another man. In the cane lounge, the downturned magazine, the dusty sun-glasses, there was evidence that she had really sat there, but when he held the sun-glasses in his hand he experienced the same struggle against a pressure of blankness, then the same sudden, helpless floundering of concentration, as when he had picked up her ear-ring.

Behind him, Theo Cass said, 'Good God! She's been wearing her husband's dressing-gown.'

David laid the sun-glasses on the window-sill. Theo was standing by the bed, a look of perplexity on his face, holding between a thumb and forefinger a sleeve of the dressing-gown. 'And the poor bastard just dead,' he indignantly muttered.

David picked up the other sleeve of the dressing-gown, fingered it, then dropped it. 'Theo,' he said, 'hadn't we better fix a date for seeing her?'

'What about Monday?'

'Very well. Monday.'

Theo was scanning the room, still looking perplexed. 'Queer woman, this. Looks like an angel, lives like a pig.'

'It's not our business how she lives,' said David in his mildest voice.

'It might be our business what she's like. I had old Sheila on the phone today, and do you know? Purdy won't even see her.'

'Mrs. Jack can be overpowering.'

'Admitted. But Purdy oughtn't to mind being overpowered when Sheila's footing the bill for all this. Yours and mine, laddie, yours and mine.'

But David was already at the door, and it was to his back that Theo grumbled, 'Women like her, no kids, what do they do with themselves all day?'

Charlie Hannaford had not moved, but he said, 'There's no two ways about it. Jobs or kids, women have got to have one or the other or they go bad. What are they, otherwise, these married women with nothing to do? I'll tell you. They're a harem of one.'

David murmured politely. Aimlessly moving about, yawning and looking at his watch, he had the strained and stoical air of a traveller waiting for an overdue train. But Theo had opened a drawer, and with his first real interest was examining cheque butts. 'Went through some cash in his time,' he said in a voice tinged with respect, then slammed the drawer shut and announced with resolution, 'Look, I'm getting out of here. Promised Betty I'd pick up some tucker at D.J.'s on the way home.'

'You won't get there, son,' Charlie said comfortably, 'not before they close, you won't.'

'Got to. People coming. Promised Betty.'

'Walk into this and you might as well jump in a cold bath.'

But Theo was squatting before a bureau, where he had discovered a pile of old newspapers and magazines. 'Hold a wad of these over my head. Plenty more here, if you fellers want some.'

'I'll wait,' said David.

Charlie knocked his hat from his eyes and looked at the window. 'Same here,' he said.

'Hello hello hello, what have we here?' Theo was holding a small notebook, swiftly turning the pages. 'Must be hers. No, Purdy's. Same writing as the cheque butts. Bits of everything. Sums. Money. Dates. Bits of scribble.'

'Anything of interest?' asked David, and Charlie, suddenly official, sat up and said, 'You can't take that off the premises, Mr. Cass.'

'Eh?' Theo was far away, absorbed in reading. Once he laughed abruptly, and several times he drew a contemptuous nasal breath. Then, like a man suddenly waking, he blinked and said, 'That's okay, Charlie. I'm not taking it away.'

'Anything of interest?' David irritably repeated.

Theo grinned. 'Listen. "When you tread on an ant, it is no doubt a very important moment in the life of that ant. But it is of no cosmic importance. I am an ant, I tell her, and so is she."'

There was a silence, broken by Theo's laugh. 'And here's another bit. "Suicide is self-assertion in its best and purest form." How's that? We might use it to prove that he held life cheap and all that. Here! Over to you.' He tossed the notebook to David. 'I'm off.'

David opened the notebook. 'Ring me when you've fixed a time for Monday.'

Theo placed a hand on his heart. 'Time . . .' he said in a dying voice. 'But time is of no cosmic importance.' Pleased as a child by Charlie Hannaford's laughter, he gave a little skip and put the newspapers over his head, clasping them daintily under his chin like a sunbonnet. 'There's some lully little bits of pornography in there,' he said.

'In there, is there?' said Charlie with interest. David did not look up; he was reading.

Theo made a little slapping movement in the air with his free hand. 'Oh, what dirty minds!' he cried in a petulant falsetto. 'You men are all the *same!*'

David turned a page. 'Bloody fool,' he murmured amiably.

Ogling, delicately wiggling his fingers, ''bye now,' Theo quavered. He vigorously hooked the door with his foot, slammed it, and they heard him clattering down the uncarpeted stairs.

Into the silence, Charlie Hannaford said, 'Mr. Cass enjoys a joke.' He cleared his throat, looking at the notebook in David's hand. 'Is it . . . ?'

'One moment, Charlie.'

David took the notebook to the streaming window and stood with his back to the room. Richard Purdy's writing was small, upright, and clenched. Pages of figures and such memoranda as: 'Write Eldrich before end of May' were followed by notes — laconic, often incomplete, and with no apparent relation to one another. David could not imagine why Richard Purdy had put such things down. He saw no point in making a note of: 'Addie told me I was an old-fashioned nineteenth century diabolist,' or: 'In the end, beauty is dull. No amusement in it. The end of Thelma's nose bulbous and rubbery. Mouth like a goldfish and wet noises when she talks. She calls me Dicky.'

'James lachrymose over gin,' he read on the next page. 'Asked me why I dragged her beauty in the dirt, talked about his mother, wanted to hit me, then made a pass at her in the kitchen.'

'Isobel,' thought David with certainty.

Behind him, Charlie Hannaford coughed significantly. 'Nothing much in it, Charlie,' said David.

Encouraged instead of rebuffed by this, Charlie came and

stood at his shoulder. 'Rain hasn't eased a bit,' he remarked, obliquely lowering his eyes to the open notebook.

'No moon at Bagshot that night,' David was reading. 'Darkness purple like old grapes. Power failure. Tripped over her by the roadside. I mean literally. Even barked my shin on her suitcase. She sitting on it waiting for bus. Got talking. Who said what first? Can't remember. First time I touched her she shied off. Remarkably easy after that. Couldn't see faces. She told me the old man had chucked her out. Your father? said I. Oh no, said she. My easiest ever. Splendid transaction. Lying in bushes by side of road when bus passed. Things you never forget. Squares of light passing over her face from bus windows. Eyes looked yellow. Saw she was beautiful then, but knew it before. Sensed it? Smelled it? Let's die now. She said that a week later. Kept saying it. Love. There we were. Funny if moralists . . .'

'Just a sec.,' Charlie Hannaford put a finger on the page David had been about to turn. When he had finished reading he said, 'Mrs. Purdy.'

David turned the page. There was nothing more. 'I don't see how you come to that conclusion, Charlie,' he said.

'Oh it's her, all right.'

David's voice was strained. 'There's not one thing to identify her.'

'No, except that it sort of sounds like her. And there was that part about her being beautiful.'

'There are other beautiful women in the world. And how do we know the whole thing isn't a fiction?'

'A fiction? You mean a story?' Charlie sounded unimpressed.

'A fancy. A daydream. How do we know?'

'Oh, I could be wrong, I *could* be,' said Charlie in the generous tone of one who knows he is right. 'Whoever it was,' he went on, 'he rolled her over pretty smartly. Or was there an hourly bus service in those parts?'

David was flicking over the remaining pages, both balked and relieved to find them blank. 'He was mad,' he said.

Charlie laughed. 'You did get my point about the hourly bus service?'

But David had turned back into the room and was pacing distractedly about. 'Where did Cass find this thing, do you know?' he said loudly.

Charlie pointed to the bureau. 'He must have been kidding about the pornography. I mean, there's nothing exactly... That's all right, Mr. Byfield. Anywhere in there will do.'

But David, shutting the bureau, hesitated. Charlie Hannaford at the window was opening the half-drawn curtains. David plunged his hand among the newspapers and searched with frantic haste until he found the notebook. It fell open at the right place. He read it through swiftly and with pointed concentration, then raised the newspapers and carefully inserted the book beneath them.

'Hey! That was sudden. It's stopped.'

Into the room surged the darkly golden light, exposing the bleary surfaces of plush upholstery, the coarse gloss of varnished wood. David rose from the bureau, one hand extended to shield his eyes, while Charlie Hannaford dropped the curtain and took a bunch of keys from his pocket.

Theo had left his pile of wet newspapers on the footpath, from where they had blown against the mudguard and the bonnet of David's car. 'You know, it's funny,' mused Charlie, as he helped David to pick and peel them off. 'That Mrs. Purdy's a sloppy sort of woman, but she looks like a lady and she talks like a lady. It just proves that you can never tell.'

. . . . .

'Have you ever heard of a place called Bagshot?' David asked his mother that night.

'Bagshot? Bagshot? Why, of course, quite near London. There's a heath, I think, or downs. Why?'

'Nothing of importance,' said David.

They were ascending the stairs, going to bed, and at the door of her room, with her hand on the knob, Daisy suddenly said, 'Max Dobie is capricious. Cruel and capricious.'

Her tone cut across David's thoughts, aroused him to interest. 'I thought you were enthusiastic about the Dobies. Max, especially. You've always said that he was one of the few civilized people in Sydney.'

'Did I?' Daisy made a grimace, oddly self-deprecatory. 'Perhaps I meant one of the richest.'

'Has he changed his mind about the Swinnerton place?'

'No, no. We were there today. Everything's splendid. But the rain was rather tiresome, and Possie pounced on me as soon as I got home to tell me she's written to apply for some job that was advertised in the *Herald*, looking after an old woman . . .' Daisy allowed her voice to trail away; she put one hand to her forehead. 'I think I must take my sleeping pills tonight, after all, though this must be the last time.'

But David, who could usually be depended on to make some critical remark about her habit of taking sedatives, said instead, 'Is Possie serious about this job?'

'I hope not, dear boy,' lied Daisy, 'but if she is, we must not stand in her way.'

'I think we must. I think we must find out why she is dissatisfied here.' He hesitated, aware that he was about to encroach on a province that had always been regarded, by unspoken consent, as his mother's. Tentatively, he asked, 'Mother, how much do you pay Possie?'

Daisy pressed a hand to her head. 'David, you must realise that it's not a question of wages. She has pocket-money and keep, and if there's anything else she needs she has only to ask. It's all very difficult, she's so very touchy about money, and I think you must leave it entirely to me. There's no hurry. She can't go yet. I can't have the distraction of finding new help until Max's job is well under way. I've told her that. I had to be quite firm about it. So you see, there's plenty of time.'

'In that case . . .' said David.

But Daisy noticed, with some irritation, that he looked unconvinced.

Chapter Seven

THE three stone steps that led down into the interviewing room at the prison, and the winter coldness cast from its walls, gave it the atmosphere of a cellar. But in the afternoons there flowed through its high western window a shaft of sunlight, bold as a searchlight and full of drifting dust. This light struck full on Isobel, moving in her ashen hair and exposing the blue and rose that lay under her skin like the imagined colours in a pearl.

For David the sad newspaper photograph had overlaid the memory of her beauty, so that its impact was almost as unexpected as at his first sight of her. She did not remember him, which may have piqued him in other circumstances, but with Theo at his side, and his lie to support, he could not help but be relieved.

Her hands were folded decorously on the table that separated her from the two men, and she sat very straight, her head alertly poised, her smile mechanical. David thought she resembled not Charlie Hannaford's lady as much as a professional hostess, paid to be pleasant, but in spite of this he found himself approving this conventional 'niceness'. It shifted the emphasis from her beauty and sensuousness, making them seem merely added graces.

But he wondered for how long she would be able to sustain this front. They seldom did, for long.

Because he had determined from the start that his own front would be one of cool and friendly interest, he kept his eyes mostly on the table before him, where his notes lay. Beside him, Theo Cass shifted in his chair, already oppressed by the atmosphere. Stifling yawns, he appeared to be holding an egg in his mouth. In a square opening in the door there was set, in military immobility, the profile of a warder.

Listening to Isobel with attention, David found himself impressed by her story. He had learned to dread the long, involved, tumbling stories of the nonprofessional criminal, and the sad jokes that so often accompanied them. ('The food's a bit rough in this pub, but it's the best rest cure I've ever had.') He liked her gravity and simplicity, her quiet voice saying, 'I did hurry down the stairs. It might have been called running. I really don't know.' And: 'I have no idea who heard or saw me going out. I didn't notice.'

He said, 'You filled in four hours. How?'

Theo Cass did not listen to her reply. 'So this is Byfield's so-called brilliance,' he thought. 'The gold-panning technique. Sift a ton of dirt and find a speck of gold.' Laboriously he creased and uncreased the crown of his hat. Like David, he seemed reluctant to look at Isobel, but when he did his glance was oblique and vivid, a spy's look. Sometimes, lowering his eyes from her face, he smiled to himself.

Isobel was saying, 'It turned cold in the park, so I went to an Espresso bar and had a cup of coffee. After that I went to the local cinema, but I only stayed about an hour, then I went home.'

David asked, 'And during that time did you see anyone, speak to anyone you know?'

'I saw a few people we know, but I avoided them.'

'Why?'

Startled by her first failure to reply, he looked up quickly, directly into her eyes. In the moment of silence a swift, exploratory look passed between them. Then she raised her hand to shield her eyes from the striking sun, but not before David had observed that they were grey, the pupils spoked with gold.

'Move your chair,' suddenly advised Theo Cass. 'The light's in your eyes.' He laughed. 'This is no third degree.'

Neither she nor David looked at him, but she moved her

chair a few inches, and David looked down at his notes, frowning. 'Do you always avoid people?' he asked.

'Yes, I think I do.'

'Why?'

'I really don't know.'

'A pity, in this case. But perhaps the waitress in the coffee bar will remember you. It may help if we could get someone to say that you were calm, that you showed no agitation at that time.'

'But I may have shown agitation. I was agitated, in fact.'

'Undue agitation,' Theo interposed, and David looked up in time to see her give him a brief, expressionless glance. 'She doesn't like him,' he thought.

'And what is undue agitation?' she asked with a touch of mockery.

'A good question,' David said dryly.

'Better try the coffee bar and the theatre,' said Theo to David, and David nodded, cleared his throat, then said briskly. 'Now, Mrs. Purdy, did your husband . . . '

'Just a moment, Mr. . . .'

'Byfield.'

'Mr. Byfield. Don't you ask people' — she put one hand flat on her chest — 'if they are innocent or not?'

David lifted the top page of his notes and studied the one beneath it in a preoccupied way. 'Not necessarily, Mrs. Purdy.'

'I see. Yet I am innocent. I didn't do that, not that.'

'As if she had done something else,' thought David. He said pleasantly, 'Then it's up to us to persuade other people of that fact, isn't it?'

'He committed suicide,' she said.

'Very well, let's take that as our starting point.' David leaned forward, his forearms on the table, his fingertips exactly together. 'I take it that he had moods of despondency.'

She did not reply, and the quality of her silence was such that she seemed to be holding her breath. David felt that he had come up against some obstacle. 'A man doesn't commit suicide without a reason,' he pointed out.

She said reluctantly, 'He didn't have moods.'

'What, then? Describe it yourself.'

'I think he was despondent all the time.'

'That will do.'

'And most despondent when he was very gay.'

'Oh.' He smiled at her. 'That won't do.'

'Won't do for what?'

'It would be better if you just said he was despondent, without qualification.'

'You mean in court?'

'Yes.'

The sunlight dropped abruptly, with the effect of a notch slipped, below the window sill. Theo Cass rose from his chair and went sighing to the window. David waited, then prompted her. 'Well?'

'Oh, all right. He was despondent.'

'That's better. And would you say this despondency was worse lately?' And David looked reprovingly at Theo, who had returned to his chair and was now giving a series of yawns like abbreviated yelps.

She frowned, looking down at the table and tracing with a fingertip an old scratch in the shape of a letter S. The electric light came on, and when she raised her eyes to the exposed bulb he was shocked to find in them a complete betrayal of her alert pose, her matter-of-fact voice. They were inattentive, incurious, all their vivacity sucked away by some deep inner preoccupation. He repeated his question in a slightly cautious voice.

'Would you say this despondency was worse lately?'

'Must we slander him?' she said suddenly.

Theo burst into a disbelieving laugh. 'Oh, I say ... Now, look here ...' And David broke in with: 'Mrs. Purdy, in a court of law ...'

She raised her voice. 'But you make him sound like someone else. He was so quick, so variable. And funny, too.' Her smile, almost maternal, dwelt on this. 'He was funny,' she said in a lower voice.

'Funny,' David flatly repeated, and looked at her with bewilderment and some hostility. 'And so he may have been. But does his funniness serve our purpose in any way? We must ask ourselves that.'

'But if it's the truth they want . . .' she began.

He almost laughed. 'It's not possible to tell the whole truth, you must know that. But we can at least exclude the false.'

'Well, then——' she said eagerly, but he broke in strongly with: 'If we begin to quibble about these things, we'll never find a starting point.'

Theo Cass, banging the side of his chair with a loosely swinging fist, gave his braying laugh. 'Only common *sense*, Mrs. Purdy.'

Isobel did not look at him, nor shift her frowning glance from David's face. 'You're trying to prove him a lunatic,' she said.

David looked at her in silence. He was retracing their conversation, wondering at what point it had changed from an examination to a contest. It was, of course, at the first mention of her husband's character. 'We are trying to prove nothing,' he said, 'not even your innocence. We are merely trying to cast what is called a reasonable doubt on the evidence that will be submitted by the Crown. In your case it seems that the best way we can do that is to offer the alternative suggestion of suicide. We can't prove it, but perhaps we can show that he was unstable enough to commit suicide. Not mad. Not a lunatic. But unstable.'

She dropped her eyes — a concession, thought David, and went on firmly. 'Did he often speak of suicide?'

'He talked of everything. He was a talkative man.'

'Quite so. But I understand that he actually expressed an intention to commit suicide.'

Her lashes moved, but she did not raise her eyes. 'He was also a fanciful man,' she said angrily.

'Even so, if he repeatedly expressed . . .'

'He used to say that the only victory one could gain over life was to throw it away.'

'Oh? And to whom did he say that?'

'To a number of people, I imagine. And at other times he would say that only a fool would kill himself, since time would do it for him in any case.'

Theo Cass rolled his eyes, appealing to the ceiling, and David said, 'Still, both statements imply an active interest . . .' But something stubborn and withdrawn about her stillness and her downcast eyes made him break off and snap at her, 'You're wasting my time. You know that, don't you?'

'I'm sorry,' she said scornfully.

This angered him still more. 'Do you understand why this court will be sitting?' he asked.

Against her continued silence, his voice became hectoring. 'I see that you don't. Let me enlighten you. It will be sitting for one reason, and for one only — to ascertain whether or not you killed Richard Purdy. Not, I repeat, *not*, to make an intricate analysis of Richard Purdy's character, interesting though that may be.'

This was David at his worst. In the silence that followed he heard her draw a deep breath, and realised with some shame that she was steadying herself, but his voice was no less hectoring when he said, 'I want the names of anyone to whom he may have spoken about suicide.'

She looked up, but her eyes, vague and staring, seemed to see through and beyond him. 'I can't remember,' she said, and raised a hesitant hand to her mouth. And as if the touch of her hand had released a spring, an ugly spasm at once passed over her face, wrenching her mouth and eyelids askew. It was over in a second, but it left a little pulse fluttering, lightly and rapidly, at one corner of her lower lip.

David saw, and thought he could feel, this final disintegration of her composure, shard after shard of stiffness falling away from her. He found himself almost unbearably moved by the sickness and distraction that now appeared in her eyes. He had pitied many people before, his pity touched with contempt. 'Poor wretch,' he had said, or, 'Poor bastard.' But pity like this, which answered pain with pain, was new to him.

But he said, 'You can remember them. Give them to me, please. And don't crack up. I've no time to nurse you along.'

'Take your time,' he said a minute later, when she had still not spoken nor removed her fingers from the pulse at her mouth. He took off his spectacles, pushed the papers away from him, and leaned back in his chair.

Isobel's sick eyes roved the room. They did not come to rest on either of the two men, not on Theo Cass, who was looking tactfully at his shoes, nor on David, polishing his spectacles, but on the little window, at which she stared as if in appeal.

'Getting late,' murmured Theo.

She gave in suddenly. Folding her hands on the table before her, she gave him the names in a low shaking voice.

Without a word he put on his spectacles and began to write. He discovered that his hand was trembling, and it was only then that he knew how much greater than his pity had been his need to make her submit. He had needed her agreement to Richard Purdy's defects not only for her defence, but for himself as well. But it was a poor triumph. Wrung from her against her will, it left him still dissatisfied. It had been a kind of rape. Accomplished, it was less than what he wanted.

He was appalled by this perception in himself of a lawlessness that had no relation to the law in which he dealt. It was more than his usual worldly caution that now made him attempt to gather himself up, to retreat from her into his safe world of known boundaries.

Her voice was gaining strength but losing tone. Like a dull child reciting a lesson, she told him that Richard Purdy had attempted suicide a year ago. 'He cut his wrists. I came home and found him. That was last September.'

'What doctor attended him?'

'He wouldn't have a doctor.' And she added defensively, 'The cuts weren't deep.'

'Who else knows about this?' David's voice was cold and weary.

'I don't know. I told nobody. But there were the bandages. They must have been seen. And wait, one of the cuts festered. He showed it to a chemist.'

'What chemist?'

'Washington Souls at Double Bay.'

'Ah!' said Theo Cass. He slapped his knees, rose from his chair and went to the little window, where he flung back his head to look at the sky. David sent a critical glance at his back, then carried the same glance back to Isobel.

She must have been watching him all the time, for their eyes met at once. 'Help me,' she silently mouthed.

Disguising his shock, he briefly hooded his eyes and pulled down his upper lip, and she gave a smile that was both contemptuous and embarrassed and began to brush slowly at the lap of her skirt. He felt himself dismissed, and found he could not bear it. 'Certainly I shall,' he said.

As soon as these words were out he felt such relief that he longed to babble them again and again. 'Certainly I shall, certainly I shall.' But at his back swelled Theo's presence, the more potent because unseen. He clenched the hand resting on the table between them and smiled at her instead.

'And I shall try . . .' she said in a stifled voice. The little pulse no longer beat at the corner of her mouth, but he had the odd feeling that it was like an animal shamming death, and that it would reappear at any moment at some other part of her face. Behind him, he heard Theo Cass whistling between his teeth, and without taking his eyes from Isobel's face, he said, 'Theo.'

As he gathered his notes he heard Theo's steps approaching, his voice saying, 'Had enough?'

David stood up. 'Enough for today.'

He grasped the back of Isobel's chair and eased it from behind her knees as she rose, a courtesy that lent to the occasion some semblance of a social encounter, and which she met with a return of her mechanical hostess manner. She calmly offered him her hand and smiled as she said, 'I think I understand now what you want. Next time I shall have thought of all kinds of helpful things.'

'And tea will be served,' Theo silently mocked, moving back a little to get her legs in perspective.

David's hand lightly touched hers. 'The Inquest is set down for the twentieth of September. Try not to worry.'

'Oh, I'm not *worried*,' she said, and he thought for a moment that she was about to begin her balking and hair-splitting again, but she turned instead to Theo Cass, who stood waiting for her look, and whose eyes at once engaged hers in a look of such unmistakable sexual challenge that she involuntarily raised her hand in the beginning of a protest, then said tightly, 'Goodbye, Mr. Cass.'

Theo's smile was triumphant. 'Until next time,' he said, and bowed with ironic gallantry.

As they left the prison Theo did not notice that David's face was rigidly set, his walk stiff with anger.

They had both come in David's car. Theo flung himself into the front seat, but did not slam the door. He had a great respect for cars. 'A man could get a good lay there, if he were fool enough to buy into it,' he cheerfully announced.

Reaching in his pocket for his car keys, David did not answer.

'Ah yes, ah yes,' said Theo softly, 'if a man had nothing to lose.'

David started the car; they drove through the gates.

'Easy, too, I reckon. Don't you?'

'I have not the least idea,' David said coldly.

Theo liked a surface amiability; he recoiled from the snub. 'What's the matter with *you*?' he asked resentfully.

'This,' said David. 'I think you made that thought too plain back there. Mrs. Purdy is a client . . .'

'What the blazes are you talking about? What did I do back there?'

But David went on as if he had not spoken. 'She is a client, and ought to be treated in the manner due to a client.'

'Oh, Lordy, listen to this,' muttered Theo to the roof of the car.

David's eyes were arrogantly hooded. 'Moreover, I saw nothing in her conduct to invite such behaviour. We shan't speak of justifying it . . .'

'You'd think I'd knocked her down and raped her.'

'. . . because nothing could justify it. But even if she had given you a lead, surely it's up to you, as her attorney . . .'

But Theo was intent on his own monologue. 'Like bloody Purdy did,' he almost shouted.

There was a sudden silence in the car, then David said in his normal voice, 'What?'

Theo said sullenly, 'The first time he met her. You read it.'

David was now forced to slow down before joining the highway, and although natural skill and much practice had long ago made his responses to traffic automatic, it was not until this operation was complete that he asked, 'What's this I'm supposed to have read?'

'In that notebook at her flat. The bit about picking her up on the road at night.'

David looked puzzled; he shook his head.

'While she was waiting for a bus,' Theo said impatiently.

'Oh. Yes, I did read that, but I didn't connect it with Mrs. Purdy.'

'Well, I did. There were remarks and references that made it pretty clear, to my mind.'

David smiled. 'Remarks and references. I see. I must have missed them.'

'Some old bloke had chucked her out.'

'Yes, I remember that. During a power failure, wasn't it? But I don't recall a name.'

'I didn't say there was a name.'

'A description of her, then?'

'I can't remember it word for word,' blustered Theo. 'All I know is that I got that impression.'

'Ah!' cried David, as if pleased that they were getting somewhere at last. 'So you got an impression.' This appeared to amuse him; he smiled. 'An impression,' he repeated. 'I see.'

Theo said angrily, 'There's something about her, let's face it. Then there are the things one hears.'

'From infallible sources, I take it.' David still sounded amused.

Anger disabled Theo's mind. The crushing retort he longed for would not come. 'Where there's smoke there's fire,' was all he found to say.

Feeling kinder now that Theo was cornered and lashing out so feebly, David said in a friendlier tone, 'Not in law, old man, not in law.'

Theo settled back in his seat in a huffy silence, but he was slightly mollified, and relieved as well. He did not wish to fall out with David, for although he did not need him professionally, he had lately been impressed (though a little mystified) by the respect with which so many people spoke of him, and he liked to be able to say negligently, 'Old David? God, yes, known him all my life. Nice feller.'

Presently David said, 'Moreover, I think it's possible that she's innocent.'

'She's as innocent as Jack the Ripper,' hooted Theo.

'I noticed no discrepancies in her story.'

'No, she's staying with it. They won't shake her. But the jury won't like her.'

'I thought good-looking women always got off.'

'I thought so, too. But not when they're so damned disdainful. Take it or leave it, that's her attitude. She'll get their backs up. She got yours up, didn't she?'

David laughed easily. 'She did,' he said.

'They'll want to cut her down to size. I wanted to, back there. So did you.'

'You're mistaken. I wanted those names.'

'Well, you got them. Had to twist her arm though, didn't you? Funny the way she jacked up as soon as you mentioned Purdy.'

'She told about that suicide attempt of her own accord.'

'Ah! Verify that, and *that* might get her off, not her looks. You know one trouble with those Englishwomen? They don't tub. And look, what about that notebook? That blah he wrote about suicide might help.'

'No, nothing there to help us. Nothing at all. All too ambiguous.'

'But look here, there it is, in his own hand . . .'

'Not if we can prove a former suicide attempt. And don't forget we have Mrs. Jack. She's well known, reputable, and we can bolster her with all these other people to whom he spoke of suicide.'

'Hearsay. You said yourself that it may be disallowed.'

'Extremely unlikely. And it certainly won't be disallowed at the Inquest. Anything goes in the Coroner's Court.'

'What? We're going to show all our cards at the Inquest?'

'I suggest we feel our way. It would save everyone a lot of trouble if the Coroner refused to commit her. Let's leave it in abeyance until we've rounded up these witnesses.'

Theo gave an indifferent shrug, and they drove in silence until he suddenly exclaimed, 'She loves that man. By *God*, she loves that man!'

'How can she love him? He's dead.'

'Dead, yes,' mused Theo. 'Well, I must have meant loved.'

It was not until he had dropped Theo in the city and was driving home that David found himself thinking, 'All three of us recognised her at once. Charlie Hannaford, Theo, and myself.'

And as he brought the car into the kerb at the front of the house, he muttered to himself, 'She fits in nowhere.'

He did not know it, but he sounded like Theo Cass.

He let himself into the hall, which seemed very still and tranquil with its squares of weak sunlight on the tiled floor and its faint smells of winter roses and floor polish. He did not see Possie come from the rear of the hall, and was half-way up the stairs before he heard her.

'Is that you, David?' Her voice was high with forced brightness.

Leaning over the banister, David made a gesture with one hand. Not quite a wave, not quite a warding-off, it said plainly, 'Yes, I am home. Please leave me alone.'

He was dining out, and had not much time. While he was shaving he heard in the corridor outside the variable and beautiful cadences of Daisy's voice. She was talking to Possie, whose drone took over whenever she stopped. The noise of David's shower obliterated this, but the first thing he heard, when he turned it off, was Daisy exclaiming, 'Oh, do as you please, Poss.'

'Possie is having second thoughts about this job she's applied for,' she told David when he knocked on the door of her room. Clearly in a wonderful mood, she still wore her hat and was removing her fur jacket.

'You must dissuade Possie,' he said, 'not tell her to do as she pleases.'

'There's no need to worry. Who would employ her? Let her dream. You've been out at the jail today, haven't you?'

'Yes. Look, Mother, I haven't much time.'

'I know. The bar and bench dinner.' She nodded approvingly. 'But do tell me! Is this woman as beautiful as they say she is?'

'Rather lovely hair,' said David judiciously, 'and one of those English skins.'

'Ah, those dew-fed English skins!' sang Daisy. She took off her hat and shook out her short grey curls. 'Or do you mean the kind of English skin that's red and wind-chapped round the eyes, like Angora rabbits?'

David roused himself from the painful contemplation of a dew-fed face upturned, while square after square of light sped over it from the passing bus. 'Surely it's the eyes of Angora rabbits that are red,' he said, 'not the skin around them.'

'Oh, don't be pedantic,' said Daisy.

. . . . .

The terrible symptoms of deprivation, such as drug addicts are said to suffer, had only now set in for Isobel. At first it had been relief that had prevailed, and a sense of freedom at being rid at last of her passion for her husband, a passion so intimate and closely fretted that its very staleness could only create a tighter bond.

She lay face downward on her bed. Her throat ached and her head rolled feverishly from side to side, but she could not cry.

She forced herself to think of David. She had once again forgotten his name, but his handshake, which she had scarcely noticed at the time, now seemed to repeat itself and to offer a ghostly comfort.

His face she saw as a carefully prepared mask, not quite alive, the result of much ritualistic washing and clipping and brushing and grooming. He reminded her, she did not know why, of a dentist. She even imagined that his fingertips would have a faintly aseptic smell.

From that other poor, darkened face she turned her thoughts resolutely away. She considered David's hands, the fingertips exactly together, and heard his low-pitched voice saying, 'Of course I shall.' But it was not until she heard his other voice, hostile and bullying, that she thought, 'Yes, he will help me,' and burst into tears.

Chapter Eight

On the morning after David's visit to the prison, Myra drove to the city early. She had quarrelled with Hughie the night before, and they had not been reconciled that morning. Estrangement from Hughie could still leave her drained and bereft, but there had lately been added to this feeling an undertone of disgust. She was beginning to see her physical dependence upon him as a wretched thing.

Their quarrel had been provoked by her suggestion that since they had to move, they should buy one of Horace Dangerfield's home units. 'It's absurd,' she had said, 'this enormous house for two people.'

But Hughie clearly did not wish to part with this enormous house. 'Suppose we had children,' he had objected. 'What kind of life would they have in a flat?'

Myra did not know why this remark had made her so angry. She herself often longed for children. She was at her best when pregnant. Her walk lost its rather angry gusto then, and she moved slowly and with delicate care, looking like a flamingo. But perhaps she had begun to discern a similarity in her longing for children and her longing for love. In both it was the first rhapsodic flush that attracted her, her elevation to a plane where she both lost and augmented herself. It was when the flush faded, and the donkey-work of marriage or of rearing children began, that she found herself ill-equipped.

While she was locking her car in the parking lot she saw David's car sliding in on the far side, his profile appearing at intervals in that mass of glass and duco as if on a silently moving lathe.

Myra at once began to dodge round stationary cars to get to him. She was so certain he had seen her that when he turned his back and walked away she stopped for a moment in bewilderment, then followed him at a slower pace, unable to comprehend that he was deliberately shunning her. What brought this home to her at last was his walk. There was a constraint about his saunter; he was willing himself not to hurry.

Since her divorce and her much-criticised desertion of her sons, Myra had become both touchy and belligerent, and had alienated herself from many of her friends by unfairly accusing them of coldness. In the taxi that took her downtown she sat hard-faced, with tears in her eyes. If she had been a little roly-poly woman she could no doubt have cried in public, but her height, her lean and worldly good looks, demanded congruous behaviour. Myra, crying in public, would have looked not pathetic, but eccentric.

'People seem to be dropping me,' she said coldly and loudly to the group of women with whom she lunched. She did not think their protests loud enough. She had a poor head for alcohol, and was a little drunk. She leaned back in her chair, apart, while her friends sat in a cluster of pretty hats, twittering like birds.

'If vultures can be said to twitter,' remarked Myra bleakly to herself.

She ascended the stairs in a softly jostling group of women and burst into the painful glare and noise of the street. Walking down Martin Place with Sybil Esterhazy, she saw herself reflected in shop windows — loping along, she thought, like a hungry wolverine. 'I'm not coming with you, Sybil,' she said suddenly. 'I'm going to see Daisy Byfield.'

'*Are* you? Then don't let her sell you a Grinling Gibbons-y mirror. I have to dust mine with a glue brush.'

'She won't sell me even an earthenware pot.'

'Oh, Daisy doesn't sell *pots* any more. She's much too grand.'

Daisy's shop was in a little street, closed to all but pedestrian traffic, which pitched sharply downhill from east to west, and as Myra, who entered it from the west end, was toiling up it, she saw Daisy coming downhill. But she was not alone; she was with Helen Dobie.

Myra, who never counted on people being busy, was drunk enough to be daunted by the sight of Helen. She slipped quickly into the doorway of a shop, where from behind a display of prints she watched their progress down the street — or, rather, Daisy's progress, for it was only Daisy who turned the heads or quickened the glances of passers-by. And no wonder, thought Myra. Even she, who was used to her, could not help admiring afresh her light, disciplined swagger, her erectly carried head, and her air of being oblivious to everyone but her companion, for whose benefit alone she seemed to be going on with all that laughing and pointing and talking at the top of her wonderful voice.

'They probably think she is some visiting actress,' thought Myra, with amusement and affection.

Daisy and Helen said goodbye at the door of Daisy's shop, and as Myra watched Helen continue downhill she observed that she was still buoyantly smiling, as if not yet freed from Daisy's presence.

By the time Myra entered the shop Daisy had disappeared, and it was Willy Macaulay, her assistant, who advanced upon Myra from a background severely lustrous, making as he came an O of surprise with his mouth. Willy walked well, disappointing those who expected him to flounce.

'Why, hell-*lo!*' breathed Willy.

'Hello, Willy. Where is Daisy?'

'Why so accusing? *I* haven't hidden her.'

'Upstairs in the workroom?'

'No.'

'Oh, do stop playing games, Willy.' But Myra's face suddenly cleared. 'I know,' she said, 'her little room at the back.'

'I'll tell her you're here,' offered Willy, dodging about in front of her.

'No, you won't.' Myra could also be arch, and with splayed fingers she pushed him in the chest, for he barred her way.

'She'll kill me for letting you into her cubby hole,' Willy called merrily after her.

About half of Daisy's cluttered back room was occupied by an enormous desk, floridly carved and inset with panels of pearlshell. Daisy showed what she thought of this desk by using it as a step-ladder, and when Myra squeezed through the door (it was blocked by a crate, and would open only twelve inches) she found Daisy standing with one foot on the desk and the other in a pigeon-hole, rummaging in a cardboard box she had taken from a high shelf.

She gave Myra an oblique look over her shoulder. 'So it's you, dear girl? How did you get past Willy?'

'I pushed him in the chest.'

'Goodness. I shall hang a notice in the shop. "Customers will please not push Willy in chest."'

'I'm not a customer,' said Myra. 'And I wish you would come down from there, Daisy.'

'As soon as I've found this sample.' Daisy saw that Myra (not a customer) was taking off her jacket, and her eyes became wary, for she was busy. 'Now that you have forced your way in,' she said pleasantly, 'do sit down.'

Myra had already done so. 'It's summer,' she said. 'My sweater is prickling me.'

'Let it prickle. Even officially it's only spring, and tomorrow will be cold again. Never rush into summer clothes. That's a mistake only very young people make. All the girls in my workroom do it. It makes me so sad to see their poor vulgar goose-fleshed little arms.'

'Something very odd happened this morning,' Myra said casually.

'Ah, my rosy-tan silk!' And Daisy held up the little sample.

'David snubbed me,' said Myra.

'Goodness.' Daisy climbed down, dusted her hands, and kissed Myra. 'Where have you been all these weeks, dear girl? I never see you any more. Is it true you're moving?'

'Daisy,' said Myra, 'did you hear what I said?'

'That David snubbed you? Oh, but you must be mistaken. He's been preoccupied lately, very busy. And touchy, I'm sorry to say.'

'Like me,' challenged Myra.

'As you have just demonstrated,' laughed Daisy.

'You're wrong, Daisy. And oh, curses, my head has begun to ache . . .'

'You poor darling,' Daisy coldly interposed.

'Oh, the ebb of this midday drinking! But you're wrong, I'm not touchy. I'm hurt, really hurt. I've known David for a long time, and I'm fond of him.'

'As I'm sure he is of you.' Daisy's tone was mechanically soothing. Foreseeing one of those interminable discussions on nebulous offences, fancied slights, she would not hide her boredom. She was relieved when the door was thrust open and Willy's moon face appeared in the aperture.

Willy's eyes conveyed news. 'The Lister-Brocks,' he mouthed confidentially at Daisy.

Daisy clasped her hands. 'Not the Pembroke table?' she whispered.

Willy gave two slow, ecstatic nods.

'Oh, bliss,' murmured Daisy. 'Myra, I shall have to go.'

With a deep groan, Myra began to rise, but at the door Daisy turned and stopped her with an imperatively outflung hand. 'No, don't go. Wait for me.'

'Why?'

But Daisy would only repeat her command to wait. 'What *can* she want so urgently,' wondered Myra, as she meekly sat down again.

In a big album on Daisy's desk were photographs of her interiors, and Myra, looking through these while she waited, played with the idea of engaging Daisy to decorate her new house, or flat. But she did not really like Daisy's designs. They were too spirited and emphatic, too hard to live up to.

Voices and laughter reached her from the shop. 'It sounds more like a party than a shop,' she thought. 'What a high old time she and her silly Willy have here.' And she looked rather enviously round the cluttered room: at the swathed bales of cloth, at the cardboard boxes, at the pile of dusty bric-à-brac in a corner, and at Daisy's pretty blue and white teacup, which had a shelf to itself and was protected from dust by a glass dome, which (Myra told herself) Daisy had probably stolen from a grave.

'She belongs to a world of *things*,' Myra suddenly thought.

Daisy's voice, raised now, detached itself from the other voices in the shop in harmonious and somewhat remorseless patterns and sequences of sound. 'Purdy,' Myra heard her say, then her laugh, and the words: 'Yes, a criminal brief. Presumably for a change.'

Knowledge pierced Myra suddenly. 'David was afraid I would tease him, so he ran away. David is in love with Isobel Purdy.'

And she at once believed she had known this all the time, ever since her party. It was Hughie who had confused her. By hinting at the same thing, he had forced her to oppose him. She was pleased with her prescience and with the dramatic situation she had thus uncovered. It took her only a very few seconds to estimate the dangers and difficulties that such a situation must hold for a man like David, and to guess how strong his resistance must have been. That he had fallen in spite of this resistance seemed to Myra, who had lived by love, a much-needed affirmation of her creed. In those few seconds she took her vow, pledged herself, and offered to David her whole-hearted support.

In the shop, farewells were being made, and presently the door opened to admit Daisy, to whom Myra presented her quietly glowing face. 'And did you sell the thingummy, Daisy?'

'I certainly did.' Daisy was also glowing. 'And that little chair as well. You must have seen it in the shop. A little mongrel chair . . .' She smiled, sketching it with her hands. '. . . but good, very good. Such pleasant people, those Lister-Brocks. They know nothing, but they're willing to learn.' She hesitated, then said lightly, 'Knowledgeable people can be difficult.'

She was recalling Max Dobie's foxy and fastidious face. She had not yet been able to find a starting point for his house. All her starts had proved to be over-confident little rushes, ending in bafflement. It was odd; it was unprecedented; but Daisy was not yet worried. That necessary, primary theme would present itself suddenly, she believed, while she was not looking. So she was now waiting, her head turned away, trying not to peep.

And to Myra it had occurred that Daisy might know about David and Isobel Purdy, and had asked her so urgently to stay in order to discuss it. It seemed wildly improbable, but Myra was curious enough to ask in an interested voice, 'What did you want to see me about, Daisy?'

'I?' Daisy looked surprised.

'You asked me to wait,' Myra reminded her.

'Oh yes.' Daisy drew from a plastic bag a little hat of blue feathers, which she respectfully lowered on to her grey curls. 'I thought as we were both going the same way you could drive me home.' Then, as Myra was silent, 'You did bring the car?' she asked.

'Yes, Daisy, I brought the car.'

'Ah. Then come along, dear girl, come along.'

Laughing weakly, Myra got up. 'What a terrible woman you are,' she said.

'Oh I am, I am,' Daisy agreed with enthusiasm. She paused at her desk, touching the album with a forefinger. 'You've been looking at my pictures?'

'Yes. Do you mind?'

'Not at all. Did you like them?'

'Yes. For other people.'

'And why not for you?' asked Daisy, looking her in the eyes, her forefinger still on the album.

'Now, Daisy, you keep your hands off my house.'

Daisy laughed, and gave the album an off-handed flip. 'Daisy Byfield drumming up trade,' she said.

In the shop, Myra stood to one side while Daisy gave instructions to Willy. Feeling rejected, shut out by their absorption in their common interest, work, she watched them with some envy and found herself thinking that they were not unalike, both so narrowly built and rigidly confined in their dark suits. Nor was that all. There was some other resemblance, too, as elusive as those floating resemblances of blood, which Myra tried and failed to identify.

'Daisy darling, do stop carping,' Willy was saying. 'Do go. I'm capable, you know. I can cope.'

'Wait.' Daisy grasped his wrist. 'If you see Hal...'

'I shan't, you know. He's at a party.'

'Still? How long do these parties last?'

'Oh, days and days. Hal's terribly gay.' Willy turned to Myra. 'This is a very dear friend of mine, Mrs. Magaskill. He's an artist. He has heaps and heaps of talent.'

'Ah yes, art,' murmured Myra, with a gasping little yawn, while Daisy said, 'He's clever, in a lightweight sort of way. But really, Willy, he seems an unreliable boy. Where *am* I to get hold of him?'

'Why not ask Mrs. Dobie?'

'Helen?'

'Yes. They're carrying him off for the week-end. Didn't she tell you?'

'She did not.' And Daisy looked rather wildly round the shop, while Willy quietly smiled, and Myra called from the door, 'Daisy, I'm going.'

'I'm coming.' Daisy sounded distracted. 'Look, Myra. Here is the chair that the Lister-Brocks bought.'

'That squat little bandy one,' said Willy. 'Isn't it heavenly?'

Myra, who thought it rather a sinister little chair, said nothing, but Daisy leaned over it, laughing, and stroked its upholstery. 'Goodbye, my darling,' she crooned.

'Look at her,' teased Willy. 'Torn between love and avarice. She'd like to keep them all and live in a warehouse with them and run round all day stroking and petting them and nursing them when they are sick.'

'And so I should,' laughed Daisy.

'Daisy, I shan't wait another second,' declared Myra.

'I'm coming at once.' But Daisy turned instead to Willy. 'Do you think Hal could design screens?'

'Screens?'

'For windows, silly boy.'

'Not for the Dobies' house, I hope?'

'Don't be fantastic. I was thinking of the Lister-Brocks.'

Willy found a drape to adjust. 'Hal does so like to get *paid*. In money, I mean.'

'I should like to put it to Hal myself, Willy, if you don't mind.'

Willy gave a beautiful shrug of indifference, and Myra called vigorously from the doorway. 'Daisy, the Dobies may live in a tent in the bush for all I care. And so may these Lister-Brocks, whoever they may be. I'm going home.'

'At once, at once.' Daisy joined her at the door. 'If you see Hal, Willy . . .'

'Never fear, Daisy dear, I'll tell him.'

In the street, Myra said, 'Is Willy really so capable?'

'He's wonderful. Before I had him I hated to leave the shop.'

'This very dear friend of his . . .' Myra began.

'Oh, I don't think Willy is actually an invert, you know, I really don't. One is not inquisitive about these things, but I've always considered him almost a neuter.'

'A neuter,' Myra repeated, giving Daisy a sidelong look that was most certainly inquisitive, for she was thinking of the odd similarity she had detected in Daisy and Willy.

'It's my opinion,' Daisy went on, 'that poor Willy is

simply a specialist in ideal friendship. For one thing, he's never jealous, not a bit.'

'And this Hal . . .?'

'Now there,' said Daisy severely, 'is a *naughty* boy. Myra, why don't you buy pictures?'

'Because I don't like them,' said Myra.

'You would like Hal's, I'm sure of it. I've never denied his talent. You would love his wonderful little pen and wash drawings. You especially.'

'Why me especially?'

Daisy put a hand on her arm. 'They're so witty. People of discernment are becoming most interested in them.'

'Well, Daisy,' Myra said weakly, 'I don't know.'

'Perhaps I could arrange for you to see some of them.'

'I suppose I could look at them.'

'Then leave it to me.'

Myra, who felt she could safely do this, now hailed a taxi to take them to the parking lot. 'I hope you are going to pay for this taxi, Daisy,' she said sternly, as she ushered her into it.

'Certainly not, dear girl. I am your guest.'

And at the driver, who was looking at her with an appreciative grin, Daisy dropped an eyelid in what may have been a wink.

In Myra's car, Daisy communed with the contents of her handbag, tch-tching over scraps of paper on which she had made notes and giving Ohs and Ahs of comprehension when she succeeded in deciphering them. And although she said several times, 'Do excuse me, dear girl,' Myra was by no means appeased. 'I might be a taxi-driver,' she thought, 'except that she winks at them. Daisy is an opportunist. She doesn't treat Helen like this.'

They were past King's Cross before Daisy shut her handbag, and Myra was sure enough of her attention to ask, 'Daisy, does David ever talk to you about his work?'

'Now you're going to pump me about that Purdy woman,' said Daisy.

'*I* am not above a bit of sensation,' Myra said lightly.

'Nor is anyone else, it seems. Helen was talking about them today. She knew them slightly in London.'

'I knew them slightly here.'

'Odd, how *slightly* everyone knew them. Helen says she's wonderfully pretty. In that newspaper photograph she looked rather German and pudding-y.'

'Pretty is hardly the word,' Myra said carefully, 'and pudding-y certainly isn't. She's the most beautiful woman I've ever seen.'

'Then she must be very foolish indeed,' Daisy said crisply, 'to start with such an asset and to end as she has done. The reason is obvious, of course. In those cases there's only one answer. She must have been silly about men.'

Myra was on the point of saying again, 'Like me,' but remembered that she would be accused, with some truth, of being touchy, so she said instead, 'I suppose you mean she fell in love.'

'I suppose I do,' Daisy mildly agreed.

'She can hardly be blamed for that.'

'I don't blame her for falling in love any more than I should blame her for catching influenza. But when people catch influenza and take no steps to cure it, when they lie down and die of it or allow it to weaken them for life, *then* I should say they were foolish, very foolish indeed.'

Myra gave a sudden shout of laughter. 'Oh, Daisy, do you really believe that love is a disease?'

'A malady,' said Daisy. 'A temporary obsession. And, moreover, often an imaginary malady.'

Myra was silent for a while, then she said quietly, 'Funny, *funny* Daisy.'

The complacency and amusement in her voice made Daisy turn sharply to look at her, but Myra's profile was set steadily to the road ahead, her burnished, austerely-cut profile from which the big, wet, disorganised mouth so strangely blossomed. Daisy was repelled by Myra's mouth. Her eyes instinctively shrank from it and came to rest on the beautiful, consolingly-tailored collar of Myra's suit. 'How well those rich plum colours suit you,' she remarked with genuine warmth.

But Myra brushed this aside to say, 'How odd if I had married David. I almost did, you know. How would you have liked me for a daughter-in-law, Daisy?'

'None better, dear girl,' said Daisy, since it was quite safe to do so.

'No, it wouldn't have done at all, since we were in love. Diseased. Two very sick people. And love's no basis for marriage, is it, Daisy?'

'You believe it is. I believe it isn't.'

'Then tell me what is,' challenged Myra.

'Oh, *some* physical attraction, I suppose. And for the rest, common ambition and . . . I am being quite frank with you . . . money . . .'

'Expediency!' Myra broke in triumphantly, as if the very word were condemnation enough.

'Yes, expediency,' Daisy equably agreed.

'I do think that's rather low, Daisy.'

Daisy gave a good-humoured laugh. 'I know that poor expediency is in very bad repute, but I can never see why. It's simply another name for common sense. It's good enough for most of the affairs of life, but when it comes to choosing a husband or a wife we must throw it overboard. We feel a positive obligation to make up our minds when we're in an abnormal, besotted state. And all because of a romantic fallacy, a fiction for the most part, a phantom . . .'

But Myra broke in again with her condescending laugh. 'Oh, Daisy, there's a whole world of which you know nothing, so many things you don't take into account.'

'Such as love, love, glorious love,' sang Daisy.

'You will never understand,' Myra grandly declared, and: 'Never,' Daisy contentedly echoed.

They were on the crest of a hill. Below them lay the radiant harbour. Myra turned the car and they swooped down towards it. Neither spoke until they were near Daisy's house, when Myra said reflectively, 'Mrs. Purdy has rather a remote air. Not at all the kind of person one would expect to do murder. Not,' she added hastily, 'that I take it for granted she did. I think it's too bad the way everyone seems to do that.'

'Naturally. Murder is so much more exciting than suicide.'

'So David believes it was suicide?'

'I have not the least idea,' said Daisy. She thought it incredibly tactless of Myra to ask such a question.

'*Haven't* you? I should have wormed the whole thing out of him by now.'

'Then you would need more curiosity than I have. And more time, too. You wouldn't believe how seldom David and I have time to talk. We rush, both of us.'

Myra drew into the kerb and shut off the motor. 'Then your lovely house is nothing but a private hotel.' And she ducked her head to peer up at Daisy's house, so beautifully set on its gentle green slope. 'It has such a genuine look,' she said.

'So you see that?' Daisy, remembering that she hoped to sell Myra some of Hal's drawings, checked her look of surprise. 'Very few people see that. It takes discernment. It's a reticent house.'

She sat back, beaming at her reticent house. 'And you're right, Myra. I've allowed it to become nothing but a private hotel. I had such plans, too, but one gets into a groove. Never mind, I shall give a little dinner party soon. For some very dull people,' she added with a sidelong glance at Myra, whom she did not wish to invite.

Myra yawned. 'That will be nice.'

Daisy got out of the car, then bobbed down to smile at Myra. 'Thank you, dear girl,' she said in her warmest voice.

But the sound of a car approaching behind them had made Myra turn her head. 'And here is David,' she said softly.

'Who snubbed you,' smiled Daisy. And to David, who had left his car and was approaching them, touching his hat, she called, 'This girl says you snubbed her, David. She demands an explanation.'

But she was at once aware of their embarrassment, as if she had made a tactless remark, and when David bent to the car and said, 'Hello, Myra,' she felt excluded by their air of gravity. Disturbed by this, she pondered it as she entered the house and went to her bedroom, from where, as she drew the blind, she could see Myra's car, in the front seat of which David and Myra now sat together.

She remembered Myra's laughter on the way home, and it seemed to her now to have been secretive as well as complacent. 'Have they revived that old thing?' she fearfully wondered. 'How very bad for David if they have. He can't afford a thing like that. Not now, not while he's still getting there.'

Behind her, Possie's voice said, 'That job fell through.'

Daisy turned from the window. 'How very disappointing for you, Poss. But I'm sure you'll get another if you keep trying. And probably much, much better than that one.'

'I was sorry,' David said again. 'Even as I walked away I was sorry. On the way downtown I almost turned back to find you, but I had to be in court by ten.'

'It doesn't matter.' Myra was smiling, regarding him with tenderness. 'And if she is acquitted . . .' she began, but he broke in to say, 'I sometimes find myself hoping that she won't be.'

All softness left her regard. 'Can you mean that?' she cried dolefully.

He turned in the seat, very deliberately, until he faced her. 'Myra, you've asked me to be honest with you. I've just been more honest with you than I've ever been with anyone in my life before. Perhaps you don't realise just how honest . . .'

'Oh I know, I know. But can you mean that?'

'Can I help it if I do?'

'No. But oh, I feel sorry for her.'

'So do I,' he retorted gravely.

'If you're her only hope, with your slightly less than grand passion.'

'Ah, so it's grandeur you miss?' He cocked his head, Daisy's gesture, and looked at her with irony. 'I ought to toss away everything I've ever worked for. I expect you would like that.'

'No,' said Myra, then suddenly flashed out, 'But I should like you to be *capable* of it.'

He lowered his forehead to a hand and gave a long low laugh of resignation and amusement, while Myra smiled and took his free hand in hers, delicately circling his wrist with a forefinger and thumb. This hand she lightly shook. 'But at least let me hear you say you love her.'

'You're going too fast,' he said. 'Sometimes I think I do, sometimes I know I do. But at other times I forget the whole thing in a spell of work, then remember it suddenly, and at those times what strikes me is its sheer improbability. I ask myself then how I can — a woman like that.'

Myra noticed how he hovered about the word 'love', never alighting. 'A woman like what?' she asked.

'Darling Myra, don't ask me. I don't know.'

She released his wrist and intertwined her fingers with his. 'These things resolve themselves,' she said soothingly, 'if you let them.'

'You mean if you give in to them.'

'Isn't it sometimes pleasant to float with the stream?' Myra almost dreamily asked. She herself had often done so, and did not choose to remember, for the moment, how battering and bruising this floating could be. '*I* will help you,' she promised in the same dreamy tone. 'If you ever need me, *I* will help you.'

'You help me by letting me talk.' His grasp on her fingers tightened, then became spasmodic, and suddenly he found himself kissing her, there in the parked car, in the daylight, where anyone could see. Nor did he kiss her lightly, but with sensual blindness, and though astonishment at his own behaviour was also present, it did not cause him to stop. It was Myra who broke away, and who even had to struggle a little to do so.

They sat in silence for a while, then he turned to her and put a shaking hand on her knee. On the lateral planes of his forehead two swollen veins were evident and the skin was taut about his eyes, but he smiled as he said, 'I believe I've proved a point. The whole thing is improbable. It happened because I need a woman.'

But without looking at him, Myra retorted, 'Darling, you've proved nothing.' She herself had been astonished by the breakdown in David's usual caution, but it was the locale that had astonished her, not the kiss. She was familiar with the overflow of the first stage of love. 'It often happens that there is some left over for other people,' she explained, but when she saw that he did not understand she broke off, laughing, and slapped her hand down hard on his.

'You're innocent, David. I've never realised it until now. Your work has left you room for nothing else. You're innocent.'

Chapter Nine

'You must be David,' said Hal Bonniface.

David nodded. 'Where's Mother?'

'Out in the kitchen, frightfully angry because Flossie or Dossie or someone has gone out.'

David nodded again, and was about to go when Hal said, 'How's Frau Purdy?'

Hesitating, with his hand holding open the door of Daisy's sitting-room, David asked, 'Who are you?'

'Hal Bonniface.'

'Ah yes, of course.' David's glance took in the sketches spread on the floor and on his mother's desk, but before he could speak Daisy appeared at his side, bearing a kitchen tray on which there was a plate of cold meat, a saucer of pickles, and a percolator of coffee.

'David dear,' she said in greeting, at the same time pushing rather angrily past him.

'Isn't she being tried tomorrow?' asked Hal, who had ignored Daisy's entrance.

'You're a little confused,' David replied. 'It's the Inquest on Richard Purdy that will be held tomorrow.'

'Oh, is that it? I knew Richard well. He was quite marvellous. Oh thank you, Daisy. I adore pickles.'

'Then eat them, for Heaven's sake, and shut up about your stomach. David, get yourself something, will you? Possie's out. Not at my desk, Hal, if you don't mind. I'm using it. Get yourself one of the little tables.'

'I hate those bloody little tables.' And Hal lowered himself on to the floor, cross-legged, the angle of the tray he held not altering by a degree: a very neat boy.

Although David recognised this as one of his mother's crises, he did not go, but lingered in the doorway, his abstracted glance resting on Hal's plate of food.

Hal offered it. 'Have some, David.'

Daisy shot her son a droll look, which changed to one of amazement when he advanced into the room and took a piece of cold meat in his fingers.

'This is very Bohemian,' he said in a bantering voice, and was instantly made uncomfortable by Hal's and Daisy's unshared, quickly curbed smiles. He chewed the meat thoughtfully, then wiped his fingers on his handkerchief and asked, 'Why do you call her Frau Purdy? She's not German.'

'No, but she looks it.'

Daisy bent to her work. 'Purdy Purdy Purdy,' she crossly babbled.

'Richard was marvellous,' said Hal again, 'and terribly clever. He could have done anything.'

'So in the end he did nothing,' snapped Daisy. 'David, don't take the boy's food, or I shall have to go and get him some more. All he's done since he came here is eat.'

They both ignored her. 'What kind of things?' asked David.

'He wrote poetry once,' Hal said tolerantly, 'but he cured himself of that by going to the reading room of the British Museum and other places like that and looking at the stacks and stacks and stacks of books by dead people. Salutary, he said, especially the smell.'

'But wasn't that a *joke*?' asked Daisy.

'No, Daisy, it wasn't. If you said it, it would be, but Richard always said exactly what he meant.'

'A negative type of thinking,' David suggested.

'Oh yes,' Hal agreed with enthusiasm. 'Richard was always negative. He was the least vulgar person I've ever known. Just filling in time until he died.'

'Why live at all?' asked David.

'Well, he didn't, did he? I adore these cheap pickles, Daisy. My mother used to keep a jar of them for the washer-woman.'

'Thank you, Hal.'

'Oh *why* do you always think I'm joking? I meant that.'

David said carefully, 'Then it would be quite in character for him to kill himself?'

'I suppose so, David, but you needn't think I'm going to come and say that in court, because I'm not. But Isobel wouldn't do it, she adored him too much, and God, how she bored him. She's a slave type.' He finished the last slice of meat and added with detachment, 'Lovely colours she has, all pale and pearly.'

Daisy said firmly, 'If you have finished eating, Hal, I should like to show you what I have for Helen's bedroom. Goodbye, David.'

When he had gone, Hal said, 'He's not bad, your David. He's a bit like Lawrence of Arabia, only taller. You know why Lawrence liked those Arab robes, Daisy? Because he had short legs. I saw a picture of him once, in little leather *leggings*, with buckles.'

'Quite so,' Daisy said coldly. 'These panels are to be natural wild silk, Hal, the moulding gold and white, and the carpet the one I showed you. Do be careful not to make it orange. It's apricot, the pink predominant.'

'All right, Daisy.'

'What do you think of it?'

'All right, Daisy.'

'It's traditional, of course, but Helen likes that.'

'That's right, Daisy. I'll do it tomorrow at my place.'

'No you won't. Do it here, now. The work you take home never gets done.'

'I hate working on this potty little desk,' Hal complained, but sat down and began, all the same, while Daisy walked about, looking anxiously at the sketches spread on the floor. No primary theme had presented itself; she had been forced to start without it.

'I'm still not happy about the drawing-room,' she remarked, and noticed as she spoke how strain had flattened and thinned her voice.

Hal agreed without raising his head. 'Such cowardly colours, Daisy.'

Daisy dropped her shoulders and rotated her head, deliberately untensing herself. 'Do you mean those?' She pointed to the sketch Hal was doing. 'Or the drawing-room?'

'Both. But I suppose there's nothing much you can do about this one, since Helen wants it built around that tatty bit of brocade she's going to stick on the bed.'

Daisy made her voice cool and ironical. 'Then perhaps you have some suggestions for the drawing-room?'

But Hal promptly replied, 'No, Daisy darling, that's your business. I'm just here to do the sketches.'

Daisy picked up the sketch of the drawing-room and took it to the window. After she had looked at it for a long time, she said, 'I'm so happy they liked your design for the gazebo, Hal.'

'Yes, they're mad about it,' said Hal, not as if he cared.

'Though why they insist on calling it a gazebo, I really don't know.'

'They're calling it a folly now, Hal's folly, then looking at me as if they expect me to simper. They make me sick.'

Daisy occupied herself in opening the window, partly to draw the deep breath she needed, and partly to cover her lack of a ready answer. She had observed some time ago that the Dobies made Hal sick (though no sicker than anyone else did), but she was yet greatly impressed by his effrontery in making such a remark to her, whom he must surely know for an enemy. Could it be, she wondered, that he thought her influence with Helen and Max of no account? And could it be, she wondered next, that he was right? 'I believe he thinks himself quite safe,' she marvelled, for she had not yet quite taken the measure of Hal's effrontery, nor realised that he did not care how she used her influence with the Dobies, or with anybody else.

'So they make you sick?' she asked, casually enough.

'God yes. Helen's a silly old totty and Max is just as bad. They've got all that culture. They've got so much culture that they can never see anything as a *thing*, alone. It always has to remind them of something else. "Look at those gorgeous Carpaccio colours," says Helen. And Max pretends to lose his temper and says, "Carpaccio? Carpaccio? When did Carpaccio use a blue like that, Helen?" And she says, "But you *must* remember the one with the perfectly gruesome dirty-green canal and all the boys with their ballet legs and the curling-pin curls on their foreheads? Oh Max, you *must*!" And she goes on and on like this until in the end bloody old Max thinks he just *might* remember a blue cap or a feather or something that Carpaccio, whoever he was, probably put in when he was drunk anyway. But he rather thinks it was a *warmer* blue, Helen.'

Here Hal flicked paint from his brush on to the carpet. 'The way they go on, feeding each other lines, you'd think any of that stuff *mattered*.'

From the window, Daisy said, 'Why not do as your friend Richard Purdy did, Hal? Go and stand in an art gallery and cure yourself of drawing? And Hal, would you mind very much not flicking paint on the carpet?'

Hal sucked his brush instead. 'I can't cure myself,' he said gloomily. 'I need the money.'

'Why?'

'To eat.'

'Why?'

'Jokes again, Daisy?'

Possie, who had come in by the back path, was now passing the window, trotting quickly and looking askance at Daisy. Her guilty air irritated Daisy. She did not respond to her wave, but only called, 'David is home, Possie,' before turning to Hal, who was saying, 'And now they want me to go to Europe with them next year.'

'And will you?'

'I said I might if they didn't make me talk about bloody culture all the time.'

'And what did they say to that?'

'They laughed. They're terribly humorous. And when

they'd stopped laughing Max said, "Each man kills the thing he loves." He put on his speechifying voice to say that, so I suppose he was quoting, but don't ask me from whom, I wouldn't know.'

'If they're so repulsive to you, why go to Europe with them?'

'I won't, if I've got any money at the time. But if I haven't, I might as well.'

'Then get some money.'

'*You* give me some, Daisy darling.'

This was perilously near a joke, Daisy thought. 'I was speaking to Myra Magaskill about you,' she said. 'Myra's rather rich. I think she may buy some of your drawings.'

'What's she like? Another old totty?'

'No doubt you will think so. But she's not cultured, I can promise you that. She's emotional, over-sensitive, rather given to striking attitudes...'

Hal gave a deep groan. 'Oh God! I'll tell you what, Daisy. I'll give you a pile of drawings, and *you* show them to her.'

'Very well. Bring them to the shop tomorrow.'

'You can take a commission if you like.'

'I don't want a commission.'

'No,' said Hal, without animosity, 'you'll only want these sketches for nothing, and you'll hope that when I get the money from this mad friend of yours I'll go off on a party and ditch the Dobies.'

There was a short silence, then Daisy said, 'How nicely you put it.'

'Yes, Daisy; but I'm not interested in how I put things, only in the things I put.'

Daisy stood behind his chair, looking over his shoulder. He was working with a pen, in a line nervous and biting, fluid but never glib. And Daisy felt, as she always did, that her own hands commanded the pen, yet knew that they were incapable of it, and that the aching response of her fingers to each line was merely a message from her mind. 'I'll pay you, Hal,' she said, 'of course I shall. And I'll see what I can do about those drawings for Myra, though I can promise nothing.'

It suddenly occurred to her that if Myra would not buy the drawings she could buy a few herself, and add the cost to Max's bill. It would be worth it to send Hal off on a party. 'I'm sure I can find some way to help you,' she said. 'After all, the drawings are splendid.'

'If you like that sort of thing,' said Hal.

'I'm surprised that Max and Helen have bought none.'

'They keep saying they *must*, but of course they won't until they see how I turn out. If they get sick of me they'll pension me off by buying a very small one.' Hal laid down his pen and sat back. 'Now that Flossie's home, Daisy, do you think I could have a hot pie or something?'

He was the most formidable boy she had ever met, Daisy decided as she went to the kitchen. Here she found Possie, who was drinking tea, and who added to her irritation by putting down her cup with a guilty clatter.

'I got caught up,' Possie nervously explained.

'Yes, you did.'

'I asked David if he wanted anything, but he'd had it already, and now he's working.'

'Yes, he had to get it himself.' Daisy was looking in the refrigerator. 'I expect you've been out applying for another job.'

'In a way. Yes, I did go . . .'

'Any success?'

'Well, I could have got it,' lied Possie. 'They wanted me. They were *most pressing*, but I had to tell them that I couldn't start for a while, and that was no good because they wanted someone next week.'

Daisy was silent.

'You told me I couldn't go until you'd finished that house. Remember? You did say . . .'

'Yes, I know. But it's no good leaving everything until the last minute, is it?' Daisy had taken a basin of curried meat from the refrigerator. 'Perhaps I could heat this. I've a boy in there working.'

'You just give that to me.' Possie rose eagerly and grasped the basin, then made a great clatter in taking a saucepan from the cupboard, while under cover of this noise she said, 'Of course, I mightn't go at all.'

'Take it in to him, will you, Poss, when it's hot?'

'Would you mind if I didn't go?'

'We must think about that,' Daisy said pleasantly. 'And Poss, there's a tray in my sitting-room. You might collect that; I forgot it.'

'I didn't actually *resign*,' cried Possie.

But Daisy, who had raised a hand to her left cheek, was now probing its hollow with her fingertips. 'No, not exactly,' she murmured. 'Is this toothache, I wonder, or neuralgia?'

'I've got some Aspros here.'

'I've some upstairs, thank you, Poss.'

'But look, I've got plenty. Look.'

But it was to Daisy's back that Possie was offering the Aspros, and Daisy's only refusal was a dismissive downward gesture of her right hand. Her left hand still probed her face, where she felt, as she ascended the stairs, a single, sharper pain.

At the open door of David's room she stopped. 'Possie is home, David, if you want something hot.'

He raised his head and gave her the bemused look of a man unwilling to relinquish his train of thought. 'No thank you, Mother.' Then with a sharper glance he asked, 'What's the matter?' for she had put her hand to her face again and her eyes were full of tears.

She said slowly, 'Either toothache or neuralgia. Neuralgia, I hope.'

'And toothache, you think,' he said crossly. 'You ought to have had all those top teeth out last year when Cairncross advised it.'

'I can't think what you mean by *all* those top teeth. I have only four. The rest are false. And you know how busy I was last year.'

He laid down his pen, reluctantly. 'Ring Cairncross. Or shall I?'

'There's no point in ringing him. He will want to take them out, and I certainly can't have them out now. I can't be incapacitated at this stage of my work for Max. I'll have to get something strong to take.'

'You already take far too many drugs.'

She laughed. '*Drugs?*'

'Those sleeping pills.'

'Oh, those. Yes, I must stop them.' She dropped her hand. 'You see, it's gone now. It will come and go.'

'It can only get worse.'

'I shan't let it get worse. I shall keep it at bay until it's convenient for me to have them out. And, David, I've just had a talk with Possie. If I can't stop her leaving, I think I may try to get the Hastings' wonderful Latvian couple, the woman for the house and the man for the garden. They say Brian Hastings can't last another month, and Anne will certainly move to a flat. What do you think of the idea?'

'Can't it wait? You can hardly approach Anne now. Brian isn't dead yet.'

'Dear boy, I can prepare the ground. I know it sounds ghoulish, but we must make up our minds.'

David directed a longing glance at his work. 'You handle it, Mother.'

'So easy, after all,' marvelled Daisy. Aloud she said, 'Is that the Purdy brief you're working on?'

'No,' he said, wondering why he lied.

'Her Inquest tomorrow.'

He sighed. 'Not *her* . . .'

'Oh I know, I know. The Coroner's Inquiry or some such thing. Of course I shall give Possie a cheque when she goes. I shall give her a hundred pounds.'

'So shall I, if she goes,' he murmured, and pointedly picked up his pen.

Daisy stood there a moment longer, looking at the top of his head and fingering her cheek again, though the pain had not returned. So cold he seemed, so prim and oblivious of her, that she suddenly felt a temptation to carp, like the mothers she most despised. 'At least have the courtesy to give me your attention,' she wanted to say. 'When I think of the sacrifices I have made for you! Grace Stuckley *begged* me to stay in London, but because I thought you may turn out too small a fish for that pond I came back. I've worked and slaved and all I get in return is rudeness and snubs.'

But she could not allow herself such an outbreak. It was not appropriate to her self-image; it was not her style. She allowed herself only a light coolness. 'I am disturbing you, I see.'

After taking several Aspros in the bathroom she went to her bedroom. 'Flowers Brian. Ring Anne,' she wrote on her memorandum pad. Then she removed her upper plate of false teeth and carefully examined the remaining four with the aid of a small mirror.

There were two molars on either side, all pitted and crowned, all standing high from the shrunken gums. Daisy had never looked at them in her life before, and she could not help thinking that they resembled rotted mooring posts abandoned by the tide. They were so ugly that for a moment her business-like attitude to her appearance failed her. She had to force herself to wipe the misting glass and examine them again.

'Cairncross was right,' she decided at last. 'I must have them out as soon as I've tied Max down with a contract.'

As if for consolation, she tapped with a forefinger the row of sound teeth in her lower jaw. Then she put her false teeth in her mouth again, and at once felt a return of confidence.

David worked late. He was worried about two of his witnesses. Of the men whose addresses Isobel had given him, only these two were prepared to state that Richard Purdy had frequently talked of suicide. Some of the others, whom David had weeded out alone (for Theo had virus influenza and was lying comfortably sick), had been what he termed 'quite decent fellows'. But the quite decent fellows wouldn't play, and David was left with these two, raffines of the worst type, who seemed to welcome the chance of exhibiting themselves in public. Forcing himself to friendliness, enduring their bragging and affections, David had tried to weigh the impression of unreliability they must make against their value as proof of Richard Purdy's own unreliability, for by claiming intimacy with him these men would force the conclusion that like had been attracted by like.

When Theo had at last risen from his sick bed ('Very weak, laddie, very weak') he had said, 'Jesus! Is that the best we can do? Thank God for old Sheila.'

And David, who was not usually influenced by Theo, had begun to vacillate, one day deciding to have these two on hand at the Inquest, the next day deciding against it.

He had at last decided for it. There was now nothing else to do but wait, but he could not wait in peace. Since he had first surprised himself thinking that if Isobel were convicted he would have no problem, guilt had driven him to turn over again and again each scrap of evidence. Even rumour engrossed him. He made guesses at the character of the janitor, as it would show itself in court, and above all at the character of Miss Morrison, Isobel's neighbour, she who had claimed to overhear Isobel's threat to her husband. Such speculation wearied him more than he had ever been wearied by intensive working with facts. Facts moved with their own weight; facts created their own momentum. But character was an unstable element; character was prone to show itself different from day to day.

About midnight he went to his window and received on his face a flow of air fresh yet warm. 'Summer will be early,' he thought, and found his mind wandering to pleasant things. All anxiety left him, and a feeling of resignation, almost of indifference, took its place. Supporting himself with an elbow against the window frame and yawning as if he would never stop, he assured himself that he was doing his best. 'And no man can do more.'

Chapter Ten

THE day of the Inquest was a summer's day so sudden that only the young girls were dressed for it. They shuttled through the sober city crowd in a brilliant and unbroken thread, their bright hair bouncing, their bare arms swaggering, and their legs snipping and flickering beneath short tight skirts. This was their weather, and they made the city under this weather their scene. They compelled the attention, and with their image still imprinted on his vision David found it strange to be confronted with Isobel. In her softer, older, more voluminous clothes, with her tired grace and her tender flushed skin, she seemed not only foreign to the place and climate, but to the age.

'I didn't know you in that thing at first,' she said, and David touched his wig and did not know what to say. The carelessness of her tone told him that in the past weeks, when neither had seen the other, their intimacy had yet advanced. He knew that while he had been thinking of her, so had she been thinking of him. Their preliminaries had been played out in absence and silence.

From the echoing courtroom above their heads he heard the dragging of a chair. 'There's one point I should like to make,' he said.

She smiled. 'What?'

She was pinning her knot of hair, and he thought the white undersides of her arms very beautiful, emerging from the sleeves of soft tan silk. 'I'm not asking you to weep when you go up there,' he said. 'I'm not asking you to put on an act. But on the other hand I don't want you to look as if you couldn't care less. You have a habit of looking indifferent. Try not to.'

But her answering shrug was indifferent. 'I can only do my best.'

This was so much an echo of his own feeling of resignation and irresponsibility that he almost laughed as he replied, 'Well then, we must both simply do our best.'

And in the courtroom an hour later he whispered to Theo Cass, 'Yes, I spoke to her about it. She promised to do her best.'

'Is that her best?' Theo gloomily responded, for Isobel, touching her hair and looking expressionlessly about her, had an air not only of indifference, but of disdain. She touched her hair, she examined her nails, and when she yawned Theo said softly, 'Ouch!'

'I could only tell her,' said David, stifling a yawn of his own.

The doctor was telling his story in a hurried conversational voice, inaudible to the spectators, who were showing restlessness. Those of them who had come expecting drama were dismayed by the shabby little courtroom, the casual-seeming troupe of actors, and by all the mumbling and cross-talk that went on. And Isobel herself was the worst disappointment of all. Because the newspapers had called her beautiful, dazzlement was expected of her. But Isobel's beauty, so much a matter of delicate moulding and textures, of muted and exquisite colours, was not the kind that carries far. All they saw was a tall pale woman dressed in an old-fashioned suit of brown silk, who shed no tears and who seemed to be thinking of other things, who even yawned, and whose chief concern, indeed, seemed to be with her hair, which tended to slip from its knot.

Only a minority of the spectators, all elderly men, sat quietly with folded arms, and sometimes sagely nodded. These were the old hands, the courtroom connoisseurs. Familiar with the rules of the game, they would give their approval only to finely scored points. But the others, the amateurs, awaited sensation.

It was not until late that afternoon that Miss Morrison gave it to them. Standing there in the witness box, thin, her cropped grey hair stiff as a toothbrush, she suddenly screamed. Everyone looked up. Everyone was still. And into the silence she released a second scream, abbreviated but wilder. These were opening chords; the torrent followed.

'What's true and what isn't? How do I know? How do I know? They've got me confused. I can't remember. It's too far back. God sees everything.'

'Miss Morrison . . .'

'Last night I prayed, and a voice said, "God sees everything." And Edie's been at me, telling me I'm always imagining things. Nobody but Edie thinks that, but it might be true. How do I know? She said it's because I never liked them, with their drink and their dressing-gowns. And *that's* true. She never even said hello. The English aren't like us,' screeched Miss Morrison above the babble of voices and the orderly's cry.

Beat down at last by this cry, she collapsed into sobs. They led her away, but as she went she gasped back into the courtroom, 'I didn't do wrong. Everyone knows she killed him. But Edie says . . .'

Who was Edie? Nobody knew. In all his guessing David could never have arrived at the hidden factor of Edie. On the table before him was a stack of books. He lifted the cover of the top book, held it, then let it heavily drop, while Theo said in his ear, 'One doll down.'

'There seems to be a certain amount of sympathy brewing for your gorgeous client,' Daisy remarked that night.

'What makes you think so?'

'The chattering of tongues, dear boy.'

'What do they say?'

'I shall tell you if you promise not to be testy.'

'Of course I shan't be.'

'Well, they're saying that they *suppose* she did it, but that *really* the police ought not to have charged her without a stronger case.'

'Do you call that sympathy?'

'You're right. It's indignation. But sympathy follows. Sympathy hovers. I can sense these things. I can pluck public opinion from the air. It's always been a wonderful asset to me in business. What a pity you haven't inherited it. I can't think of anything more useful in politics.'

'Do these talkative friends of yours realise . . .'

'You promised not to be testy.'

'. . . that only part of the evidence has been heard? I'm not testy.'

'You sound it. I don't know whether they realise that or not. And in any case — who knows? — there may be a swing against her tomorrow,' said Daisy cheerfully.

'I shall trust you to keep me informed.'

'By all means, dear boy, by all means.'

On the following day David offered evidence of Richard Purdy's former suicide attempt. The chemist said yes, he remembered the cuts, one shallow cut on each wrist. He had suspected the explanation Richard Purdy had given, which had been something garbled about broken glass. 'I could never follow him,' rather whined this neat young man. 'He always sounded silly or drunk or both.'

Richard Purdy's two friends remembered the bandages, and to one of them Richard Purdy had extended his wrists and said, 'Botched it again.' But he had not taken much notice, this man said, and when asked by the prosecutor why he had not, he shiftingly admitted that it was because he suspected Richard Purdy of putting on an act.

'You thought him a fake?'

'In some ways, yes.'

'He would talk of suicide?'

'Yes.'

'But not commit suicide?'

'Well, they don't usually, not when they talk about it first.'

'When he spoke of suicide, did you think there was any danger that he would commit suicide?'

He had to say it. 'No.'

Both these witnesses, unexpectedly awed, suppressed their braggadocio and answered briefly and hesitantly, making neither of the impressions David had hoped for. Only Sheila Jack stood firm, speaking loudly and with great emphasis, her only fault being a tendency to directly harangue the Coroner. 'He was crippled, mentally crippled. He wasn't to blame. He was a poor, crippled man.'

Her manner was in direct contrast to David's, whose curious feeling of yielding to events had caused him to adopt a manner low-toned, careless, and tired. He began by resignedly thinking of it as his poor best, but before the day was out he knew that he had by accident alighted on the best, the very best, manner for the occasion. He seemed to be offering a truth too evident to need emphasis, and Theo Cass, narrowing his eyes, admitted to himself that Byfield could put it across.

'Might pull this off,' he said to David, 'now that Purdy's stopped yawning.'

For Isobel, who had begun the day stiffly enough, had been beaten down by the words of David's succession of witnesses. Down, down, she drooped, like a plant slowly losing sap, until in the end she presented no separate features, only this wounded posture that was confirmed rather than contradicted by her prosaically clasped hands and by the neat and obedient placement of her feet. These were relics of her former composure, forgotten by her. Between them, her body flowed into collapse.

Yet it was embarrassment rather than sympathy that this attitude aroused. Pride was still apparent, and her wound a private one. Voices seemed unnaturally quiet or too deliberately loud. There might have been a corpse in the room, forcing unwilling observance.

And it was in almost the same attitude that David and Theo found her in an adjournment. She would look at neither of them, and would only say, 'When does it end? When can I go back there?'

'Will she last it out?' asked David in the corridor. 'She looks sick.'

'I'm scared to look at her,' Theo replied. 'Eyes right, that's me, or you say I'm leching.'

They emerged into sunlight, and Theo clapped his hat on his head. 'But by *God*, I could go for her.'

'And what are your voices in the air saying today?' David asked his mother that night.

'Oh, *today*! They are rather amused today. They are saying that to get away with murder there are two things you need — good looks and a smart lawyer. Meaning you, I fear. I have never cared for that word, *smart*. It suggests trickery, charlatanism.'

'I've heard you called smart.'

'So I am, dear boy. But you and I are travelling different roads. I can afford to be called smart. You can't, at least not too often.'

'You've very strict ideas of what I can afford and what I can't.'

'I admit it,' said Daisy, and fastidiously probed her cheek. Pain had broken through her barrier of drugs. But her gesture was unnoticed by David. He had forgotten her teeth. And when she said, 'I shall see Cairncross tomorrow,' he only replied abstractedly, 'Do that.'

It was Cairncross who told Daisy of the Coroner's finding. He spoke in small bursts, between probing and peering. 'That son of yours — is a smart lawyer — Mrs. Byfield — Don't close up. Open — I've not known that — to happen for years.'

'Wha?' Daisy angrily gasped.

'Usually it's — a foregone conclusion. Yes, yes . . .' Cairncross took his probe from her mouth and said briskly, 'Three of them must come out. There's no point in leaving one.'

'No. One out, all out. What's a foregone conclusion?'

'That the Coroner will support the police charge.'

'Didn't he?'

'He found that the fellow had died from gas poisoning, but whether self-administered or otherwise he could not say.' Cairncross laughed appreciatively. 'They had the stove there in the court. It was very smart work. I'll take an impression of your mouth and we'll make up a study model. Can you have them out next week?'

'Goodness, no. Not until November.'

'I strongly advise . . .'

'Mr. Cairncross, I said November.'

Cairncross shrugged. 'Please yourself, Mrs. Byfield,' he said coldly.

. . . . .

'I had to go. Cleo's having her pups,' said Sheila Jack, 'but thank goodness I got back in time to take you home.'

Isobel sat on a bench in the police room, her shoulders hunched, her feet together, and a small suitcase on the floor by her side. To Sheila she had yielded her hands as if they were two detached objects, nothing to do with her, and Sheila, pressing and squeezing these lifeless objects, exclaimed that it was too wonderful. 'I never dared to hope for this. Never.'

'I thought there was to be a trial,' said Isobel, dull and puzzled.

'No trial. You're free, my dear, free. And you can thank Mr. Byfield and Mr. Cass.'

Isobel transferred her gaze to the two men. No gratitude was evident. David stood with his hands clasped at his back. Theo bowed.

'And you can bring a charge for wrongful arrest,' Sheila cried happily. Her consolatory purpose forgotten, she now pumped Isobel's hands up and down. 'And *that* will settle the business once and for all.'

'It's not important,' said Isobel.

'Not *important*! Mr. Byfield, persuade her.'

'No, Mrs. Jack.'

'Then you must, Theo.'

'God, no,' laughed Theo. 'Let well enough alone.'

Sheila was still holding Isobel's hands, but absent-mindedly now. 'What's the matter with you all? Isn't this thing *good*?'

'It's very good indeed,' David said quickly. But he wondered why there was no triumph, only this sense of bewilderment and even of defeat. It was Isobel, of course, he thought resentfully, she was one of those people who selfishly impose their own feelings on those about them.

'Well then, well then,' wailed Sheila, and suddenly turned again to Isobel. 'Isobel, for your own sake, you must bring that charge. You're tired. You're sick. But that's why I'm here, to do your fighting for you.'

But Isobel averted her head and pulled her hands from Sheila's grasp. 'Go away, Sheila,' she said. 'You smother me.'

It was Theo who broke the silence that followed this. 'Mrs. Jack was only trying to help you,' he said.

'It's all right, Theo.' Sheila sent him a smile. 'She's sick. She's not herself. Come home with me now, Isobel, and we'll talk this over in the morning.'

'I'm not sick. You believe everyone is sick. And I'm not coming to your house with you. Please go away.'

Sheila looked rather helplessly round at them all, even at the Sergeant, who stood with his back to them, looking in a filing cabinet. 'Then where will you go?' she asked.

But Isobel would not reply to this, and at last Sheila began to make her way falteringly to the door, which David, intercepting her, quickly opened. Ushering her almost surreptitiously into the empty corridor, he said in a low voice, 'I'm sorry about that.'

'I didn't expect gratitude, Mr. Byfield. Helping others ought to be its own reward, and that's how I try to look at it. It's not myself I'm worried about, it's her. She can't go back to her flat, not in that state. Where will she go?'

It was with this question that David addressed her as soon as he returned to the police room. 'The rent of our flat is paid until the end of the year,' she coldly replied. 'I shall go back there.'

Theo was sitting beside her on the bench, his elbows on his spread knees, his hands rotating his hatbrim. 'I've been offering her a lift,' he said in a joking tone, looking not at David, but at her.

She looked at neither of them. 'I'll get a taxi,' she said.

'Can't let her do that, can we?' Theo asked in the same joking tone.

David crossed over to them. 'It's out of Mr. Cass's way, but it's not out of mine. Perhaps I could drive you,' he casually suggested.

'Very well,' she said, so promptly that David moved to the window to avoid Theo's amused glance. It was not until he heard the door close that he took a place on the bench, about a yard from her. They had still to wait until the spectators and photographers should grow tired and leave the outlets of the building, and during this hour David ignored her completely, but talked with almost feverish amiability to the Sergeant and to the other policemen and clerks who came and went.

. . . . .

'I'm glad,' said Myra, 'so glad she got off.'

'Female trade unionism,' said Hughie. He was in a good mood. They were driving to a party, and he was pleasantly conscious of their knees; his in worthy black, Myra's in light and lifting chiffons. He was pleased, too, that the car was upholstered not in plastic, but in leather. In this light there was no difference to the eye, but in any light there was a difference in Hughie's mind. 'You can't beat quality,' he said to himself.

Myra said, 'And I was right. The police *do* make mistakes.'

'Who said they made a mistake?'

'The Coroner and I,' Myra said smugly.

'Sweetie, he did no such thing. He merely found that the evidence wasn't strong enough to support the charge.'

'Is that how you interpret it, Hughie?'

'That's how most people will interpret it,' said Hughie.

Myra was silent. She averted her face to gaze through the window, which was sometimes sheeted with light, but which sometimes, when backed by darkness, gave her back her grave and pensive face.

'Dud Henderson rang me today,' said Hughie in a gratified voice, 'especially to ask if we would be there tonight.'

He was amazed when instead of replying to this Myra said loudly and flatly, 'Let us be kind.'

'Kind?' echoed Hughie.

She struck her knee with a clenched fist. 'Let us be kind!' she cried. 'At least let us be kind!'

They had stopped for a red light, and Hughie saw that the occupants of the car abreast of them were both amused and startled by this ringing plea. 'Shush,' he said. 'Later,' he pleaded.

'Now what's the matter?' he asked, when they were moving again.

'Nothing,' she said dully.

But presently she began to cry, and they had to pull into a side street, where Hughie, telling her she could not *possibly* appear like that, dried her eyes and tenderly repaired her make-up.

She was a little softened by these ministrations. 'And yet,' she said restlessly, 'sometimes you're nice.'

'That's my girl.'

'I don't want to go tonight. Not tonight. Let's go home.'

'There's nothing I should like more,' said Hughie with carefully calculated regret. 'But Dud said he wouldn't go unless we did. Can't let Dud down.'

'No,' sighed Myra. 'Not old Dud.'

· · · · ·

In David's stationary car, Isobel said, 'I'm sorry about all that.'

'Don't be,' David responded, as stiffly as she.

'I thought I could. But when we got there, I simply couldn't.'

'I understand. But you do realise that those people at the door will have gone by now?'

'Yes, I suppose so.' But she sounded as if she did not believe this, as if she fancied that the small but unmistakably avid group, and the running figures, carrying cameras, that had instantly detached themselves from it, would be there for ever.

'Then shall we try again?' asked David.

'Tomorrow, the next day. Not tonight. I can't.'

'Then where can she go tonight?' David wondered again. He thought of Myra, then of Hughie, and dismissed his half-formed hope.

Since Isobel's cry of panic as they neared the block of flats they had driven a long way in silence: he wondering where to take her; she sleeping, or perhaps only stupefied. They had stopped once, when David, hoping to revive her, had gone to buy sandwiches and tea, which he had brought to her in the car. But even while eating and drinking she had seemed half-asleep, and he himself had been able to eat nothing, so harassed he had been, so nervously aware of the passers-by and of the light of the full moon striking into the car, revealing her chin, mouth, and wearily-moving hands.

But here the moon showed only, far below them, the unfaltering curve of a yellow beach. It was only when he had stopped here that she had emerged from her stupor and had begun to talk in this staccato way, while he sat as far away from her as the width of the seat allowed, aware of the tension of unfulfilment rising like a thorny hedge between them, longing to broach it, yet dreading to begin.

'I wish you felt able to go to Mrs. Jack,' he said. 'Perhaps you do, now?'

Isobel sat with her head bent, meaninglessly plucking and pulling at the skirt tautened over her thighs. 'I can't,' she said stubbornly.

Through David's mind there flitted the thought that for someone in her position she was pretty damned choosy. He sat humped and silent, watching her hand, abstractedly at first, then with such a rush of irritation at its silly, feverish plucking and pulling that he reached over and roughly stilled it with one of his.

Touch at once performed its magic, so quickly dispelling the tension between them that it seemed not only easy, but natural, to move along the seat and put his arms around her.

He drew two deep, sighing breaths, and they sat quite still for a long time. Then he began to rub his cheek against her hair, almost thoughtfully at first, as if to assess its texture, then with increasing force and momentum until the doubt raised by her lack of response caused him to stop, to put a hand on her forehead and press her head away from his so that he could see her face.

Because his body blocked the low-striking moonlight, her face was only dimly visible, but enough to show him that her eyes were closed, and to show him also his own dark, skeletal hand laid so incongruously across her forehead, between her pale soft hair and her pale soft eyelids.

At first sight both face and hand looked utterly unfamiliar to him. Then, with one of those abrupt transposals experienced by children when, having seen that the stain on the wall is shaped like a bird, they can no longer see it as anything but a bird, face and hand became most intensely her face, his hand; each member the essence of each self.

It was then that the first real shock of contact with her took place. He murmured incoherently and said her name, scarcely noticing and not caring that she did not move nor respond, until she jerked her head impatiently away from beneath the pressure of his hand. His voice died uncertainly away then, and he released her. Yet he was not at all surprised when she at once moved her head blindly towards his and set her mouth with gentle skill against his own.

. . . . .

'I think I had better take you home with me,' said David.

He had offered to pin up her hair, but to attach each loose strand to that great central knot was harder than he had imagined. She sat still, her neck bent submissively to his hands. 'Do you live alone?' she asked.

'No, with my mother.'

'Will she mind putting me up?'

'I think she might, but it doesn't matter.'

It was wonderful how easily soluble the problem of where to take her had become. 'You ought to get this stuff cut,' grumbled David, then added quickly, 'I don't mean that. Don't get it cut.'

Her laugh surprised him. Low and sustained, it was a laugh of pleasure, not of mirth. Thinking of this laugh, he said, 'You know, I've a hell of a lot of things to ask you.'

She did not reply, and though she sat perfectly still, he felt that she had withdrawn herself from him, as she had done at the prison.

'I'm not much good at this hair business,' he said, 'but it's better than it was. Turn round.'

But she only half-turned, and looked not at him, but out through the windscreen of the car.

'No. Look at me.'

She turned unwillingly, and they exchanged a long look, of calculation on his part, of caution on hers.

'Just tell me one thing,' he said.

'What?'

But he only said helplessly, 'Oh, my dear girl,' and they fell silently and spontaneously into an embrace, each with a hand on the other's shoulder, their bowed heads lightly touching.

'Thank you,' she said formally.

. . . . .

'Did he say anything about having dinner out?' asked Possie.

Wearing a plastic apron, she stood in the doorway of Daisy's sitting-room, where Daisy sat at her desk. From a tall lamp at her side the light fell upon the accounts she was checking and upon her wrinkled, disciplined hands. She did not speak or look up until she had finished sorting these accounts into two bundles, on the smaller of which she then placed a hand and said, 'People think I have money to burn. But look at these. All these I must regard as hopeless.'

'You mean they won't ever pay?'

'Never.'

'So much for the rich!' declared Possie with sycophantic indignation. 'They've no principle,' she cried.

'It's not the principle of the thing, it's the money. I might as well tear them up.'

She did not do so, however, but put them carefully to one side and busied herself with the others.

Possie said, 'What about his dinner?'

'Don't fuss. He's not a child. Go to bed if you're tired.'

'Oh, that's all right,' Possie said quickly. Having asked Daisy if she might stay with her, receiving no pay and drawing the pension, and having received no reply except that it did not seem a *frightfully* good idea, she felt that she could afford to take no chance of displeasing. Her venture into the labour market had terrified her. 'It's you that should be in bed,' she said, 'with that toothache.'

'My teeth aren't aching, not a bit. I got some magic pills from Doctor Hollis.' And with a gesture that plainly said, 'Interview over,' Daisy picked up her pen.

This preoccupation was assumed. As soon as Possie went she laid down her pen, touched her cheek, and frowned. An hour ago, she had learned that the Dobies had gone to Melbourne. 'How like Max,' she thought, 'to get me to rush those designs through, then to run away without looking at them.'

Hal had also disappeared, but Daisy refused to connect the two events. All she would allow herself to think was that Hal might have had the grace to leave those drawings for Myra before going off on one of his parties.

She now had the reckless idea of making a design for the gazebo herself — much, much better than Hal's — and presenting it to Max when he returned. But the fact that Tina

Grey would have to do the sketch discouraged her, though not as much as her suspicion that she was incapable of doing a design even as good as Hal's, to whose inconsequential talent the notion of the gazebo was so well suited.

She stood up, unbuttoned her jacket, and took several deep deliberate breaths, raising her arms with each intake. Then, bending from the waist, she allowed herself to droop until her loosely swinging hands just touched the carpet. She stayed like this for a full minute, telling herself firmly that she was relaxed, relaxed, that she was a rag doll. Then she drew herself upright, feeling refreshed in spite of the stab of pain caused by the rush of blood to her head.

This rush of blood had also deafened her to the footsteps on the path outside, so that she was still buttoning her jacket when David appeared in the doorway, a woman at his side. He raised a hand, flicked on the concealed lighting, and said, 'Mother, this is Isobel Purdy.'

Only the shortest of silences followed this, and even that Daisy was able to account for by a short-sighted look, as if the pause were merely to allow her to focus her eyes. Once aware of the need to gather her forces, to brace herself, she could always do so quickly. There was no fumbling as she finished buttoning her jacket and advanced towards them, on her face the lively little smile, with its hint of enquiry, that she used when an unknown customer walked into her shop. And although in this case it was not Isobel's spending power she was questioning, but her very presence, she put on her richest voice, as she also did on those occasions.

'How do you do, Mrs. Purdy,' she almost sang.

Isobel, advancing with David's hand at her back, murmured the customary reply. She had slept heavily in the car on their return journey, and now looked about her like a sleep-walker, stunned and uncaring.

Daisy did not shake hands with those strange customers. For a handshake she had no precedent. By the time her hand had touched Isobel's, and had fallen lifelessly away, their enmity was established.

The longer, denser silence that followed this exchange was broken by Daisy, who sent into it one of her little laughs. 'But do come in and sit down. You look so very tired. David!' This last was an admonishment, for David also seemed stunned, standing there so tentatively, looking about the room as if some recent experience had estranged him from it. 'David,' she repeated, 'perhaps Mrs. Purdy would like to take off her coat.'

If it occurred to David that his mother was stressing the brevity of Isobel's visit by letting her take her coat off in the sitting-room, he gave no sign of it. He obediently turned to Isobel. 'Yes, let me take it. It's warm in here after the car.'

As soon as their attention was withdrawn, Daisy's eyes, always wonderfully rapid in appraisal, darted over Isobel from head to foot. The removal of the light coat revealed a shabby suit of tan silk. It was not even well-cut, Daisy decided, but at the same time she had to admit that on Isobel it had a kind of perverse appeal. Its absence of pride gave her astonishing beauty an air of being casually carried. Fortified by art, it would have been almost too emphatic.

It was a beauty that Daisy at once associated with the eighteenth-century miniatures of France: the enormous eyes, the delicate brows, the small, curling mouth, the white arms. But it lacked the smiling ease of the miniatures, their air of independence, levity, and wit.

Isobel was vaguely smiling. With a weary gesture she removed her hat and handed it to David; and: 'My God!' thought Daisy. 'What hair! One forgets the appeal of long hair.'

'You have very beautiful hair, Mrs. Purdy,' she said.

Isobel responded to this by smiling politely. She touched her hair. Their eyes met for a moment. Daisy's were inquisitive; Isobel's were blank. 'She is one of those women who drift with the tide,' Daisy found herself thinking. 'She's supine, a person to whom things happen.'

Feeling herself threatened by hysteria, she turned to her desk, where she collected her accounts blindly but with apparent dexterity. 'I wish you would both sit down,' she said.

David settled Isobel into a chair as if she were a big doll, but Daisy was interested not so much in his solicitude as in his efforts to disguise it with jocular remarks. Alarm and humiliation contended for possession of her mind: alarm at their intimacy, the secret smiles they exchanged; humiliation at her own folly in fearing Myra. David's recent outbursts, moods, and silences now shuttled about and fell into place, forming at last their undeniable pattern.

'Mother,' said David, 'may I see you for a minute?'

Blinking at him, Daisy slowly closed the drawer of her desk. 'Certainly, dear boy. Mrs. Purdy, perhaps you would like a drink?'

Isobel raised a hand, but no words came. She lowered the hand and closed her eyes.

'Has she fainted?' Daisy asked sharply, halting in front of her.

David leaned over her. 'Isobel.'

She opened her eyes. 'I'm all right,' she said.

'Reaction,' said David. Very lightly, he touched the back of her hand with his. 'Mother,' he said, with a jerk of his head towards the door.

They went into the hall, David leading the way, while Daisy, as she walked behind him, said meditatively, 'Well, well. A bloody fairy princess.'

David had never heard his mother swear before, but he did not turn his head, and she allowed herself a flash of spite as she addressed his moving back. 'But rather a bedraggled one. Did someone leave her out in the rain?'

He stopped and turned to face her in the darkness of the hall, for though the light switch was near at hand, he did not turn it on. 'I feel very sorry for her,' he said.

'And you call her Isobel?'

'Yes, I call her Isobel.'

He sounded so matter-of-fact that for one moment Daisy wondered if she could be mistaken after all — a hope that died so quickly that her voice was sardonic when she said, 'Then it was pity that made you bring her here?'

He hesitated. 'Not entirely.'

'Then why?'

David sounded trapped, she was pleased to hear. 'Surely you could see for yourself,' he said.

'Yes, dear boy, but I long to hear you say it.'

'It's unnecessary.'

'Are you ashamed of it?'

'Certainly not.'

'Uncertain of it, then?'

Very coldly, he said, 'I am in love with her.'

A little hoot of laughter escaped Daisy. In the darkness, she felt his eyes upon her, and imagined their expression, the outraged one with which she was so familiar. 'I'm sorry,' she said, 'but it was such a chilly declaration. And really, I can't believe you mean it.'

'I do, Mother,' he said unhappily.

'Listen,' Daisy began. She put a hand flat against his chest, and suddenly felt not only panic, but a sense of loss. It was with an effort that she kept her voice light and cajoling. 'Listen, you want me to put her up, don't you?'

'Yes. She went back to her flat, but when it came to the point she couldn't go in. I've had a devil of a time, Mother, wondering what to do with her.'

She knew that if she did not respond to this appeal she would certainly alienate him. 'Yes, yes,' she murmured, and patted his chest consolingly, at the same time sending glances around the hall, from which, as her eyes became accustomed to the darkness, objects began to emerge: the drawing-room door, a fall of drapery, white tiles. But these familiar objects brought neither help nor comfort. Moreover, David was saying, 'And could she have something to eat, do you think, before she goes to bed?'

'Now just a moment,' said Daisy. 'You can't expect me to take this in all at once. I'm not a conventional woman, you know that. It's not the murder charge I'm thinking of,

121

although of course that must be taken into account. To ignore it would be childish. But what amazes me, what has quite thrown me, is that you should choose such a woman, such a . . .' She broke off and began to laugh in such faithful imitation of mirth that its gasps and gurgles impeded her next words. 'Do forgive me, Davy dear, but she's so very *dead*, such a big *doll*.'

'You make no allowance for the ordeal she's suffered,' he said curtly. 'And in any case, the only issue at the moment . . .'

But she would not let him continue. Peal after peal of laughter, a great relief to her, rang through the hall.

David grasped her arm, but refrained from shaking it. He brought his face close to hers and said angrily, 'The important thing now is to get her to bed.'

Daisy let her laughter subside. 'Yes, of course,' she agreed in a voice convincingly weakened by laughter. 'I'll get Possie. I do hope *she* hasn't gone to bed. She will be thrrr-illed.'

They parted just in time, for Daisy could not have sustained this pose much longer, and it was with a set and serious face that she mounted the stairs. 'David is innocent,' she decided with real astonishment. 'Yes, innocent. People have brought their troubles to him. He has listened to stories of greed and passion and treachery. But those were other people's experiences, and other people's experiences have no bite.'

Fear possessed her, and after fear, fury. Halfway up the stairs she halted, leaning on the banister as if she could not go on. The ruthless demands of self-improvement had made her life like a play in which she was both actress and director. Whatever she did, she watched herself doing. But now this consciousness of self was suspended for a moment. Resorting to an early, long-suppressed idiom, she whispered, 'The hide of her, coming here! The *hide* of her!'

Light suddenly flowed down to her. 'Were you calling?' quavered Possie from above her.

'Poss,' said Daisy, and climbed the last few steps. 'Oh, Poss.'

'I know,' whispered Possie. 'I saw them come in.' As Daisy had predicted, she was thrilled. Her eyes were most eagerly scandalized. 'The way they were walking,' she went on, 'I could tell it wasn't just, wasn't only . . .'

Daisy put a hand on her wrist. 'Oh, Poss,' she wailed.

Certain now of Daisy's stand in this matter, Possie flung an arm round her. 'Never you mind! He'll come to his senses.'

'But she has to have something to eat.'

'A murderess. It's a shame.'

'Shush, Poss.'

'Her coming here!'

But Daisy was already regretting the temporary weakness that had made her seek Possie's support at a time like this, when Brian Hastings was all but dead, and the wonderful Latvian couple were almost hers. 'Well, since she's here, we must feed her,' she said. 'What is there, Poss?'

'Never you mind that. I'll get her something. Oh, the cheek! I can't get over it.'

All this indignation did nothing to prepare Daisy for Possie's meeting with Isobel, which took place a few minutes later. It was like a falling in love. Forgotten was all Possie's moralizing, all her plans to use the incident for her own ends. Isobel was so beautiful, in such obvious distress, that Possie capitulated instantly. With a joyful cry of, 'Oh, you poor thing,' she almost ran to the kitchen, where she excitedly heated some soup, into which she beat an egg while sippets of bread browned in the pan.

The soup revived Isobel. Absently but with grace, she thanked Daisy and apologised for her former stupor. 'It was the effect of your very pretty room. It was like hacking one's way through a jungle, then coming suddenly to a clearing.'

David, who had been watching her rather broodingly, recognised this as her professional hostess manner. He was pleased, and shot a glance at his mother, who was answering Isobel most pleasantly.

'You're looking much better, Mrs. Purdy. But please don't get up in the morning. Possie will bring you a tray. Won't you, Possie?' she added sardonically, for the sight of Possie hanging over Isobel, clucking with pleasure and anxiety, irritated her very much indeed.

When Isobel had gone to bed, attended by Possie, David looked at his mother. 'Well?'

She shrugged. 'A *talking* doll.'

'You're grossly unfair,' said David. But he was still looking pleased, still smiling.

Daisy raised a hand and looked haughtily at her fingernails. 'Like shopwomen used to do,' she suddenly thought, and folded her hands firmly behind her back, wondering why this old extinguished habit should have returned to her. She said, 'Yes, she's very beautiful, and she walks and talks. Also, she's slovenly, dresses in shocking taste, has no money, and has been charged with murder.'

'The charge was withdrawn.'

'She was charged, charged, charged. Nothing will ever alter that fact.'

Both were silent for a while. Daisy tidied her desk with unusual fussiness, while David stared over his steepled fingers, not at her. Presently he said, 'People forget these things.'

'Not the people you need. They can't afford to. They have to play safe. Climbers, the lot of them. Like you, dear boy. Like me. Climbers.'

David laughed, brought his hands to his knees with a decisive slap, and got up. 'I think you're warped, and I think you're hard.'

'Certainly I'm hard. Softness is not admirable, in my opinion. Look about you. Look at the soft people. Possie is soft. Myra is soft. And your Isobel, she is soft.'

'Yes,' agreed David, with a look so transported that Daisy gave an exclamation half of amusement, half of disgust.

'You're quite besotted,' she snapped.

He smiled. 'I'm damned hungry.'

'There's a casserole. Will she leave in the morning?'

'Not until she has somewhere to go. She can't go back to that flat.'

'And you take my consent for granted?'

'Certainly. Or I shouldn't have paid you the compliment of bringing her here.'

'*Very* adroit,' murmured Daisy, touching her face.

'Have you seen Cairncross? You're looking ill.'

'I? I have never been better in my life. It's *you* who is ill, my poor boy.'

Isobel went to bed in a rather bare bedroom, from which Daisy had recently sold the dressing table and a cedar chair.

'Sorry it's not nicer for you, love,' said Possie, 'but after what you've been through I daresay you'd sleep any old place.'

In a white nightgown, with her hair down her back, Isobel looked like an angel, Possie thought. 'She can't have done it,' she decided.

She clapped her hands together. 'Now into bed with you,' she cried.

When Isobel was in bed, Possie looked critically round the room. 'Just a jiff,' she said. But by the time she returned with a vase of flowers from her bedroom Isobel was asleep.

Possie stood by her bedside for some time, murmuring 'Poor love,' and treating herself to a daydream in which Isobel and David were married. She gave them three blond children and a serene house that would be a haven for her own old age.

But as she returned downstairs, into Daisy's orbit, she thought, 'It's no good. She'll never let them.'

She found Daisy in the kitchen, heating the casserole.

Into the accusing silence, Possie said, 'It was only common humanity, after all.'

Daisy placed a tablespoon delicately on the sink. 'Possie, there is one thing I will *not* stand, and that is disloyalty.'

But she had hardly finished speaking before she recognised this as another voice from her past. 'That's exactly what I used to say to those girls when I was head of China and Glass in Bently and West's,' she recalled with horror.

Two hours later, lying stiffly in bed, Daisy said to herself, 'How very tasteless of David.'

The sound of David's footsteps in the corridor, the sibilant whispers, the softly closed door, had filled her with a sense of outrage which she was now trying to transform into indignation at a breach of good taste. She could be tolerant of sex in the abstract, but she hated and shied away from its direct manifestations.

She lay quite still, even keeping her breathing light and shallow, but heard no further sound.

'But were those David's footsteps?' she wondered next.

Urging herself on against her own distaste, she got out of bed, carefully opened the door, and padded down the corridor.

David's door was shut, but Isobel's stood frankly open, the moonlight lying in a clean swathe across the foot of the unoccupied bed.

'Turning my house into a brothel!' pronounced the voice from Daisy's past, to be stifled at once by the voice of her urbane overlay. 'So! An *aggressive* odalisque! She will gobble him up.'

A long low laugh of pleasure reached her from David's room, but Daisy was by now braced against further shock. 'Perhaps she also *sings*,' was all that she would allow herself to think.

Chapter Eleven

DAISY's eye sometimes impeded her emotions. She could not help but see Isobel in terms of painting, for the pink billows of bedclothes contained her like an inverted shell; the shell, the separated serpentine strands of hair so strongly suggesting some fanciful Renaissance Aphrodite that the bed, a Queen Anne reproduction, seemed grossly out of period.

'And yet,' mused Daisy, 'she is not quite Florentine.'

Isobel opened her eyes.

'I knocked,' said Daisy. 'You didn't hear. Did you sleep well?' She made the perfunctory nature of this question quite clear by standing barely on the threshold of the room, retaining her hold on the knob of the half-open door.

Isobel murmured that she had. She was not yet awake, Daisy noticed without surprise. She had expected Isobel to be lazy-fleshed, a slow waker. 'Splendid,' she said. 'It's half past nine. David has gone, and now we must see about your breakfast. I expect you would like to make an early start.'

'An early start?' echoed Isobel.

'Yes, you must be longing to get home. But we can't allow you to leave without breakfast. I'll get Possie to bring you a tray.'

'You're very kind,' murmured Isobel in a slightly puzzled voice. She clambered rather clumsily from the bed and stood raising her hair from the back of her neck with both hands. She yawned. 'Long hair is so hot,' she sleepily remarked.

Her white nightgown was soiled at the armpits, Daisy noticed. Isobel's negligent magnificence, her bewildered but satisfied air, her private smile, all angered Daisy, while at the same time she could not help thinking that in different circumstances she would have enjoyed taking her in hand, restoring and redecorating her. 'I should give her a whole summer in white, nothing but gold and white. Plenty of silks, very fine cottons, and a few linens for texture contrast. No velvets — she's too plushy already.'

Isobel had picked up a blue comb and was combing her hair with such absorption that Daisy felt herself dismissed. She had gained her point; Isobel would leave the house. But as long as she wore that private smile Daisy could not feel triumphant. She tightened her lips and clasped her hands. 'And *did* you kill your husband?' she suddenly rapped out.

Isobel's eyes widened, but she went on combing her hair, and it was with curiosity and some hostility that she returned Daisy's look, certainly not with confusion. 'Rich people always think they can be as impertinent as they please,' she said.

'So you think I'm rich!' Daisy triumphantly exclaimed.

'And you think *David* is rich.'

'Aren't you?'

'No. Neither is David. We both work hard.' But even as she said this, Daisy knew that the diversion had been a mistake, that Isobel did not care about money.

Isobel pulled hair from her comb, dropped it into the ashtray, and went on meditatively combing her hair. It was an advantage to have something to do with one's hands, thought Daisy. She herself, having suppressed an impulse to put her hands on her hips, could only stand clasping them primly at her waist, aping a self-possession she did not feel.

'You must have heard me go into David's room,' said Isobel.

Daisy looked startled.

'Something must have happened to put us on this sudden footing of intimacy,' Isobel explained, 'and I can't think what else it could be.'

'I did hear you,' Daisy admitted. She meant to be as calm

as Isobel, but was not prepared for the surge of fury that propelled from her a single exclamation of disgust. 'Pah!'

Isobel very slowly blushed, an ugly purplish blush against which her hair looked white.

'So you have the grace to blush!' cried Daisy.

Isobel put a hand to her cheek. 'I think I'm blushing for you.'

Daisy looked at her in complete misunderstanding, then gave several little nods, slight and rapid, resembling the tremors of the aged. 'All very well, all very well, but none of this answers my question.'

'But I've no reason to answer it, and you've none to ask it.'

'Perhaps we may take silence for consent?'

'You may not. Silence simply means that I will not be bullied like this by any woman.'

Daisy was accustomed to dealing with artifice, but not with honesty. She suspected Isobel's candid gaze, her patient and expository speech, of being a refined and perfected form of artifice. She made no attempt to disguise these thoughts, but looked at Isobel with such calculation that Isobel gave a half laugh and said, 'Wouldn't it be simpler to believe me?'

Daisy nodded, not in acceptance, but because another idea had just occurred to her. 'I believe I can place you now,' she said. 'Yes, the coffee shops and clubs and pubs of cheaper Chelsea. That classless and really quite interesting scum. Artists, racing motorists, theatricals. Some of them quite clever but none in the first rank.' She nodded again. 'Yes, your husband, too.'

Isobel was no longer combing her hair. Standing with her hands hanging at her sides, she said, 'I can't think what you mean.'

'I could be wrong.' Daisy now sounded as if she were talking to herself. 'Your assumption that I was rich, for example. Yes, I could be wrong. Those people can smell money.'

'Do you always try to place people?' Isobel asked with real curiosity.

'Yes. So does David, you'll find.'

'Does he?' Isobel frowned. 'But don't you find that some people are simply . . . people?'

'Detached individuals, floating about alone? No.'

'No,' Isobel agreed. She was combing her hair again, very slowly. 'But I wasn't detached, until recently.'

'You mean you had your husband?'

Fear flickered in Isobel's eyes. The comb, meeting the obstruction of a knot, jerked to a halt.

'But what about before you met him?' demanded Daisy.

During the following silence comprehension came to Daisy. It broke into her face, her eager eyes. 'Or didn't you exist until then?' she cried.

To her amazement, Isobel began to cry. Shielding her eyes with her raised forearms, she wept, while Daisy, loosening and tightening her clasped hands, exclaimed disbelievingly, 'A whole world in a man!'

Isobel turned her back. She stood stiffly, her feet together, but did not lower her arms nor let go the comb, which from Daisy's angle of vision stuck out like a clumsy blue plume from her head. There was no hysteria in her weeping. These were the deep, reluctant sobs of grief, each torn painfully from its base. They gave her pause enough between them for a monotonously murmured accusation, which to Daisy sounded like: 'You said it. You said it.'

Daisy advanced into the room and gave her a policeman's tap on the shoulder. 'What did I say?'

Isobel did not reply, nor need to, for Daisy then said, 'David won't be able to do that, you know. Even if he wanted to — which I doubt — he would never be capable of it. He simply isn't the kind of man that drowns himself.'

Isobel did not turn round, but her sobs grew quieter, and Daisy sensed that she was listening. 'So if it's something as whole-hearted as that you're looking for,' she went on, 'if it's a replacement . . .' Her voice, trailing away, gave the effect of a shrug. She looked at Isobel's freshly combed hair, inches from her, and thought, 'Very rare, that cloudy effect. Marie Laurencin.'

'He has helped me,' said Isobel.

'Yes, but he's not a bottle of medicine, you know. And I don't think he'll be at all pleased to find out that you're simply using him.'

Isobel dropped her arms and walked away from Daisy. 'I'm using him, he's using me. What does it matter?'

'It will matter to David, I fear,' Daisy said pleasantly.

Isobel got into bed, turned away, and drew the sheet up so that only the top of her head showed above it.

'But I have rung for a hire-car to call for you at eleven-thirty,' Daisy protested.

'Very well, I shall go.'

Daisy would have liked to believe that these were words of capitulation, but Isobel's voice, stubborn even in agreement, told her quite clearly that they were nothing of the kind. She hesitated in the doorway, feeling the scene incomplete, reluctant to go. There were many more questions she wished to ask Isobel; for example: if, when she had said she would not be bullied by any woman, she had meant that she would accept the same treatment from a man? Daisy rather thought she would, but knew that she would get no answer to that or any other question from Isobel. She had, indeed, the curious feeling that Isobel was no longer there.

It was not until she was putting on her hat in her bedroom that Daisy realised that she had not manipulated Isobel as she had intended. She had been betrayed by her anger into showing direct antagonism. Nevertheless, now that it was done, she felt only relief. She had taken her stand, and was glad of it.

. . . . . .

'We shan't have those dried grasses in the window, Willy, if you don't mind.'

Daisy had just arrived at the shop. She still wore her hat and was shuffling through her letters as she spoke.

Willie said, 'I put them there especially as a surprise for you.'

'Very well, I'm surprised. Now take them out.'

'I thought they looked rather heavenly.'

'By noon you'll find they look less than heavenly. They'll drop those little hairy bits all over the place.' She suddenly turned on Willy her best and warmest smile, 'Now do take them out, like a good boy.'

Willy did so, but he was unappeased, Daisy observed. Standing with the bronze urn in his hands, looking angrily at her through plumes of grass, he demanded, 'What about my rise, Daisy?'

Daisy took one step back. 'See, they're dropping already. Please don't let them moult all over me, Willy. Maria said her cheque was in this mail. I'll sue her. I mean it this time.'

'My rise,' said Willy.

'Didn't we say the end of the year?'

'No, Daisy, we didn't. And I've been offered another job.'

'Oh? Where?'

'Merricks.'

'Heavens! A department store. You won't like it there, Willy.'

'I'd get more money, and there's chances for promotion.'

'You sound like a public servant. Here, give those to me.' Daisy tucked her handbag and the letters under one arm and took the urn from his hands, holding it carefully away from her dress. 'They're really very pretty, but I think it's quite an art, drying them so that they don't shed. No, you'll hate it there, Willy. The ladies in the corsetry department with their big black bosoms and purple hair — they'll make a pet out of you.'

Willy flushed. He was sensitive, and was becoming more so as he more indulged it. For some years he had lived in a confined area, travelling only from his flat to the shop, sometimes visiting nearby but careful to expose himself only to people who would offer him no affront. And the more he clung to this safe little world, the more formidable the outside world appeared. He seldom ventured into it unless fortified by braver company. Merricks stood on the edge of this outer world, and Willy knew it, but thought it very unkind of Daisy to remind him of the fact.

'I do think that was uncalled for, Daisy,' he said.

It was Daisy who now peered through the plumes of grass, her eyes hard and appraising, as if for the first time she took no account of Willy's decorous exterior, but was looking into some ugliness beyond it. She said, 'Willy, for your own sake, I should hate to see you make such a mistake. You would be very unhappy. I may manage a rise at the end of the year. Max's job will be nearly finished by then.'

Willy gave a little shrug, not of resignation. 'I heard from Hal this morning,' he remarked.

Daisy carried the urn to the back of the shop, halting before the closed door of her back room. 'Do open it, Willy,' she said impatiently.

Willy opened the door, carelessly, and Daisy weaved into the room, past the crates and bundles, and put the urn on the desk. 'And where has Hal run off to?' she asked.

'Oh, he's in Melbourne. Didn't you know?'

'No. And I do think he might have left those drawings for Myra before he went. Is he seeing anything of Max and Helen there?'

'Heavens, yes. They're not coming back for a month.'

'I know,' lied Daisy. 'Did Hal say when he was coming back? I need a new sketch for a drawing-room. I've made some changes.'

'He didn't say. But he asked me to tell you that he wants his money as soon as he returns.'

Daisy looked amused. 'Are you his agent, Willy?'

'Why do you have to be so horrid, Daisy?'

Daisy shook one of her pain-killing pills out of its bottle. 'I'm not being horrid, Willy. And Hal shall have his money, of course he shall.' She swallowed the pill, looking thoughtful, then made her way once more along the encumbered path to the door, where she stood looking confidingly up at Willy, her hands resting lightly on his shoulders. 'I shall make out a cheque and you may send it to him, if you'd prefer that.'

'When he comes back will do.' Willy did not want to admit that Hal had given no address. He was, moreover, baffled by Daisy's willingness to part with money. 'You'll pay what he asked?' he suspiciously enquired.

'But of course.'

Willy, who instinctively felt that someone was being cheated, but who could not think who, or how, looked at her meditatively. He saw then how exhausted and even feverish she was, in spite of her smile, her strongly ringing voice. He was on the point of saying, 'How ravaged you look.' But because he imputed his own sensitivity to other people, he never wantonly hurt them. He was sometimes waspish, but never cruel. So all he said was, 'Thank you, Daisy.'

'Now what about the bed we sold Liz Vaughan? Did she ring?'

'Yes. I wish I knew what to do about Merricks.'

But Willy was not Hal. He was not dangerous, did not have to be bribed and placated. Daisy was very sure of him. 'Yes, it's a problem,' she said sympathetically, 'but one that you must decide for yourself. Is Liz having the canopy?'

'No, and she wants the posts cut down.'

'Truncated posts. They'll look absurd.'

'She said would you think of some jiggers to put on top of them. To finish them off, she said.'

'Street lamps, possibly. Is she persuadable?'

'She might be.'

'I have ideas for that canopy, Willy. We could use the stuff we used for Mary Wilson's Venetian room, with the braid we got last week.'

Willy looked doubtful, then, seeing it, pointed a finger at Daisy and breathed, 'With the brass and ormolu. Oh, Daisy, *yes*.'

Daisy pointed her own forefinger, met the tip of his. They had these moments. She said, 'Liz will spoil it, of course, by lying in it.'

Willy broke into laughter. Stamping softly round the shop, he crowed, 'In a pink nightie, with a *hairnet*.'

'Nothing is perfect in this world. What time is Liz coming?'

'About half-past eleven.'

'Half-past eleven.' Looking at her watch, where the hands stood at eleven o'clock, Daisy thought of Isobel, inevitably connecting her with the richly canopied brass and ormolu bed. 'So she is Venetian, after all, if that matters. In half an hour she will be gone.'

And for the rest of that day Isobel mattered not at all. Buoyed up by work and by the challenge of pain, Daisy all but forgot her. It was only in the evening, when the taxi was bearing her home, that she allowed herself to think of David's certain anger. But she still had the feeling of being set to a course, and was confident that the momentum she had already established would carry her along.

. . . . .

David said into the telephone, 'But I feel she can't stay in that flat.'

'Now wait,' said Myra. 'I don't quite understand. Why did she go back there in the first place?'

'She didn't. I told you. She came here.'

'Here?'

'Home, home. I'm ringing from home.'

There was a long silence, then Myra said weakly, 'Good Heavens!'

'I had no alternative, and I'm not sorry it happened.'

'What about Daisy?'

'Oh, she could have been worse, though she did put it all on the line. From her point of view, of course.'

'Her point of view is quite fantastic,' said Myra with sudden severity. 'And I can't say how pleased I am, David, that you wasted no time in making a stand.'

'It didn't happen quite as intentionally as that, Myra.'

'All the same, you made it. By taking Isobel . . .'

David interrupted. 'What about the extensions at your place?'

'What about them? Oh, I see what you mean. But Heavens, I'm quite alone, and you're ringing from home, where surely there are no more secrets.'

'Crossed lines,' he said unhappily.

'Oh, to hell with crossed lines. The only conversations *I* ever hear like that are about someone's arthritis or someone's Auntie May.'

'But you do hear them,' he pointed out.

Her sigh was audible. 'Very well, I'll be crafty. Go on.'

'Good. Now here is what happened. When I came home this evening Possie told me that she had returned to her flat. I believe Mother had something to do with this. I know how she dreaded going back there, and I want to get her out of it as soon as possible. I was wondering about your place at the beach. With Hughie's permission, if that's necessary,' he added diffidently.

'Some friends of Hughie's have it at the moment. I *am* sorry. But if you've really made a stand, if you don't care about secrecy, why not bring her here? I'll put her up for as long as you like.'

'Myra, I don't think she would come.'

'Persuade her.'

'It's wonderfully kind of you. I'll think it over.'

Myra did not like this. She had hoped for splendid defiance, decisive action. 'You don't sound enthusiastic,' she said.

'Frankly, I'm not. I feel I need a little time. And Myra, wasn't it you who told me these things resolve themselves? Wasn't it you who suggested that I float with the stream?'

But in Myra's imaginary stream there had been no cross-currents. 'Very well,' she said resignedly, 'float away. But be careful she doesn't drown while you float.'

He was silent for a moment, then he said rather formally, 'I shall certainly try to persuade her to come to you.'

'Do, David, do. She mustn't be allowed to hide herself. She can't run away for ever. Besides, it's too ridiculous. Nobody cares as much as that. It will all be forgotten in a week.'

'No, that's childish. It won't be. But I'll do my best. I'm going out there now.'

'Where? To Auntie May's flat?'

He did not laugh at this flippancy. 'I'll ring you in the morning,' he said.

'Do that,' said Myra.

But when she replaced the receiver she left her hand upon it, tempted to ring him back quickly and ask, 'Look, what *is* all this? The legal charge has been dropped. What impediment is there now? Have you charges of your own?'

But she knew that he would hedge, grow frosty, and pretend to be puzzled. Or, worse, perhaps he would really be puzzled.

'Better not,' she decided.

. . . . .

When Daisy arrived home she found Possie sitting at the kitchen table eating her dinner. Many things contributed to Possie's look of guilt, the lamb cutlets she was eating among them. Cutlets were expensive; she had hoped to finish them before Daisy came home.

'Has David been home?' asked Daisy.

Possie looked at her sideways, then gave one of those deliberate nods that imply so much more than mere affirmation.

'He's been and gone, is that it?' Daisy's voice was sharp.

Cutting the meat from the last cutlet, Possie put it delicately into her mouth. 'He did go out again,' she admitted.

'Cutlets,' said Daisy.

'Hogget,' said Possie, for who could prove otherwise, with only bones for evidence?

'Did he go immediately?'

Possie said slowly, 'He made a phone call first.'

'Where did he go?'

'He didn't say.'

'Oh, do stop hedging. He came home, found that woman gone, and went straight after her. Isn't that what you mean?'

Possie was silent, but looked dignified. 'Torture me. Torment me. My lips are sealed,' her raised head and drooped eyelids seemed to say: a message perfectly understood by Daisy, who gave an exasperated laugh, then bent over the table and presented to Possie her determined face.

'Isn't it?' she asked again.

Finding it difficult to chew and look dignified at the same time, Possie convulsively swallowed a mouthful of potato. 'I don't carry tales,' she said.

Daisy laughed outright at this. 'No, you want the pleasure of revealing them and the glory of concealing them. So you conceal them with your words and reveal them with your manner.'

Possie capitulated. Laying down her knife and fork, she burst into tears. 'And he blamed me for letting her go,' she wailed. 'The way he spoke you'd think I'd been put to guard her.'

Daisy straightened up, looking relieved. She liked to know the strength of the opposition. 'You must admit you gave that impression last night,' she said. 'And do stop crying. What is there to cry about?'

'I don't know,' sobbed Possie, who could think of a number of things to cry about, now that she had started.

'Oh stop it, stop it,' Daisy wearily begged. She took a folded handkerchief from her handbag. 'Here,' she said without kindness, offering it to Possie.

The little movement of the shoulders with which Possie rejected it was meant to be proud, but looked merely petulant. From her apron pocket she took her own crumpled handkerchief, while Daisy, sighing elaborately, returned hers to her handbag. 'Tell me what David said,' she then demanded.

'He only asked if you told her to go, and of course I said I couldn't say.'

'Don't bother to shield *me*, Poss. I did.' Daisy bent as she spoke to take from the floor the crumpled paper that had been withdrawn with the handkerchief from Possie's apron pocket. 'Didn't Mrs. Purdy tell you so?' she asked.

'No. She's a silent, queer woman, you have to admit.'

'Certainly I shall admit it,' said Daisy. She had smoothed the paper out on the table and she now slowly read aloud, 'A. Healey, grocer.' Then, on a rising note of interrogation, 'Double Bay?'

Possie gave her nose a last wipe. 'Eh?' she said.

Daisy contemptuously dropped the bill on the table, and Possie, picking it up as if it were hot, began to stammer, 'What... what... I can't imagine...'

'With whom do we deal at Double Bay?' Daisy coldly enquired.

Possie pretended to be puzzled. 'It can't be ours.'

'No, it can't be, since it's made out to someone named Purdy. So you went out there with her?' Daisy sounded cool and amused. 'And you took your apron. To do her housework, I expect, while this house is as neglected as ever.'

'I didn't want to go,' said Possie.

'Then why did you?'

'Out of common humanity. It's not right to treat her,' cried Possie without thinking, 'as if she's committed some crime.'

Daisy flung back her head and laughed.

'Oh, I know what you're thinking,' Possie accused her, 'but how do you know that she did it?'

'I don't. I surmise. And nor do I care.'

'You're hard as hard.'

Daisy looked interested. 'How hard is that?'

With a baffled and angry movement, Possie rose from the table and carried her plate to the sink. 'Always mocking,' she muttered.

But at the same time she was wondering how she could placate Daisy without abandoning too abruptly her former hauteur. The Isobel of that day had been very different from the distressed angel of the night before. Alone with her in her flat, Possie had felt not only ill at ease, but even a little frightened. She had had the strange feeling that between Isobel and herself there floated some substance that blocked communication. She had not recognised Isobel's remote and indifferent air as that of an exhausted traveller, who, sated with changing scenes, loses at last all sense of surroundings. She had suspected callousness. By the time she had cleaned the flat and had received Isobel's absent-minded thanks, she knew that she had risked Daisy's displeasure for what had proved to be merely another illusion.

She said sullenly, 'I picked up that bill when I was sweeping, from behind a cupboard along with all the matches and cockroach dirt. That flat of hers was so filthy I was disgusted.'

'Rather like this house.' Daisy spoke with the false friendliness that is so much more threatening than anger. 'You know, Poss, I think it's just as well that you and I are parting.'

'And she had a bath when we got there,' Possie cried desperately. 'And do you know what she changed into after it? You'll never guess. An old dressing-gown of her husband's. How could she!'

Daisy did not bother to reply to this. She was turning the bill in her hands. She knew that it offered the perfect excuse to get rid of Possie without fuss or recrimination, but she wished that she knew exactly when Brian Hastings was to die.

Possie was watching the bill revolving in Daisy's hands. 'And what's more,' she went on, 'she came into that kitchen, where it happened, as if it was any old place. It made me think.'

'What did it make you think?'

'That she did it. I tried not to, but I couldn't help it.'

'Possibly, but it doesn't really matter. She was charged, that's what matters.'

'Oh you're right, you're right. That's what matters. Mud sticks.'

Accomplices in meanness are each other's mirrors. As if she saw her inhumanity reflected in Daisy's eyes, Possie averted her own and began to shift things about on the table, while to herself she made her usual excuses that she had meant no harm, and that she just hadn't thought. 'But come to think of it,' she said miserably, 'it must matter whether she did it or not.'

'To whom?'

'It must matter to God.'

'God.' Daisy repeated the word idly, as if it meant nothing to her, which, indeed, it did not, though it sometimes evoked for her the splendidly outflung arm of Michelangelo's airborne man. 'I don't know about God,' she said. 'I think it may matter to David for a while, until he comes to his senses, which I am convinced won't be long. But in the meantime it's most important that no rumour of this aberration of his should get around. So I must warn you, Possie, not to gossip about this thing when you leave here. It will be a temptation, but if you don't think of David, think of yourself. Your new employers won't be impressed by gossip from your last place. It will merely make them mistrust you and could even cost you your job. Nobody will employ people they can't trust.' She had neatly folded the bill as she spoke and she now offered it to Possie. 'Here, Poss. This belongs to you.'

'Well and good,' said Possie. 'Well and good.' She took the bill and put it in her apron pocket. 'And when do you want me to go?'

'I expect my new help to start in about six weeks, though of course if you get something before then . . .'

'Don't worry, I'll be out of here in six weeks. Have you told David about all this?'

'I told him you were leaving. He said he would like to give you a cheque. And so should I, Poss.'

'Well and good,' said Possie. 'Well and good.'

She could hardly have chosen more inaccurate words. There was nothing well or good about it. She had already proved that she had little hope of getting a job. She regretted having boasted to Daisy about the wonderful jobs she could have for the asking, but she knew it was useless to withdraw these boasts now. Against this implacable pleasantness of Daisy's there was no appeal.

. . . . .

David, who had thought he had so many secrets to wring from Isobel, at first found himself as content with her inconsequential disclosures as she seemed to be with his. The combined glow of moonlight and street lights entered her bedroom, and it was very pleasant lying in this incomplete darkness, the first strangeness behind them for ever, their hands idly playing or lying interlocked between them. Their conversation was relaxed and murmurous, and though it was concerned only with trivial things he did not at first have any feeling that they were skirting dangerous subjects.

She rolled over and put her forehead lightly on his bare chest, her arms encircling his head. 'I once thought you were like a dentist,' she said.

He put a hand on her hair. 'Why a dentist?'

'I don't know. Because you were so clean.'

They laughed, and she flung away from him and lay with her hands clasped behind her head, leaving her feet and ankles entwined with his, so that they resembled one of those divided trees that grow from a single root. Smiling, lazy, and warm, there was yet a drift of melancholy about her. 'This is the best part,' she said.

'Yes, if it could go on for ever.' Her movement away from him had broken their mood enough to allow to obtrude his unfulfilled promise to Myra. He took her hand in his and they lay without speaking until he felt it safe to ask, 'Do you remember Myra Magaskill?'

'No. Who is she?'

'You went to a party of hers at the end of last summer.'

'Oh. I remember a thin dark woman at some party. But I was taken there by other people. I don't know her.'

'That was where I first saw you. I even spoke to you.'

'Did you? I don't remember.'

Against the wariness in her voice he had to force himself to go on. 'I remembered you, but that's not the point at present. Myra's very kind, very decent, one of my oldest friends. Now if you want to get out of this flat, she will put you up until you can find another place. How about it?'

'But she's a stranger. I don't know her.'

He wanted to say, 'But do you know anyone?' Instead he said, 'She wouldn't be a stranger for long. She's easy to know.'

'I couldn't,' she said. 'Now that I'm here, please let me stay a little while.'

He found it flattering, this implication that she was his to dispose of as he pleased. 'I thought that since you dreaded coming back here . . .' he said.

She sat up abruptly, resting her chin on her raised knees. 'I know I did. And when your aunt — is she your aunt? — when she went home I walked round and looked at everything, waiting for something to happen. But nothing happened, nothing at all. It was just another place.' Her voice took on a puzzled and slightly complaining note. 'Tables, books, chairs — they did nothing to me. They were only things.'

He wondered by what effort of will she had been able to disassociate Richard Purdy's surroundings from Richard Purdy himself. Was it because she was accustomed to a series of rented rooms, on which no single, personal imprint had been made, but only the fused imprints of many occupants, each cancelling the other? Yet surely there was something personal about Richard Purdy's dressing-gown, in which she had greeted him without embarrassment that very evening. But perhaps, he reflected, it was this boldness that gave him the measure of her need to escape. She had set herself to defy these objects, to exorcise them by re-establishing their familiarity.

Pleased by this explanation, he was not prepared for the counter argument that instantly followed it. 'In that case, why will she not mention his name?'

Sitting there so still and withdrawn, she frightened him. His wish to know the answers to these questions yielded to the more urgent wish that she should come back to him. Tentatively, he put out a hand and picked up a strand of her hair. 'Isobel,' he said.

She did not move. 'Yes.'

'Do one thing for me.'

'I know what it is.' Her voice was listless but stubborn. 'You want me to leave here.'

But David, having kept his promise to Myra, was really rather relieved by the result. 'No, not that,' he said, and gathered her hair, strand by strand, into the loop of a thumb and forefinger. Then he said in a light and friendly voice, 'Let me buy you a new dressing-gown.'

She was already sitting so still that it was odd that her silence should give the effect of an even greater stillness, of a held breath. He involuntarily tightened his grip on her hair, not knowing what to expect, and was almost surprised when at last she coldly replied, 'Very well.'

'A blue one.' Pulling gently on her hair, he felt her resistance. 'Blue is my favourite colour. My mother says that the favourite colours of all uncomplicated men are blue and red, in that order. And tell me, how did you get on with my mother?'

But she ignored this opportunity to tell him what had passed between herself and Daisy, though whether from delicacy, indolence, or another of her morbid fears he could not guess. But he was pleased enough to accept her silence, and when she said, 'My own favourite colour is blue, so that means I'm uncomplicated,' he immediately laughed and said, 'Oh, you are.'

He did not believe this for a moment, but was so pleased that she had resumed her conversational tone that he would have agreed to anything. 'You're large, uncomplicated, and very beautiful,' he declared, still holding her hair. 'The only complicated thing about you is your hair. Do you ever plait it at night?'

No longer resisting his gentle tugging, she allowed her head to drop back. 'Never,' she said.

He did not know what made him tug her hair with such brutal force that she gave a cry of pain as she fell back beside him. He rolled over at once, putting his forehead on the pillow beside her head. 'I love you,' he said.

But she only laid one hand gently on his head, as if in consolation. 'Instead of a blue dressing-gown,' she said, 'may I have one of those Chinese ones? A kimono?'

He knew that she was offering this show of interest as an apology. 'If you like,' he rather stiffly agreed.

It was now she who was cajoling. 'I had one once. Let me tell you about it. I bought it in Hong-Kong.'

'When were you in Hong-Kong?'

'I was there — oh, a long time ago,' she replied, so evasively that he found himself amending her statement to '*We* were there'.

But he did not move his forehead from the pillow, nor ask any of the questions that were forming in his mind. Lying quite still, allowing her hand to move firmly over his head, he lapsed into his now familiar resignation to an unalterable course of events. 'Was it blue?' he asked idly.

'Yes. And all around the hem there were irises growing.'

'Irises.'

'Yes.' Her hand lay quite still now, and seemed heavier. 'But the other side was green, the inside, so pale that it was hardly coloured at all. I liked it. On the green side there was one bird. One bird. And the silk had such a funny . . .' Her voice trailed sleepily away, then she said with an effort, 'One bird.'

When her inert hand had slipped from his head, and he knew that she was asleep, he got up and moved around the room as quietly as he could, finding his clothes. After he was dressed he drew the sheet and blanket up over Isobel's bare shoulders. Then, because his hands seemed to have a life of their own, which urged them to violence, he released her hair from beneath her shoulders with great gentleness, spreading it out over the two pillows. A thread's gleam between her lids showed him that her eyes were incompletely shut. In spite of her heavy breathing, she was sleeping shallowly, scarcely submerged.

In the living-room he went straight to the bureau, where he found Richard Purdy's notebook still inserted between the newspapers, where he himself had hidden it on that rainy day. Squatting before the bureau, he held it in both hands, unopened, while his eyes searched the room for a more secure hiding place. No effort of Isobel's will, he felt, would succeed in pushing it into the same category as the tables and chairs. He was afraid of what it might do to her, and as much afraid for himself as for her. Yet, because it did not belong to him, it seemed a lawless act to take it away and destroy it.

When he heard her laughing his heart gave a sick thud. He lifted the newspapers once more and inserted the book between them. She was still laughing when he reached the bedroom, although she was, as he had guessed, at least half asleep.

He sat on the edge of the bed, bringing his mouth close to her ear. 'Isobel.'

She stopped laughing abruptly, and he took her hands, discovering as he did so that their palms were damp. 'Listen to me,' he said.

'What is it?' Her voice was wide-awake, but very quiet.

'Do you answer the door?'

'No.'

'The telephone?'

'No.'

'Very well. Now listen. When I ring, I'll let it buzz four times, then ring off, then ring again. Answer it then.'

'Four times, then again,' she obediently repeated. Her hands began to struggle in his. 'But will you only ring? Won't you come?'

'Yes. Tomorrow, if you want me to?'

'Yes. Tomorrow. Whenever you can.'

He hesitated, then said lightly, 'Why do you want me to come?'

But still she would not say it. She released her hands, grasped one of his, and held it to her cheek. 'Oh, how I hate going to sleep,' she said.

There was a moment of silence, then he said, 'Whenever I come, I'll ring first, so that you'll open the door.'

'I'll look for the other key,' she said.

'Yes, that would be better. Can you go back to sleep now?'

'No, not yet.' Her eyes moved restlessly round the room. 'Must you go?'

'Yes. It's two o'clock.'

After a moment, she said, 'Not long to daylight, then. I'll read.'

On his way out he took the notebook from the bureau. He was relieved to find that the lights were now out in the corridor and that the opposite door, Miss Morrison's, remained shut. It had opened that evening when Isobel had not responded to his knock and he had been forced to stand there importunately calling her. He had not turned when he heard the click of the latch behind him, and thought it unlikely that Miss Morrison had recognised him. But it was a warning, all the same, that until Isobel moved he must plot his comings and goings with great care.

As he cautiously trod the uncarpeted stairs, he thought that he must find out about that side entrance, and immediately he was visited by a flash of distaste, then by a flash of animosity towards Isobel.

Because he still hesitated to destroy the notebook, he carried it in his briefcase for two days. At the end of the second day he took it out and read it, very carefully, his face expressionless. Then he destroyed it.

Chapter Twelve

THE warmth that was so beneficent in September had strengthened by the end of October to a thick heat, plunging the city too soon into the real heart of summer, a summer that was to be unrelieved for many weeks by the equable nor'-easterly or the evening Southerly Buster. There was seldom a noticeable drop in the temperature at nightfall, and in this evenness of heat the days seemed to lapse unbroken into one another, calendar law suspended. Temperatures were front-page news; cold became unimaginable; and strangers conversed in shops and trains. 'The hottest since '39,' they told each other with some pride, 'and it's even worse in the country.'

Hal Bonniface returned to Sydney one very hot Saturday.

'It's just as hot in bloody Melbourne,' he snapped in reply to a solicitous remark offered by Willy.

He had just arrived; they were still standing on the platform at Central Station. Hal wore a black shirt, duck pants, and espadrilles. He carried over one shoulder, by the drawn cords, an old army duffle bag. His nose was slightly swollen, his face blotched with the sickly purples and chromes of fading bruises. Porters passed them by.

In spite of all this, Willy, who had been hiding behind a chocolate machine while he waited for the train to come in, felt quite secure now that Hal was with him. 'Did some people hit you?' he asked.

'Yes. Some pol-eese-men.'

'Goodness!'

'Let's go,' said Hal, and went. Looking straight ahead, ignoring Willy, he made his way down the platform, cutting through groups, breasting human obstacles as if they were air, while Willy, afraid to let him get too far ahead, dodged about in his wake and soothed his hindpath with apologetic little smiles.

They passed the barrier. 'Let's get a taxi,' suggested Willy.

'No. We'll walk.'

'But, Hal, it's miles, and it's so hot.'

'I like walking,' said Hal.

So they walked up Oxford Street, which was almost deserted at this time, three o'clock.

They had different ways of dealing with the heat. Willy hated to be mussed; he dabbed at his forehead and neck with a white handkerchief. But Hal indifferently sweated, never once easing the wet shirt from his chest, never relaxing the pugnacious set of his shoulders nor slackening his swift gliding pace.

Willy, drooping and scurrying, threw puzzled and imploring glances at him, sensing a change in him, a new resolution. He noticed that when people cast curious or jeering glances at them, Hal did not ignore them as he used to do, but stared hard and defiantly back at them. 'Looking for war,' thought Willy. He no longer felt safe.

'You're different, Hal,' he ventured at last.

Hal did not answer.

'It must be Melbourne that's changed you,' said Willy. Offended by Hal's continued silence, he told himself that it was too bad, when he was putting him up and had come to this perfectly barbarous part of town to meet him. 'Of course, Melbourne's a vile place,' he added crossly.

'All places are alike,' said Hal. 'All just collections of dirt and bricks and trees and rotten people.'

'Then why did you come back here?'

'To get some money out of bloody old Max.'

It was so unlike Hal to travel hundreds of miles to get some money that Willy, flabbergasted, came to a halt. 'What?' he cried. But Hal did not stop walking nor even

turn his head, and Willy had to run to catch up with him.
'What?' he said again.

'That's the last time anyone's ever going to do this to me.' Delicately, Hal touched his bruised face. 'They picked me up for soliciting, but they couldn't make it stick, because I wasn't. They just thought I might be, the swine. Then they shoved me in the peter on a vagrancy charge. They're not going to do it again. I'm going to get some money. I'm going to get a house.'

'A *house*!' gasped Willy.

'A house with a peaked roof. I'll live in the house and keep all my things in the peak.'

Willy clapped his hands. 'Oh, that will be lovely. Like in Hansel and Gretel or something.' But on meeting Hal's sidelong look he became confused, and dropped his fancy just as he was about to decide what confectionery they would use for the peaked roof. He had forgotten Hal's contempt for such talk. After giving him a minute for forgiveness, he asked soberly, 'But how will you get money from Max?'

Instead of answering directly, Hal asked, 'How's Daisy?'

'Oh, hectic. Sometimes I think she's dying, she's so gay. As if she's having one last, glorious outburst. Working like mad and doing some marvellous things. Little things, her best ever. But it's a bit trying, she simply can't stop talking. And she has toothache or something. She takes bottles and bottles of pain-killing things . . . ' With his hands, Willy indicated the capacity of these bottles — about a gallon, apparently. '. . . and sometimes she runs into her back room and simply *collapses*.'

'She'll get false teeth and make jokes about them,' said Hal.

But Willy said defiantly, 'I don't care what you say, Hal, Daisy's wonderful. And she's tremendous fun when she's like this, simply sweeping everything along in front of her. I *love* Daisy.'

Hal ignored this. 'Gallant jokes,' he said.

'She gave me your cheque, too,' said Willy reproachfully.

'Why shouldn't she?'

'She could have made you wait until Max paid her. That's *quite* often done.'

'Max won't pay her.'

'Oh, don't be silly, Hal. Max is one person who *does* pay.'

'Has she given him the designs?'

'Yes. Yesterday.'

'Does he like them?'

Willy hesitated. 'He wants a few days to think about them.'

'That means he doesn't like them,' Hal said with finality.

They were in Darlinghurst now, passing the Supreme Court, and for the first time Hal came to a halt, swinging his duffle bag to the ground and wiping his sweating hands down his trouser legs. 'That son of hers, Lawrence, will be a judge one day,' he gloomily commented, looking at the Court House.

'You mean David,' said Willy. 'David's rather scaring, but awfully nice.'

'He's like her. When he's a judge he'll make jokes.'

'No, he won't. Everyone says he's going into politics.'

'Oh, one of those.' Hal slung his bag over his shoulder once more and walked on. 'Then he'll make the kind of jokes they make in Parliament.'

Willy was hurrying to keep up with him. 'He's got lots of style, and he dresses beautifully.'

'Yes,' Hal contemptuously agreed.

'It must be awful to be you, Hal,' Willy suddenly flashed out. 'Hating everyone, even people who are nice.'

'Nice,' echoed Hal, without emphasis.

'Sooner or later you'll start hating yourself.'

'I do that now,' Hal replied indifferently.

Willy was shocked. 'Poor Hal!' he wanted to say, but a glance at Hal's profile made him change his mind. 'It must have been rather awful,' he said instead.

Hal looked at the sky. 'I'm going to be frightfully rich,' he said.

'Hal, I can't run any more. I'm too hot. Really I can't.'

Surprisingly, Hal slowed down. 'There are only two

things to do,' he said. 'Kill yourself or get rich and spit on the lot of them.'

'But I thought you only wanted a *little* house,' Willy said plaintively.

'I didn't say anything about little.' Hal swung the duffle bag from his right to his left shoulder. 'I'm going to submit some designs for the Dobies' house myself.'

'What!' Willy ducked his head so that he could peer into Hal's face. 'But you *can't*! What about Daisy?'

'What about her?'

'That's her job.'

'It's anyone's job who can get it. That's what they call business.'

Willy had to admit that it was, but he felt, and certainly looked, troubled. His handkerchief came out again, fluttered about his sweating face. 'And she was so decent about the cheque, too,' he said.

'That's why I wanted it now. I knew I wouldn't get it at all if I waited.'

'Oh, I do think that was mean.'

'No, it was business.'

'And a wee bit disloyal, somehow.'

'Business.'

'You're a dirty dog, Hal.'

Hal almost allowed himself to laugh. 'Then what does that make Daisy?'

They walked along in silence for a while, Willy sulking, until they came abreast of a kiosk, where Hal stopped. 'Let's get an almond chocolate,' he said.

'I don't want a chocolate.'

'I do. I'm hungry.'

Somewhat abstractedly, Willy bought the chocolate and handed it to Hal. 'About Daisy,' he said as they walked on. 'I don't care what you say . . .'

'I know, you love her, you said that before. But you'll have to leave her, all the same, and come in with me.'

'No, I won't. You don't understand. I was offered

another job, more money and everything. But in the end I just couldn't leave her.'

'More fool you. Come in with me, Willy. When I've finished Max's job I'll get lots of others. I'll be as cute as they like, till I get what I want.' Hal rolled the silver wrapping from the chocolate into a ball, which he catapulted from his powerful thumb and forefinger into the gutter. 'I'll even talk about art,' he said.

But Willy said suddenly, 'It won't work out like that. Other people have tried it. Artists are always trying it.'

'I'm not an artist,' chanted Hal. 'I'm a businessman.'

Willy could not help but be amused at this. 'You'll have to buy a suit,' he crowed.

Hal was eating the slab of chocolate in big mouthfuls, like a slice of bread and butter. 'No, I won't. I'm going to be eccentric.'

Willy thought about this, then said, 'Poor Daisy.'

'She's made hers. Let her move over.'

'And she's so awfully kind sometimes,' mourned Willy. 'She asked me, she asked me especially, to get you to bring those drawings for Myra Magaskill into the shop.'

'All right, she can have them. I'll go through that pile I've got stashed away at your place, and you can take them into the shop on Monday.'

'I don't know how you can make use of her like that, Hal, and then stab her in the back.'

Hal, who felt he could very easily stab anyone in the back, even Willy, did not bother to reply to this, but fell into an indifferent silence, which he maintained until they were darting through the traffic on the broad intersection at the Cross.

'I suppose this Myra Whatshername will want drawings exactly the same size,' he then gloomily remarked, 'so that she can hang them in one of those bloody little batches.'

. . . . .

On that Saturday Myra roved around the house measuring furniture. The house had been sold two days before; they were to move into one of Horace Dangerfield's home units early in December.

To Hughie she said, 'The sideboard will have to go, it's much too big. And all the pictures, every one of them.'

'They were your grandfather's,' said Hughie.

'Yes, but I believe they're terribly bad. And we really must have smaller pictures for the dining-room. I'll hang them in one of those batches.'

'You mean you'll group them.'

'Yes, that's what I mean. When I didn't want pictures Daisy was twisting my arm to make me buy some drawings. And now that I want them I expect she's forgotten all about them. I'll ring her.'

'Well, I'm off,' said Hughie. 'Pity it's such rotten sailing weather.'

'Is it? I should have thought it was perfect. Such heat.'

'But no wind.'

'Oh no, what a pity,' said Myra, and kissed him. 'Have a wonderful time, my darling.'

She watched him go. He was thinner, and dusky with sun. He had never looked more attractive.

This was Hughie's summer. He had suddenly blossomed into a yachtsman. Uffa Fox's books lay about on coffee tables, and in bed he talked of Dud Henderson, with whom he sailed. On the boat he and Dud each wore only shorts girdled by an old tie and a knitted cap with a pom-pom on top. On the run home they usually got drunk and then Hughie would sometimes bring Dud home for more drinks. On these occasions they would laugh a great deal and point at each other with their pipes, while Myra sat in a deep chair, smoking and smiling.

'What a pity I get so seasick,' she had once said to Hughie. 'I should so love to come out with you.'

'There are pills,' Hughie half-heartedly suggested.

'With me the cursed things don't work.'

Both were glad to spend this time away from each other.

Saturdays and Sundays seemed like holidays to Myra. She spent them at home, always alone. She had lately been restless, serious, and disinclined for company.

To David she had said over the telephone, 'Come to see me one Saturday or Sunday, and bring you-know-who.' And she had added, 'It's a shame Hughie won't be home, but he's mad about sailing. He never misses a Saturday or Sunday.'

But she had offered this little slight to Hughie for nothing. David had not come. And on these brooding weekends, when she often thought of him and Isobel, she would sometimes murmur aloud, 'No, he couldn't be so mean.' Or: 'It would be too ignoble.'

For it had become important to Myra that Isobel should emerge into daylight, with David openly at her side.

. . . . .

Every Saturday David came into the city at ten o'clock and worked in his chambers until two in the afternoon. The building was almost empty, and very quiet. At first street noises drifted in through his high and open windows, but by half-past twelve these began to ebb, leaving him isolated in deepening silence. All he would hear then was the occasional clang of heels in some corridor, each impact sending out concentric echoes, a sound so lonely that it seemed to emphasise rather than break his isolation.

In these four hours, free of telephone calls and appointments, he found that he could reduce his backlog of work just enough to appease the guilt that acted on him like a hidden irritant during the week, when, taken unawares sometimes by the thought of work undone, he would find himself cursing to subdue his rising panic; for the habit of industry, of occupying every waking hour, of taking only enough leisure to fit oneself for more work, is as insidious and as hard to break as the habit of sloth. The order David had imposed upon his life was not resilient enough to withstand the pressure of his passion for Isobel; it could only break.

So this new Saturday morning routine was salvage work of a rather desperate nature.

The air conditioning was turned off on Friday nights, and on this Saturday morning the heat was such that he decided to strip to his underpants. Then he took off his watch and laid it on his desk, noting with satisfaction that the hands stood at exactly ten o'clock.

But half an hour later, seeking a reason for his failure to immerse himself in work, he realised that his own bare chest was a distraction. Every object in the room seemed to reproach him for its inappropriateness to these surroundings, so that he no longer felt alone, but ringed around by disapproving spectators.

He put on his shirt, which might have been the magic, power-conferring cloak of some fairy-tale prince, so completely did his uneasiness vanish as soon as the cloth enveloped his chest and encircled his neck.

After this return to civilization he worked with increasing satisfaction until his telephone rang.

It was Possie.

'It's your mother,' she told him. 'She got home ten minutes ago, and, my word, she looks bad.'

David looked at his watch, which showed him ten minutes past one. 'Sick, do you mean?' he asked angrily.

'Yes. I wouldn't have disturbed you otherwise. To my way of thinking, she should have someone with her.'

'Well, aren't you there?'

'No, I'm in the box on the corner, on my way out.'

'Oh, I say! Must you go out?'

'I think I'm quite entitled,' Possie began, but David cut in impatiently, 'All right, all right. Now how sick is she?'

'She lay down the moment she got in, in all her clothes, and her hat fell off,' Possie said impressively. Then, rightly interpreting David's silence, she went on with a rush, 'I wouldn't have left her, only I've got to go and see a lady about a job. I've got myself to think of, too,' she rather sullenly concluded.

'Yes, of course, but couldn't you go later? Is it so urgent?'

'Urgent! Well, seeing she's got that couple starting in ten days' time, *I'd* call it urgent.'

David was frowning. 'Now wait a minute, Poss. What couple?'

'How do I know their names? All I know is they used to work for someone who died.'

'Brian Hastings?'

'How do I know?'

'She didn't tell me about this,' said David.

'You're never there to tell. And she only told me this morning. She can afford to pay a couple, it seems, when I've only been getting a pittance all these years.' Possie was becoming angrier as she spoke; her voice rose. 'So what call have *I* to stay with her when she's off-colour, bearing in mind that the whole thing's her doing?'

David took off his spectacles and blinked rapidly. 'I don't understand you. What's her doing?'

'That I'm going.'

'But surely it was your idea?'

'So it may have been,' admitted Possie, who could not remember exactly how or when she had first set foot on this incline down which she was now hurtling to disaster. She was certain of only one thing — that Daisy's firm hand was at her back. 'If I did start it,' she said, 'I didn't mean her to take me up on it.'

David knew that he ought to press her, to make her reveal the whole story. At the same time, he felt himself recoiling from these revelations; he suspected that they would force him to take action, to set up a tiresome domestic tribunal, to hear who said this and who said that.

He swivelled his chair and picked up the top page of his work — a gesture merely, for he was so distracted by irritation that the words meant nothing to him. All he could think was: 'Surely I'm not to be saddled with all this nonsense.'

He returned the paper to the pile and put his hand firmly

on top of it. 'Well, it's between you and Mother, Poss,' he said.

Possie gave a nervous little laugh. 'I've been regretting it, David.'

'Yes, of course,' murmured David, as if he had not quite heard her, or was thinking of other things. Then he said, 'Keep your appointment, Poss, and don't worry. I'll go home.'

Possie met this with a silence that quickly became strained. David cleared his throat. 'Are you there?' he asked.

'Yes,' she said dully.

'I thought we were cut off,' he said cheerfully. 'Well, the best of luck, Poss.'

He replaced the receiver almost stealthily, keeping his hand on it, looking out of the window. 'She'll probably be a great deal happier. Mother bullies her,' he told himself.

And as he dialled Isobel's number he thought, 'And I must remember to give her that cheque.'

'David,' said Isobel, as soon as she lifted the receiver.

She spoke in her smiling voice, and he at once responded with a smile of his own. 'What were you doing?' he asked.

'Sitting on the bathroom floor reading. It's the only cold place here. Are you hot?'

'Very.'

He told her about trying to work in his underpants, but when he had finished she said, 'Yes, go on,' as if she expected something more.

'That's all,' he said.

'Oh. But why couldn't you work?'

He thought her unexpectedly dense. 'Never mind,' he said. 'Did you notice that I'm early?'

'Yes, a quarter past one. Are you coming right away?'

'No. I have to go home.'

There was a silence, then she said flatly, 'You're not coming today.'

'Of course I'm coming. At least, I think I am. I certainly hope to.'

She said in a hopeless but dogged voice, 'But why can't you come at the usual time?'

He kept his own voice casual. 'Mother's sick, apparently. But I don't think it's serious. I'll ring you again from home.'

'What time will you ring? Tell me what time.'

Suddenly, he remembered the Myra of fifteen years ago, her comradely and ironical replies in similar situations. 'You must trust me to come as soon as I can,' he said.

She hesitated, as if she had a choice. 'Oh, very well,' she dully agreed.

He settled back in his chair, smiling once more. 'Tell me what you will do until I come.'

But instead of answering she cried anxiously, 'What about my books? Did you get my books?'

David had forgotten her books. 'Not yet,' he said soothingly.

'The library will be closed now.'

There was real despair in her voice. In all of David's absences she sank herself in bouts of reading. She must always have at hand an untapped cache of books, and when this supply dwindled she became alarmed. David had at first been pleased with her habit of reading, but was now troubled by it, for he had lately realised that it was not a pleasure, but an addiction.

Yet she never opened a book when David was with her, and it was this that now made him ask, 'Isobel, am I a substitute for books, or are they a substitute for me?'

But she was too intent to answer this. 'Perhaps you could bring me something from home?' she suggested.

'I've nothing but reference books. But I could go to the Cross on my way and pick up some paperbacks from the news stand.'

'If you come at all,' she said in a bitter aside.

He set his upper lip. 'Quite so. If I come at all.'

'And if you go to the Cross it will make you later than ever.'

'Take your pick.'

'Then don't get the books. Come straight here.'

'I thought books were your first necessity.'

'No. *You* are my first necessity.'

She spoke with such evident warmth and simplicity that David immediately felt a return of the joy with which he had first heard her voice. 'Look here,' he said abruptly, '**I** must go home, and I must finish some work. But I'll come. I promise I'll come. If I can't come this afternoon, I'll come tonight.'

'But you'll come, you'll come.' Delight freshened her voice. 'And David, why not do your work here?'

He turned his head and gave the work on his desk a look of calculation. 'Why not?' he said.

'Then hurry, hurry.'

'Yes. Goodbye,' he said happily.

'Goodbye, goodbye.'

He collected his work very quickly, cramming it into his briefcase without looking at it. As he strapped on his watch, he thought, 'But Mother is never ill. It will only be toothache.'

David found his mother in the spare bedroom, lying beside a kicked-back rug. The blinds were drawn, and she lay perfectly still, spread-eagled on the polished boards, wearing a loose white wrapper.

His heart bounded; his joints seemed to melt. 'Dead!' cried a voice within him. It seemed a fitting conclusion to his search, which had grown in suspense and anxiety as he had moved from room to room.

In a testing voice, he said, 'Mother . . .'

'Yes, dear boy,' she calmly replied.

Unable to speak, he came into the room and weakly let himself down to the edge of the bare mattress. He then saw the gauze pads that covered her eyelids, and smelled the astringent with which they were soaked, and as soon as he knew them for what they were, he could only wonder that they had suggested to him at first the closed face of death.

But because he did not see how she could have failed to hear his footsteps, his shock was giving way rapidly to resentment at her trickery. Moreover, he thought a woman in pain would not have the heart for such mischief, and it was in a suspicious voice that he asked, 'Are you really sick?'

'It would seem so, dear boy.'

This cool reply was somehow more convincing than the most passionate statement. Realising now that he still wore his hat, he took it off and tossed it on the bed beside him. 'How sick?' he asked.

She lifted one of the pads, regarding him with a sunken and bloodshot but still ironical eye. 'Not sick enough to cause you any inconvenience, David.'

'But why are you lying here, on the floor?'

'It's cooler on the floor.' She patted the gauze pad back into place; her face became blank again.

'Now listen, Mother . . .'

'No, you are *not* to mention my teeth. Since I've borne it so long, it would be the greatest folly to give in now, when Max has the sketches and we shall be signing the contract any day. After it's signed, of course, I shall be as sick as I please. He has made me wait . . .' Daisy's voice became a little grim. '. . . and he must also be prepared to wait.'

Thus forestalled, David could say nothing of what he had intended, but now that she could no longer see him, he stole a glance at his watch. 'Possie rang me,' he said. 'I do think she might have stayed.'

'Thus relieving you of that obligation,' she said dryly.

He settled himself further back on the mattress, as if to prove his willingness to stay. 'Is there anything I can get you?'

'No. I took one of those green pills half an hour ago. There's nothing you can do. You may go.'

But she knew — and so did he — that he could not go and leave her lying there on the floor. Such an action, though not in fact brutal, would have the appearance of brutality. By lowering his self-esteem, it would mar his afternoon. On the other hand, if she could be got to bed, if she would allow him to bring her a tea tray and surround her with medicines and magazines, he could then say a few rallying words and take his departure with his self-esteem intact.

So he said cheerfully, 'Well, we must get you to bed.'

'Why?'

'You would be more comfortable.'

'Indeed I would not.'

He laughed, and made his voice affectionate. Both were difficult. 'This is no time for your Queen Elizabeth act. Now come along, Mother. As soon as you're in bed I'll bring you a tray.'

'Food!' She made a face of disgust. 'No, thank you. And I'm as comfortable here as I can be, with this pain.'

Daisy mentioned her pain only because she perceived it as a means of keeping David with her until she had said what she felt she must say, for he had lately run away from her as soon as she had opened her mouth, and nor could she be sure that the remarks she had sent flying after him had reached their goal. But because he hated acting in a way that he could not justify to himself, she knew that he would not leave her now. He was as good as tied up.

Daisy was, in fact, suffering no pain at present, but on coming home that afternoon she had given herself up to pain so completely that for the first time in her life she had wished to die. As soon as she had expressed this wish the pain had begun to recede, as if its only purpose had been to wring from her that cry of defeat, but the intensity of it, and the drugs she had taken, had left her in an abnormal state. Her body felt sometimes heavy, sometimes suspended in air, and though her thoughts were mostly incisive and indeed of a heightened clarity, there came over her now and again a wave of lethargy and utter indifference, when she felt herself sinking, rather delightfully, into the incoherence of dreams.

Now, battling her way out of one of these troughs, she gasped with the effort of it, and realised even as she did so that her gasp must have impressed David, so as soon as she was able to speak she tightened his bonds a little by saying, 'Do go. Isobel must be waiting for you.'

'You're really sick, Mother. Lie still. Don't talk.'

'David, aren't you rather a hypocrite? You don't mind if I talk, as long as it's not about Isobel. You've never allowed me to put my case.'

'I thought you had.'

'Not fully.'

'I hope you're not going to put it fully now,' he said warningly.

She made a little self-deprecatory grimace. 'Dear boy, I long to. But I'm tired, much too tired.'

Disarmed by this, he said slowly, 'All the same, I wish you would try to understand how I feel about her.'

'Would it change anything if I did?'

'It would make me easier in my mind.'

'And that, of course, is the main thing.'

Daisy was sinking again, and not caring. She knew that David was still talking, but his voice came to her across tracts of mist, a meaningless and variable noise that at its most amplified was a soft roar and at its most reduced a cry from a mountain-top, addressed to someone else.

Presently she felt herself plummeting, and heard the rush of his voice as it plummeted with her. But as soon as she jolted to a stop and her body resumed weight, it became an ordinary conversational voice, even and light and of ironical intention.

'. . . so that I feel like the worst kind of criminal every time I leave the house,' it was saying.

As soon as she heard this Daisy felt both bored and ill-used. She had all but fainted, but he had not noticed, so engrossed had he been in himself. She touched the pads on her eyelids and murmured, 'What monsters of selfishness you lovers are.'

But David only said in the same ironical voice, 'It's not clever of you, Mother, to oppose me like this. It won't alter my course, you know that.'

'I don't oppose,' sighed Daisy. 'I'm fatalistic. I know that such things must run their course.'

'Like all diseases,' he sarcastically remarked.

'Let us say like all fevers.'

'And now you'll say that fevers are symptoms of a disease.'

'Exactly. The disease itself is this absurd fallacy of romantic love.'

Daisy was feeling so much better that she decided that the severity of her last lapse must have been salutary. She felt her powers returning to her. Half-raising herself, supporting her weight on a forearm, she turned to him and raised an oratorical finger, but because light was truly unbearable, she kept her head thrown back so that the pads should not fall from her eyes.

'That fallacy,' she said, 'has been exposed by the best and most logical minds for hundreds of years. Yet you, *you*, a man trained to the use of your intelligence, can repudiate their findings in favour of a pretty myth. That seems to me not only stupid, but wicked.'

'Dear me,' David said staidly.

'Self-deception is a wicked and debilitating vice. It cannot fail to enfeeble you. Your mind is already so enfeebled that you believe that your present abnormal state will last for ever.'

'Very well, that's your diagnosis. What's your cure?' he asked with a mockery that was not quite convincing.

'Give her up if you can, before your association with her can damage the more important purposes of your life. If you can't, get her out of your system as quickly and as secretly as you can. Let it run its course. But never deceive yourself that it won't.'

David suddenly laughed. 'How very Greek,' he said.

'So it may be. The Greeks were realists. Romantic love is a modern affliction.'

'Oh, I don't mean your theories, Mother, I mean you. It suddenly struck me that you look like a statue of Socrates.'

Daisy, who saw at once that this could be so, fell back with a laugh, touching the pads on her eyelids. 'I was entirely sincere,' she said.

'I know you were, but you present only one side of the case. There's such a number of things you don't take into account.'

Daisy remembered that Myra had once told her the same thing. She was not surprised when David continued with: 'You pride yourself on your realism, but perhaps these other things have a realism of their own.'

'That's exactly the kind of remark one expects to hear from Myra,' said Daisy.

'Myra is also sincere.'

'You defend her because you were once in love with her. And *that*,' said Daisy, 'ran its course.'

'This is different.'

'It always is. That's one of the most celebrated symptoms of the disease, present in all the worst cases.'

'You simply don't understand.'

'And that's another. Yours is a textbook case.'

'Your own disease seems to have disappeared,' David rather tartly remarked.

'By no means. But it's a temporary affliction. I know it as such, and endure it as such.'

David gave a deep sigh. 'Your arguments would be more convincing if I didn't feel that they were prompted by a personal hatred.' And he added with real curiosity, 'Why do you hate her so much?'

'I don't hate her,' lied Daisy. 'You know how susceptible I am to beauty. She's much too beautiful to hate. I've never seen a woman with so many natural assets. That's why I find her presentation of them so bewildering. I ask myself why the grubbiness? Yes, grubbiness, dear boy, you can't deny it. Why the sloppy clothes? Why the down-at-heel shoes, the disreputable look?'

'You saw her at her worst,' said David. And he added unhappily, 'She's improving.'

'Goodness, how pathetic that sounds! I expect you've been nagging her. She's very submissive, isn't she?'

'I rather like submissive women,' said David, as lightly as he could.

'No doubt. But submission has its price. Does she take your money?'

'She does not.'

'She will. She will say that such things don't matter between you two, thus sanctifying her beggary.'

'What a poisonous remark,' David said scornfully.

'How you fear the truth!' returned Daisy. 'You admit she's submissive, but you're afraid to flick the coin over and look at the other side.'

'She can be stubborn as well as submissive.'

'No doubt. Those submissive women can be very implacable. Don't be surprised if she turns out to have a touch of the sergeant-major.'

David remembered Isobel's voice pleading, 'What time will you ring? Tell me what time.' Rather grimly he said, 'I think you have more than a touch of the sergeant-major yourself, Mother.'

'Don't be preposterous,' said Daisy. 'I am a colonel at least.'

But David did not laugh; he only said stubbornly, 'No one has less of the sergeant-major than Isobel.'

'You may be right.' Daisy sounded indifferent, as if about to dismiss the subject. It seemed an afterthought when she said, 'Then, of course, there's the charge of murder.'

'That matter has been disposed of.'

'In law, yes. But who cares about the law? The public doesn't, not really. *They* haven't disposed of it. Even those who are most hot in her defence will find themselves wondering now and again if she did it or not. They wouldn't be human if they didn't. No, wherever she goes, whatever she does, she will always, always, be the woman who was suspected of killing her husband.' Daisy's voice rose; it became rich and sorrowful. 'And because extremes breed extremes, and love breeds hatred, one day you will quarrel with her. And on that day you will ask yourself...'

But David coldly interrupted. 'How I love those rolling Biblical phrases,' he drawled.

She had gone too far, she knew. Too anxious for victory, she had passed over into histrionics, and had lost him. She sat up and took the pads from her eyes, allowing him at last a full view of her bloodshot, sunken eyeballs. Blinking, she said, 'And now I expect I look like Moses?'

He was standing, his hat in his hand. 'You look very sick indeed. You must go to bed.'

She took his proffered hand, but found to her own surprise that she needed more than that. He had to thread an arm under both of hers and half carry her to her room, where she collapsed at once on the bed.

Hiding his concern, he said curtly, 'You mustn't go to the shop on Monday.'

She closed her eyes. 'I shall rest today and tomorrow. And I shall certainly go to the shop on Monday.'

He shrugged, and went to the door.

'So you are going?' she flung at him.

He halted. 'Mother, if I stay, can I relieve your pain?'

'No, it's not that . . .'

'Very well. Then there's no logical reason for me to stay. If you want me to live by logic, don't be surprised if I do so.'

Pitting her anger against a fresh spasm of pain, she clapped a hand to her cheek and cried, 'You use logic when it suits you, and ignore it when it doesn't. You want all of the prizes and none of the losses.'

'So do you. You ask me to reason Isobel out of my life, yet protest when I can also reason you out of it.'

She sank back on the pillows. 'I offer you order.' She sounded tired and peevish. 'But this love business is so *dis*orderly, so *very* disorderly.'

It was strange that after all her powers were spent, this one chance remark should strike home. On his way down the stairs, and all the way to Isobel's flat, the word 'disorderly' whispered itself again and again in his mind.

. . . . . .

David and Isobel sat on the bathroom floor, for although it was late afternoon, the heat had increased.

Isobel wore the Chinese robe David had bought for her, which was printed not with iris, but with chrysanthemums. Dropping from her shoulders and bunched between her legs, it left bare the cleft between her breasts and an inverted triangle of belly. He wore only shorts, his bare chest no longer anomalous.

They sat wedged in the narrow space between bath and wall, facing each other but a little apart; he with his back to the bath, she with her back to the wall, their raised feet on a level with the other's waist. Between them on the floor were two glasses of whiskey and water, both still half-full, though the ice cubes with which David had made them had melted long ago.

From the living-room came the ring of the telephone. It had been ringing for so long that it had taken on a note of great urgency, but neither of them moved, though their faces were turned to the door and their eyes were as wary as if they were waiting for an enemy to appear there.

When it stopped they turned enquiringly to each other.

'How many times is that?' asked David.

She shrugged. 'I don't know.'

'Who can it be? I really can't believe it's Sheila Jack, you know.'

'Neither do I. Not any more.'

'It's the kind of thing a drunkard does. Can you think of no one?'

'No. It's never been as bad as this, not even at first. Will you answer it for me next time?'

He looked away, a little disconcerted. 'Better to just let it ring.'

'Or take the receiver off the hook.'

'Very well. But if someone is so determined to reach you, they may ring complaints, and it's just possible we'll have the janitor up here with the P.M.G. men. I thought you didn't want that,' said David, who did not want it himself.

'I see. Then we'll have to forget it.' And as if to show her determination to do so, she let her head roll back to the white-tiled wall and closed her eyes. 'Nice here,' she murmured, 'so cool.'

Rather broodingly, his eyes explored her face. She had a cat's instinct for a comfortable corner, he reflected, and a cat's sensuous and deliberate way of settling to enjoy it. Having wished her to forget the telephone, he now resented her apparent ability to do so, for he himself still felt tense and irritable.

'And there's still tonight and tomorrow to do your work,' she said.

He thought she sounded like a fond mother who with affection but no understanding indulges her child's interest in some harmless hobby. 'Oh, quite, quite,' he said.

She opened her eyes. 'Why do you say it like that?'

'Like what?'

'You sounded sarcastic.'

'Did I? I'm sorry.'

'You don't sound sorry.' She offered him a hand; the curled and moving fingers begging him to take it. 'It isn't my fault,' she said cajolingly.

He gave her hand a look that was both thoughtful and detached, but did not attempt to take it until her moving fingers became still and he knew that she was about to withdraw it. Then he put his own hand, palm upward, a few inches beneath it, and she laughed and let hers drop heavily into it.

His fingers immediately closed about it in a spasm of anger and desire. He watched the flesh of her palm rise and crease, and felt the crush of her joints as the hand folded in his grasp.

'But it is your fault,' he said.

These words gave him such relief that he was able to relax his grasp and raise his eyes to her startled face. 'If a woman behaves like a doormat,' he said, 'it's her fault if people wipe their feet on her.'

'But what are you talking about?' she cried. 'I meant that it's not my fault that the telephone rings.'

'Yes, it is your fault. You're so supine that you invite disaster. You're so cowardly that you stay here instead of moving.' He released her hand, putting it back in her lap as if he no longer wanted it. 'Yet you must know that it can't go on for ever, this refusal to face facts.'

She let her head fall back against the tiles. 'I know I'm a coward.'

'Yes, you're a coward. This flat is your funkhole.'

'But you agreed that I should stay here,' she protested.

He found it easy to forget for the moment how willing his agreement had been. 'I thought you had some purpose.' He paused, giving her time to interrupt, his eyes seeking an answer in her face. Finding none, he went on, 'But if you did have a purpose, surely it's achieved by now?'

She met this with her trick of withdrawal. With her expressionless face and drooped eyelids, she seemed on the verge of sleep.

A bleak light flooded the bathroom. Sharpened by white reflections, it lay upon her upturned face, exposing two lines, new to him, that dropped from the inner corners of her eyes and surrounded areas of flesh almost negroid in colour. Her unsymmetrical mouth he had noticed before, but so fleetingly that it had seemed only a trick of attitude or light. Now, however, there was no mistaking it. On the left side her lips curved and parted as sweetly and exactly as the lips of a child, but on the right side they opened to disclose flatter planes, suggesting a little the taut flesh that springs apart from the cut of a knife.

By the continued concentration of his attention on this irregularity, it gradually imposed its expression of weariness and brutality upon her entire face, but this transformation was no sooner complete than his mind assumed its customary mastery over his eyes, and she became once again the Isobel with whom he was familiar. But he would never again see her as wholly beautiful.

The discovery of this imperfection moved him strongly, as if by reducing her value as an aesthetic object, it added to her humanity and accessibility. Moving his bare foot up the wall, he half-inserted it behind her shoulder. '*I* thought you wanted to stay here,' he said, 'to lay your husband's ghost.'

She did not move, but he felt her added tension and knew at once that he had miscalculated, that he could not expect so sudden a victory. But in spite of this he went on. 'And if that was your reason, and if you haven't done it by now, you never will, not like this. Was that your reason?'

She shook her head, not in denial, but restlessly, in evasion. 'What do you want me to do?' she murmured rapidly.

He knew that she was prepared to bargain, to cede him something in return for his continued silence. 'All right,' he said. 'I want you to go out.'

She said grudgingly, 'Why is that so important?'

'Because I'm sick of doing the shopping.'

'Oh. You want me to shop?'

'Yes, and to begin to see people. Will you?'

'I suppose so,' she said unhappily.

'Good.' He picked up her whiskey glass and put it in her hand, then drained his own, celebrating not only her decision but the defeat of his own caution, for to appear with her in public was to acknowledge her, even if that public were only Myra. 'Then I shall take you to see a friend of mine,' he announced.

She set her drink on the floor, untouched, and a look of caution appeared on her face. 'Who?' she asked.

'Myra Magaskill. You have to start somewhere, and Myra is kind, very kind. Think of this as a net to break your fall.'

Isobel took her feet from the side of the bath, drew them towards her, and encircled her knees with her arms. Laughing but pleading, she said, 'No, David, no. I can't jump.'

He put a foot on her shoulder and pushed her slowly but with force against the wall. When he had her pinned there he looked into her evasive eyes and a belligerent liveliness appeared in his own. 'You'll jump,' he told her, 'or by Heaven, I'll push you.'

'Not yet, not yet,' she pleaded.

'Not yet, not yet!' He thrust at her shoulder with his foot. 'This bloody inertia! Look, you can either live or die. Which do you choose?'

Her shoulder moved protestingly beneath his foot. 'That's absurd,' she said.

'Very well, you want to live. Then start.'

'But that isn't living,' she complained, 'seeing this Myra.'

'Yes, it is. People are life.' He jabbed at her shoulder again, half-laughing. 'At least it's a start.'

'It's very kind of you,' she said coldly.

'Yes, I know it is.' He was laughing frankly now, and looking at her with pleasure. He felt wonder, too, at his own happiness. 'I don't know why I bother with you,' he said.

She turned her face and gave him a direct look. 'Because I am beautiful,' she said in a hard voice.

The smile left his face abruptly. His foot slid to the floor, and she clumsily got to her feet, drawing her robe tightly about her, looking a little discomforted by his unbelieving stare. 'Men have always pursued me for that,' she said apologetically, 'and I've always hated them for it. I've always wanted something more than that.'

Behind his blank stare, David's thoughts were of Richard Purdy, who had met her in thick darkness. 'And did you ever get it?' he enquired coldly.

She was shifting her whiskey glass from tile to tile with one bare foot, like an uncertain chess player. He got to his feet and stood looking at her bent head. 'If you say yes, I shan't believe you,' he warned her.

She made a movement away from him, but he checked it with a hand on her shoulder. 'You seem to want a guarantee that a man would feel the same way about you if you were plain. But you won't get it, you know, not from me or from any man.'

Comprehension of many things came to him as he spoke, and he looked into her face with growing wonder. 'That's the way you were born,' he pointed out. 'We're all stuck with something, and you're stuck with that, and all its consequences.'

It suddenly struck him as so funny that he should be consoling a woman for her beauty that a burst of laughter escaped him, and she looked at him quickly, puzzled and ready to be angry.

'Look,' he reasoned, 'any woman would give ten years of her life . . .'

'They had much better keep them, those ten years,' she flashed out.

'A gift of the Gods!' he exclaimed incredulously.

'An accident of Nature,' she returned.

'So is everything. Talent, intelligence . . .'

'They can accumulate. Beauty can only deteriorate. And a man who falls in love with beauty will fall out of love when beauty goes.'

But future events, even when inevitable, are easy to dismiss. 'Ah, but by that time,' David said with confidence, 'something else will have grown to take its place.'

'Yes, I know.' She looked at him angrily. 'Habit!' she almost spat.

'And what's wrong with habit? Habit's a fine thing. It's all we have to sustain us sometimes, when enthusiasm flags. Enthusiasm for work, for example,' he added with a grimace.

'A prop,' she said scornfully.

He turned her by the shoulders, forcing her to face him. 'I didn't know you had such a contempt for props,' he said slowly.

Meeting his speculative stare, she faltered. 'I haven't . . . I . . . But oh,' she cried with sudden impatience, 'do you think that's all I want, a prop?'

Both frowning, they were watching each other with the alertness of fighters, but also with a new curiosity. The language of the body temporarily suspended, they were now using, gropingly but intently, the language of the mind; and although outwardly so much at variance, they were at that moment very near an understanding of each other: he seeing the thickets of secrecy and rumour about her beginning to part a little, and she seeing in him a better and more enduring hope than the one she had so desperately and falsely entertained.

She said uncertainly, 'You think I've used you as a prop. If I have, I was wrong. I think you're more than that. I think . . .'

She broke off and smiled at him, a little shyly, and it was unfortunate that he should have been moved by this to break once more into his importunate cry.

'Isobel, do you love me?'

Nothing is more wounding than the look of impatience or discomfort with which the less loving of a pair meets this demand. He dropped his hands from her shoulders and in the same movement bent to pick up their two glasses. 'Finish your drink,' he said curtly, 'and let's have another.'

The telephone rang as she was drinking. He saw her eyes widen over the rim of the glass, then she put it into his hand and said with decision, 'This time I'll answer it.'

'If you like,' he said.

'You're right,' she said almost gaily, as he followed her into the living room. 'I must begin some time.' But with her hand inches from the receiver she hesitated and looked at him for approbation. 'Mustn't I?' she begged.

He would not give it. 'I expect you must,' was all he said.

Determined to show no signs of interest, he carried the glasses to the kitchen, from where he could hear her voice, broken and puzzled, but could not distinguish her words. She laughed once—incredulously, he thought; and presently he heard her replace the receiver.

When he returned with fresh drinks he found her still sitting by the telephone. 'It was Theo Cass,' she said.

He set down the drinks with great care. 'Oh? And what did he want?'

She looked vague. 'All kinds of absurd things.'

'He wanted to come here, did he?'

'He seemed to.'

'Then why didn't you say so?'

'I *have* said so. You know, I believe he's rather horrid. I've never liked him.'

'Was he drunk?'

'He didn't sound at all drunk.'

David could have told her that Theo sounded most sober when most drunk. He did not do so, however, but picked up his drink and said meditatively, 'So when he rings, you don't hang up. You talk to him.'

'But one doesn't hang up,' she said.

'Doesn't one?'

'And after all, I have nothing against him.'

'No, that was quite apparent. You laughed.'

Their eyes met. On her face there appeared first disbelief, then the guilt and confusion that an innocent person so often displays on divining the thoughts of an accuser. She began to defend herself. 'I was taken by surprise. I didn't think . . .'

He nodded, as if this was exactly what he had expected from her, and made his way to the bedroom. While he was putting on his shirt she appeared in the doorway.

'David, why are you doing this? Why are you looking for something to blame me for?'

But he did not reply, and she came into the room and put a hand on his arm. 'David,' she pleaded.

'Yes.'

'Are you going?'

'Yes.'

'Why?'

'I'm going to do some work.'

'You were going to do it here.'

'So I was.' He sounded amused. 'But it's not a very good place to work, is it? You do understand, don't you, that I must work? It's a question of money. Or don't you care about money?'

He was fully dressed now, and as he passed her on his way to the door he asked casually, 'How do *you* get on for money?'

'You mean for rent, and things like that?'

'Yes, and things like that.'

'Well, I need so little,' she said awkwardly and humbly. 'And the rent — that's paid until the end of the year.'

They had halted in the living room, yards apart. 'And what will you do after that?' he asked. 'Will you take some from me?'

She watched his face. 'I suppose I would have, an hour ago.'

'But not now?'

She shook her head.

'But an hour ago . . .' he prompted her.

'Money wouldn't have mattered between us then.'

This was near enough to what Daisy had predicted to give him his victory. 'A curious kind of pride,' he scoffed, on his way to the door.

From behind him, he heard her cry of fear. 'David! Come back!' He heard the swish of silk, the thud of bare feet; then her head butted him hard between the shoulder-blades and her arms encircled his chest. 'Don't go, don't go.' And in the same imploring tone she said, 'I love you, I love you, I love you.'

He stood upright and still, staring at the door. 'Don't, Isobel,' he said.

Her babbling stopped; her grip relaxed. He turned to her with a sigh, hearing her sigh at the same time, and took her in his arms. 'It's all right,' he said. 'You don't have to say it.'

They stood interlocked for a long time, rocking slightly as if in grief. He noticed with surprise that it was dusk, and that a cooler current of air was stirring in the room.

'It's a little cooler,' he said vaguely.

'Yes,' she said, 'it is.'

They broke apart and moved with one accord to the divan. Like robots, they sat down, side by side.

'Yes,' he said, as if resuming an interrupted and rather sad conversation, 'I think you must marry me.'

She hesitated for only a few seconds. 'All right. And will you stay tonight?'

'No, I won't. I meant that.' He gave her a puzzled sidelong look. 'You don't seem very impressed.'

'By your offer of marriage. Well, I've never thought about it.'

'Neither had I, really. But I can't leave you, and I can't put up with all this sneaking and plotting and muddle. So I must marry you, if you'll have me.'

'Oh, I'll *have* you.' She laughed jerkily. 'When did you decide to ask me?'

'I didn't decide at all. I simply said it.'

She did not look at him, but clasped and unclasped her hands. 'Yes,' she said, 'it happens like that.'

David felt that Richard Purdy had made one of his backdoor entrances into their conversation, but was too exhausted to care. 'Do you mind very much if I don't come tomorrow?' he rather formally asked. 'I should like to see Myra. To arrange your debut,' he added with a smile.

'Yes, I do mind, but from now on I shall try not to show it.'

And when he was going she laid a hand on his cheek. 'It may be all right, this marriage.' She sounded worried. 'In any case, I shall certainly try.'

He thought this generous of her, in the light of his own behaviour. 'It seems we must both try,' he said.

Chapter Thirteen

THE following morning, Sunday, Daisy awoke free from severe pain, but because she knew it must return, and because she had learned to respect this new antagonist, she lay in bed most of that day, drowsing and drifting, storing strength to meet it.

Her appointment with Max Dobie was on Friday, and it was her intention to be admitted to hospital on the following Tuesday. She looked forward with longing to at least three days in bed. 'No visitors,' she decided, 'and no pills.'

She had often been bored by people who talked of having their teeth out, but now fragments of their talk returned to comfort her. 'Cairncross is wonderful,' they had said. Or: 'Cairncross popped my pretty new teeth in straight away.'

In the early afternoon David came to the door of her room. 'Mother, here's my cheque for Possie. We came in together last night. She has her job, she says. She's leaving on Saturday.'

'I know. And my new couple can't start until Anne moves to her flat, two weeks at least. Difficult. I'll have to engage one of those household services in the meantime. But don't give me the cheque, dear boy. Give it to her yourself.'

'No, give it to her with yours.'

Daisy took the folded cheque and opened it at once. 'Surely fifty would have been enough,' she said.

'I don't consider a hundred too much. Did she tell you anything about this new job of hers?'

'No. She has one of her moods. But she seemed almost insultingly pleased about it.'

Possie had not seemed insultingly pleased when she had spoken to David, and he was about to say so when his mother said, 'I see you're going out. There's no need to ask where.'

'I'm going to the Magaskills.'

'Alone, I hope?' cried Daisy.

'Yes, alone.'

'David, what a good idea!'

And David, hesitating in the doorway, decided that it would be unkind to break the news of his coming marriage while she was so sick.

Daisy felt much more cheerful after that, and when she later encountered Possie in the kitchen, she laid an arm across her shoulders and said affectionately, 'So you're off at last, Poss. Well, here is something from David and me.'

Possie took the cheques and moved from under Daisy's arm. Encased in hauteur, she held her head high and her mouth slightly pursed. When she had read the cheques she said, 'And no more than my due. Some would say less.'

She badly needed the stiffening that hostility would give her, but Daisy would not be provoked. She talked brightly and implacably about the dreadful, dreadful heat until Possie hung up her tea-towel and left the room.

Possie's new job was a fiction. Yesterday she had failed for the last time; she could try no more. 'I would die rather than tell them at home,' she had said to herself after this last rebuff, so she had rented a little yard room, and intended from now on to live on the pension.

'I'll be as free as a bird,' she thought bitterly, as she ascended the stairs to her room.

. . . . .

On Myra's verandah, where a grapevine gave coolness and privacy, she and David sat side by side in cane chairs, frosted glasses in their hands.

Their talk at first was desultory. They talked of the heat, of mutual friends, of Myra's new flat and of Hughie's sailing.

David found it soothing sitting here with Myra, whose parents he had known, whose problems did not show, and who served drinks in fine glasses. He had never liked her so well. When they fell silent he thought they might have been sea voyagers, looking out from deck chairs over a monotonous expanse of ocean, lulled by the promise of many such days before them.

Myra, too, would have been content to let the afternoon pass like this. It surprised her a little that in the companionship of this somnolent afternoon she should suddenly feel that only small talk was possible; anything else was too much trouble. Her hands were cooled by the glacial glass. She idly turned it, idly lifted it to her mouth; she felt half-asleep.

When David said at last, 'May I bring Isobel on Saturday?' they both felt the broken mood, the intrusion, as if someone foreign to their ways had suddenly joined them there.

She set down her glass. 'Of course,' she said.

'About four, if that's convenient?'

They had become very formal, she thought. 'Any time,' she said.

'Isobel and I have decided to marry.'

As he said this he turned abruptly and gave her a searching look, as if to surprise from her a true, unguarded response, but it was only joy that enlivened her face. 'Oh, I'm so glad,' she cried.

'And you think it a good idea?'

She laughed. 'If you want to marry Isobel, and if Isobel wants to marry you, why shouldn't it be a good idea?'

'You make it sound so simple.'

'Isn't it?'

'No.'

'But you told me you loved her. Though not in those words,' she added.

He was silent, and seemed to be debating this point. Then he said, 'Understand this. I'm quite engrossed in her. Or obsessed by her, if you like.'

'I don't like,' said Myra. 'I don't like at all.' She took a long drink. 'Shall we get drunk?'

'You sound as if you've just written me off as hopeless. And no, don't let's get drunk. I have to drive.'

'Yes, that's a thing about you, isn't it? The chief thing, I often think. You're a good citizen.'

'You make that sound very disparaging.'

'No,' she said uncertainly.

'You would approve, I suppose, if I took the risk of killing some poor beggar on the road.'

Myra had the air of being at bay. 'No,' she cried. 'And why are we talking about poor beggars on roads?'

'We aren't. We're talking about Isobel. And what you're really saying is that you're disappointed that I'm not quite lost to reason, because I can still see that it's *not* simple. Yet I've told you I intend to marry her.'

'Yes, David, I heard you.'

'And I do intend to, make no mistake about that.'

'I wasn't. But don't you think you might be?'

'No. I'm quite determined on it.'

She said sadly, 'You don't sound determined. You sound stubborn.'

Startled to have his attitude so accurately defined, he gave her a look of curiosity, not wholly friendly. Then he told her about Richard Purdy's notebook. In a careful, dry, unemotional voice, he quoted passages, pausing from time to time to mark the effect of these on Myra. She fished in her empty glass for slices of lemon, and while sucking these gave him encouraging little nods, but when he stopped speaking she only said, 'Well?'

'I know,' he said apologetically. 'When I'm with her it isn't important, either. But when I'm alone, it is.'

'Really?' She sounded incredulous. 'But David, everyone has a past life.'

'Not like that.'

'I expect they would all sound like that if Richard Purdy had recorded them. Mine would, I know.'

But he shook his head, not knowing how to convey to her his sense that for Isobel love had created its own climate and made its own rules, and that such total surrender was on another plane than Myra's self-consciously romantic preoccupation, which even at its deepest had never quite lost touch with life's amenities. This was vivid to him, but he could not put it into words. All he found to say was: 'The first time he met her!'

'And the first time you met me,' Myra said languidly.

He looked startled, then contemplative. Then he laughed. 'We were very young,' he said.

'So was she. She's only thirty now. But evidently we're to be allowed that excuse, while she is not.'

'Oh, one must be fair,' he admitted.

'Yes, one must, mustn't one? And as well as that, she *was* rather madly in love with him.'

'Madly in love,' David repeated thoughtfully. 'You know, one hears those words so often that they don't have much meaning. But I rather think they're accurate in this case, quite accurate.'

'Wait!' said Myra.

He thought she was about to make some objection, but instead she leapt from her chair and hurried into the house. When she returned she was carrying a basin of ice cubes in one hand, and in the other a bottle of whiskey by the neck. Meeting David's eye, she laughed, and swung the bottle like a club before she set it on the table.

'Your trouble is jealousy,' she said strongly. 'You're jealous of a dead man.'

'Yes,' said David. Then he said, 'No, it's not quite as simple as that.'

'Oh, it *wouldn't* be,' sighed Myra.

'But, listen, she won't talk about him. She won't even mention his name.'

For the first time Myra looked disconcerted. 'Never?'

'She won't. And I daren't make her.'

'I see.' Myra took a long drink in silence, then said

without much assurance, 'One can easily see why, of course. She's been so badly hurt.'

'Oh, I know all that,' he said roughly.

'And perhaps she knows how hard it is to stop at *one* revelation, how one must go on and on until every revelation is made, and things said that were better left unsaid. And the more deeply you are in love, or engrossed, or obsessed, or whatever you like to call it, the harder it would be to stop.'

Myra gave a satisfied nod. She was pleased with this explanation. 'So don't start, David, don't start.'

But when she turned to look at him she realised he had not been listening to her. Staring straight ahead, he said in a surprised voice, 'She won't talk about him because she won't deliver him up to me.'

'*What!*' Myra leaned over to peer into his face, then lay back in her chair, laughing. 'Whatever *that* may mean,' she said.

'All the same, that's the truth.'

'Oh, it's too far-fetched. And how unlike you!'

'It's the truth.'

'Pooh, pooh, pooh. Have a drink.'

'No, thanks.'

'Then I shall.'

As was usual after her third or fourth drink, Myra was feeling pleasantly careless. 'This is the last kind of thing I expected to hear from you,' she said, 'all this song and dance about diaries and past lives and delivering up dead men. I expected that if you had any objections they would all be practical, all connected with that silly murder charge. But no, not a word about it.'

'I accepted that long ago,' said David.

'I should hope so! It would be too mean to make her pay for being the victim of circumstances.'

'Oh, she'll pay. She'll pay all her life, and I with her. That's something else I accept.'

'Are we now speaking of your career?'

'It's easy for you to dismiss it so lightly, Myra. But it's not so easy for me. I've spent a great deal of time on it.'

'Too much. Far, far too much,' Myra said grandly. She had been lying back in her chair, but now she struggled upright, her weight on the edge of the light chair causing its back legs to leave the ground. Dangerously tilting, she said, 'And will it be affected, this wonderful career of yours? No, of course it won't be. Not a bit.'

Smiling, David looked obliquely down at the legs of her chair. 'Myra, let me give you some advice. Never come into court drunk. And never, never . . .' He pointed to the chair. '. . . create a diversion like that. It's like a crooked wig. It distracts attention from what you're saying.'

He reached out and forced the legs of her chair to the floor. She fell back into it. 'And about what you call my career,' he went on. 'It will certainly be affected. Let's not be silly about that.'

'No, I simply don't believe that. It's too absurd. Not all people are so narrow, so bigoted. You think they are because *you* are. But Heavens, people forgive, people forget. People are even sympathetic.'

'People, yes. Organizations, no. Organizations play safe.'

'Organizations? Organizations? What are they? Can you love them?'

Although David said nothing, Myra looked at him with sudden fierceness, as if he were hotly arguing. 'Now you have made me angry,' she said. 'Now I shall really get drunk.'

Already slightly drunk, she miscalculated the distance to the table and set down her glass with a thump. She glared at him again, then filled it. 'You ought not to do this to me, David,' she said sternly. 'You know how I loathe drinking in the daytime.'

He laughed, reflectively at first, then long and easily. 'I rather like you, Myra,' he said.

She looked at him more fiercely than ever. 'Ha! So you like me, do you?'

'Only when you're drunk.'

She laughed, her artificial ferocity forgotten, then caught his hand and held it against her cheek. 'Darling David, love this woman of yours. Love her and marry her. Believe me, it's worth more than anything else.'

'Myra, why is this so important to you?'

'Darling David, because I want you to go to Heaven when you die. And how can you, when you've never reached for it when you're here on earth?'

'Do you mean that by helping Isobel . . .?'

'No, no, no. How can you be so dense? I mean by transcending yourself, just once. Oh, let me remember that. I'm only saying it because I'm drunk. I never even knew until now that I had ever thought of such a thing. And tomorrow I shall have forgotten it or be ashamed of having said it. Isn't that sad?'

'Oh, very sad.' But David was thinking that if Myra had transcended herself in her love for Hughie, then perhaps she might have transcended herself still more by denying herself of him to stay with her children. And Myra, as if this had occurred to her also, suddenly dropped David's hand and turned away.

'But I know it's not always as easy as that,' she said quietly.

David rose with a laugh and a sigh. 'Never mind. I intend to take your advice in any case. I *must* love her and marry her.'

Myra was about to say, 'Ah yes, nothing can save you now.' But she checked the impulse in time. She looked intently into her glass, swirling the whiskey in the bottom of it. 'And you will be very happy,' she said.

. . . . .

Hughie came home sober, and without Dud Henderson.

'Hello, what's all this?' he cried, when he found Myra curled on her side on their bed. 'Not sick, are you?'

'No, only drunk. And I'm not, any more.'

Knowing how seldom she drank, he laughed dutifully, not believing her. 'What about dinner?'

'There's cold stuff in the refrigerator.'

'Don't you want any?'

'No, Hughie, I don't.'

He leaned over her and sniffed. 'I say, you've been drinking,' he said in a surprised voice.

'Yes, that's what I said.'

'Did anyone come?'

'Only David.'

'Old David, eh?' Hughie sounded disappointed, even a little envious. 'Well, well. And you got on the grog. Too bad I missed it.'

'Yes, such fun,' Myra said gloomily.

'You don't sound as though it was.'

'No, I'm frightfully blue. It was all those lies I told.'

'Hey, hey, hey! What's all this? What lies?' And Hughie sat down on the foot of the bed.

'Oh, I don't know. Perhaps they weren't lies after all.' Myra heaved herself slowly on to her back and extended one hand to him, but did not open her eyes. 'Come here, my jolly Jack Tar.'

Hughie edged along the bed and gave her his hand. 'Look here, this is a bit queer. Why did David come?'

Myra, still with her eyes closed, ran the tips of her fingers over the back of his hand. 'He came to tell me all his troubles.'

'What troubles?'

'Oh, I don't know,' said Myra.

Leaving his hand with her, Hughie turned his head to look speculatively out of the window. 'Say what you like, I still think there's something in this Purdy business. I'll tell you why. Dud knows Theo Cass pretty well, and he was drinking with him last night — he's on it again, by the way — and Cass told him that David drove her home from the Coroner's Court.'

Myra drew his hand to her lips and kissed it. 'All lies,' she said sadly.

'Oh I don't think so, you know. Dud doesn't tell lies.'

'I didn't mean Dud. I meant me.'

. . . . .

Isobel spent that Sunday alone, reading shallowly in
books she had read before, or lying in cool baths or across
her bed, never quite still, thinking of marriage to David.

To Isobel, marriage had meant two bodies enslaved and
entangled, not happily, forming a single entity that might
have been spinning in space, so truly isolated it had been.

But during the last few years she had sometimes thought of
another kind of marriage, and whenever she did so there
arose in her mind vague images of a house, a man, and a
sheltering tree.

She was not a domesticated woman, either by nature or
training, and it was with difficulty but with growing hopefulness that she now began to entertain this new ideal.

She was as unworldly as only those can be who have
dedicated themselves to a single passion. She had travelled
the world, and remembered its landscapes, buildings, and
peoples only as a confused and dreamlike background
against which she and Richard Purdy had played out their
selfish yet self-losing drama of love and hatred. Excesses of
these emotions had stamped on her memory many images,
but she could seldom give these images an exact location.
Thus, streetlights seen through misty rain, having bloom but
no brilliance, she associated with delight too great to be
easily borne. That was in Edinburgh, she believed, in their
first months. Or she remembered a cold and towering façade
of stone against which she had knelt in the dark to weep, and
how it had suddenly seemed to press against her, to threaten
her with its toppling weight. But she only thought, and
could not be sure, that this had been in Florence.

She remembered the faces of people they had known, but
did not feel that these lives had touched theirs. Only the
faces of the women with whom Richard Purdy had so
stubbornly betrayed her came to life for her. To these she
could give names and exact features.

Less immoderate women, living all their lives in quiet
villages, had more acuteness and worldly wisdom than she.

Worldly ambition, too, was both so alien to her nature

and so much outside her grotesquely limited experience that though she knew enough to guess that, in marrying her, David must relinquish or at least contract his ambition, she took it for granted that this could be lightly done, and did not give it much of her attention, that Sunday during David's absence. She saw the project of marriage with him in broad and somewhat misty perspective, as an ideal only. Detail evaded her.

That the day's absence had been a significant one, during which both had shifted their positions, became apparent as soon as he arrived at her flat that night. The absence might have been not of a day, but of a year, so persistent was the undercurrent of estrangement in their meeting, so urgent the sense of questions to be asked and answered before they could be at ease with their changed intentions. It was clear that a new phase had begun for them both.

David had brought food, and while they ate their sense of estrangement grew, for this business of food could not help but suggest much more such business in the future, and it was precisely on such details that both their imaginations balked. Both talked too much, their voices a little strained, and looked into each other's eyes with glances that were not quite candid.

It was only bodily fusion that gave them back their ease. Lying once more in the incomplete darkness, their awkwardness with each other seemed as if it had never occurred.

But later, when he was rousing himself to leave her, he asked, 'Has Cass rung again?'

There was a moment of silence before she said, too casually, 'No, he hasn't.'

He was grieved by the clumsy lie, and tempted to challenge her on it, but feared too much another quarrel, an exposure of the issues between them. He put an arm resignedly beneath her shoulders and drew her to him.

She turned to him at once, flinging a thigh over both of his, and began to talk eagerly to smother the fear, so similar to his, that had caused her to lie.

Chapter Fourteen

ON Thursday afternoon, Myra, hot and anxious-eyed, stepped through the doorway of Daisy's shop.

'Air conditioning! How lovely!' she gasped.

'Daisy's just had it installed,' Willy told her. 'She said this heat was bad for the stock.'

Myra laughed; then, because Willy continued sullen and serious, she said soothingly, 'But, Willy, she was joking.'

'No, she wasn't. I know when Daisy's joking.'

'Where is she?'

'Gone home.'

Myra was not sorry to hear this. She had been a little reluctant to face Daisy, against whom she could not help but feel she was conspiring. 'Ah!' she said. 'Then *you* may show me these wonderful drawings, Willy.'

'No, I can't. She took them with her.'

'Oh damn. Why did she do that?'

'She wanted to show them to someone else on her way home. And she's coming back here tonight. We're going to do the window. Overtime,' said Willy, 'in this weather.'

'I might catch her at home,' said Myra, to whom the drawings seemed more desirable than ever now that Daisy was hawking them round.

But Daisy was not yet home when she called.

'One never catches her,' she complained to Possie, 'She's like that ever-receding horizon.'

'She'll be home any minute, dear,' said Possie, who did not know when Daisy would be home, but who, after days of proud aloofness, was feeling too desperately lonely to part with Myra, whom she had always liked.

She ushered her into the kitchen, sat her down with much ceremony, and gave her a glass of cold lemonade. 'You won't mind waiting in here, I'm sure,' she pleaded.

'No, I like it.' Myra had kicked off her shoes, thrust her hat to the back of her head, and now sat with her elbows on the table, very much at her ease. She was amused by Possie, so nervous and garrulous, and was touched by her talk of old times. She thought Daisy very lucky to have this kindly and devoted cousin, who was loyal and discreet, and who would never, never leave her. She herself had recently lost her housekeeper, and she was just about to mention this fact to Possie when Daisy appeared in the doorway, the bundle of drawings under one arm.

'Why, Myra! How unexpected! And how delightful!'

They kissed; then Daisy said, 'Dear child, you look ghastly.'

'So do you, Daisy, I'm happy to say.'

'It's the heat. We all do.'

'Except Possie,' said Myra, who had noticed Possie's offended air, and supposed it was because she felt herself excluded.

'Yes, how *fresh* Possie looks,' Daisy agreed.

They both beamed at Possie. 'It must be wonderful to stay home all day,' sighed Daisy. 'No corsets, no rushing.'

Possie, with elaborate restraint, laid her knife and half-peeled potato on the sink. 'If you'll excuse me,' she said distantly, and walked from the room, looking at neither of them.

Myra turned enquiringly to Daisy.

'It's nothing, nothing,' Daisy assured her. 'Now give me a few minutes, dear girl, then we shall look at these drawings.'

Myra peered at her. 'Daisy, you're crying.'

'No, I'm not, silly girl. It's only that I've rather a pain, and must take a pill.' And she began to search her handbag in a nervous and distracted way, quite unlike her.

'Where is this pain?' asked Myra.

Daisy found the bottle and tipped a green capsule into her hand. 'It's nothing, only my teeth.'

'David didn't mention it.'

'No? Well, he has troubles of his own.' While she took the pill, Daisy looked searchingly at Myra over the rim of her glass. Then she lowered it and said, 'Hasn't he, Myra?'

'I expect so,' said Myra. 'You ought to have them out.'

'Yes. Cairncross is going to do it.'

'Cairncross is wonderful.'

'He had better be,' said Daisy.

She shut her eyes, clenched a fist, and beat a tattoo on her cheek with such force that Myra became alarmed. 'Sit down, Daisy,' she commanded. 'Sit down at once.'

'Yes, I think I must.' And Daisy sat down and lowered her head to her folded arms.

Myra found this unfamiliar Daisy a little embarrassing. She was not at ease with physical suffering. 'Shall I go?' she asked with constraint.

'Certainly not. I shan't be a minute.'

But a minute passed, then many more, in utter silence. Myra looked down at Daisy's bowed head and thought how hard it must be for her, who was never ill and seldom opposed, to have to deal with toothache and Isobel at the same time. She was beginning to feel more than ever guilty for her part in the affair, when Daisy sprang to her feet and said briskly, 'Thank you, Myra. Now come along.'

In her sitting-room, she spread the drawings on the floor, explaining that she had meant to mount them before showing them, but had not had the time. 'It didn't occur to Hal. He never thinks about money, the odd boy.'

She stood aside, probing her cheek, and watched while Myra walked hesitatingly up and down the row of drawings, peering and blinking in a worried way. 'Like a review of the troops,' thought Daisy, 'by an officer in his dotage.' She could see that Myra was disappointed.

'Well, I don't know,' Myra said at last. 'They're all so scrawly.'

'Don't buy any if you don't like them. *I* certainly shouldn't.'

She joined Myra, and they both stood looking down at the drawings: Myra with uncertainty, Daisy with a fond smile.

'Tell me which one you like best,' Daisy suddenly demanded, as if this were a new game she had just invented.

Myra's finger hovered, then pointed. 'That one, I think.'

Daisy turned on her a look that was both appreciative and amazed. 'Why, Myra, that *is* the best!'

'Is it?' Myra squatted, took the edge of the drawing in her fingers, and examined it with a new interest. 'I rather like,' she said, 'those tiny grey figures walking up the beach carrying fishing nets. Are they nets?'

'Yes, nets,' said Daisy with approval.

'And the boat. It looks as if it's made of gauze. Yes, and that makes the sea look so heavy and solid.'

'Exactly.' Daisy, who had not looked closely at any of the drawings, wiggled her fingers in a manner vaguely explanatory. 'That's why he made the sea opaque and solid,' she improvised. 'It's the men who are made of sea water, and the boat.'

'Yes, I see that. But why? And what are they doing among all the people swimming and sunbaking, and all the beach umbrellas? People don't fish and swim from the same beach, or do they?' She bent to decipher the pencilled title. 'Deaths at Sea,' she read aloud. 'But who's dead?'

'Probably the fish,' said Daisy.

'Or is it the men who are dead?' cried Myra. 'Why, Daisy, they're not men at all, they're ghosts.'

'I believe you're right.' Daisy put on a look of amazement at such perspicacity. She took the drawing and examined it. 'Heavens, she *is* right,' she said to herself.

Rather jealously, Myra twitched the drawing from Daisy's fingers. 'I like it,' she said. 'It's pathetic, but he has managed to be not the least bit solemn about it.'

'Oh, nobody can accuse Hal of reverence,' said Daisy.

'I see now what you meant when you called them witty.'

But what Daisy had made Myra feel was not only that the drawings were witty, but that she herself was. 'And the one of the lizard on the rock,' she said. 'I like that one. He looks so huge and prehistoric.'

Daisy nodded. 'That one is my own favourite, as it happens, though by all impersonal standards the one you've already chosen is the better. But don't buy the lizard, Myra, not if you want to group them. One will alter the scale of the other.'

'I must have it,' said Myra. 'I'll hang it separately, on another wall. And to hang with the beach one, I'll have, I'll have . . .'

And Myra moved quickly and excitedly before the row of drawings, while Daisy, standing to one side, offered her from time to time a little languid advice.

In the end, Myra selected four drawings, then sat down at Daisy's desk to write a cheque. 'I hope I like them as well when I get them home,' she said.

'You will. It's the best possible sign that you didn't like them at first sight. Buying a picture is like taking a husband or a wife. Love at first sight soon peters out, and then you hate them, and regret your money, and want to hide them in the attic. Knowledge of what you're buying — that's what pays off. And you can always love them later, if you must,' she added generously.

Myra, still fired by excitement, her guard down, was busy writing the cheque. 'Is that what you tell David?' she asked.

'So he has confided in you?'

'Yes. No.' Myra looked up, her face flushed. 'Damn, I've made this cheque out to you.'

'That's all right.' Daisy whisked it away from her and read it. 'I suppose I ought to give you some kind of a receipt for this,' she murmured, looking vaguely round the room as if wondering how one transacted such business. She did not like giving receipts.

'Pooh,' said Myra. 'What should I do with a receipt?'

'Oh, I don't know. You could put it in a little drawer.'

'Exactly.'

Daisy had been fanning the cheque dry, but now she suddenly stopped. 'Myra,' she said sharply, 'it was *marriage* we were speaking of.'

'When? I don't know what you mean.'

'Yes, you do. I compared buying a picture with taking a husband or wife. And *you* said, don't deny it, "Is that what you tell David?"'

'Did I? Look, Daisy, Willy said you're going to the shop tonight. I really must go now, and let you rest.'

And Myra almost ran to the door, but it was no use — there was Daisy at her heels. 'Myra,' she was pleading, 'you must tell me.'

'You must ask David,' said Myra in the hall. 'And, Daisy, I can find my own way out.'

But Daisy followed her to the door, where Myra was forced to turn to say goodbye, but was given no chance to say it, for Daisy at once grasped her wrist and said, 'Myra, if you're really fond of David you won't support him in this disastrous enterprise.'

Myra's face took on a closed stubborn look. 'You know I'm fond of him. I want him to be happy,' she said.

Daisy dropped her wrist. They looked each other over with great care. Then, slowly, Daisy smiled. 'Dear girl, there's no need to ask what side *you* are on. You and Mrs. Purdy are co-religionists.'

Myra turned blindly away, lunged down the shallow steps, then turned back to face Daisy. 'I wish I didn't like you, Daisy, because you're really rather horrid. And I can't think what you mean by taking sides. You ought to know that in the end David always does exactly as he pleases.'

'I wish I could count on that,' said Daisy.

'Goodbye, Daisy.'

'Goodbye, my dear.'

As Daisy shut the front door, Possie quietly let herself out through the kitchen, carrying a weekend bag. She hurried; she did not wish to be challenged by Daisy, nor to be forced to explain her flight in words. For Possie, on going to her room and seeing the row of half-packed suitcases, had suddenly decided that since she had to go, she would go now. 'One more day here, and I'll crack up.'

She had been forced to pay the rent of her little room from the time of taking it, and she could send for the rest of her bags. Her way was open and her justification plain. But so strong was her habit of subservience to Daisy that it was with a feeling of guilt that she let herself out of the door. It was useless to recall her many grievances. She felt she was leaving Daisy in the lurch.

Daisy went upstairs to rest, and as she passed Possie's room, where she believed her to be sulking, she threw an exasperated look at the closed door.

'Thank Heaven *that* will be over by Saturday,' she said to herself.

And when Possie did not appear to cook dinner, Daisy still had no suspicion of her flight. She merely shifted in her mind the location of this fit of the sulks. Instead of sulking in her room, she now supposed Possie to be sulking in some cinema, where she would make an interim dinner on a bag of chocolates.

Of more concern to her was the fact that David did not come home, not even to shower and change, as he usually did before he went to see Isobel. She now suspected him of keeping a change of clothes at Isobel's flat, an arrangement ominously domestic, and far more frightening to Daisy than any mere protestations of love.

To give him time to appear, she delayed going to the shop. Walking restlessly about the house, looking out of windows, she mistook other cars for his. But he did not come, and at last she was forced to go, with her mind still seething and her words unspent.

At the shop she found Willy sitting in her back room reading a detective story.

'Haven't you started?' she snapped.

He did not look up. 'I was waiting for you.'

'I was delayed.'

'I thought you must have been.'

'You might have started, Willy.'

He closed his book then, and looked at her. 'Daisy dear, you had better take a little pill.'

Daisy was, in fact, delving in her handbag for her pills, but as soon as she heard this she pulled out a handkerchief instead. Giving her face a token dab with this, she asked, 'And why didn't you turn on the air-conditioning?'

'What! Just for *us*!'

Daisy turned it on herself. 'Oh, of course,' said Willy. 'I forgot the stock.'

In the shrouded window, Daisy worked feverishly, as if trying to quell with speed and energy the slight but even tremor of her hands. All she allowed Willy to do was to set up a stand and to pass things, which she snatched from him with angry cluckings of her tongue.

'I'll tell you what I'll do, Daisy,' he volunteered at last. 'I'll just stand back here and say, "Ooo, that's lovely."'

Daisy shot him a twisted smile. 'You'll be interested to hear that Myra Magaskill bought four of Hal's drawings. I've the cheque here, but I've still to endorse it. She made it out to me.'

'How much?'

Daisy told him.

'Heavens, all that lovely money,' Willy said dully.

'Yes. Your terrible little friend will be pleased.'

'Oh, he'll be pleased all right.' Willy took his underlip in his teeth; his eyes were troubled. 'But Daisy——' he suddenly burst out.

'Yes, yes. What is it?'

'Oh, nothing . . .'

'Willy, I loathe that, and you know it. Pass me that Thai silk. No, not not *not* the blue. The green, boy, the green.'

Willy, who had once had a short spell as a waiter, did not like being called 'boy'. He picked up the wrong silk, then allowed his mouth to hang stupidly open as she pushed him out of the way and got the silk herself.

'All right, Daisy, since you don't need me, I'll go out and get some coffee.'

'You stay here.'

'No, not until you take a pill.'

Daisy gave him one of her droll looks, less effective than usual. 'Mutiny, Willy?'

'If you take a pill now, it might have worked by the time I get back.'

'Very well, wretched boy, I'll take a pill. Go and pamper your stomach.'

Willy rolled down his shirtsleeves, considering Daisy as he did so. 'Have you seen Max?' he asked.

'Why should I have seen him? Our appointment's not until tomorrow.'

'I just thought you might have.' Willy picked at a fingernail. 'He was looking for you.'

'What? Did he ring?'

'No.'

'Then how do you know he's looking for me?'

'Hal told me.'

'Hal,' Daisy repeated. She stood very still for a moment, then backed away from the window to consider the effect of her green and blue silks. She backed into Willy, who halted her with a hand between her shoulder-blades. 'Whoops, Daisy dear,' he said.

Surprised to find herself comforted by the friendly pressure of his hand, she leaned back slightly, enough to make him add the support of his other hand. Sighing, she said, 'Oh, Willy, Willy. Perhaps *you* ought to have been my son.'

'Daisy! Oh, Daisy, that's the nicest thing you've ever said to me.'

'Then don't sound so grieved about it, dear boy.'

'But I am grieved. Why do you have to say a thing like that now?'

'Never fear. I shall be horrid again in a moment.'

'Yes, I know you will.' He gave her a little push to set her straight. 'Coffee,' he said, wandering towards the door.

Pounding her cheek, she sighed again. 'What can Max want?'

'*Please* take that pill. Perhaps he doesn't like the designs.'

'Nonsense. I saw Helen yesterday. She was most enthusiastic.'

'Yes, but you know how they work together. She enthuses, and Max does all the dirty work.'

But Daisy suddenly bounded into the window and began pulling at the silks. 'This is wrong, all wrong. What else have we got?'

Willy, at the door, turned to her a horrified face. 'Shop!' he called softly.

Daisy ignored him. This was one of their jokes. Willy often announced in this way stray cats or pieces of newspaper blown in from the street. Kneeling in the window, cursing fretfully, she gathered up the tumbled silks. 'Don't go, Willy. Stay and help me.'

'But, Daisy, it's *Max*.'

Max was in the shop before she could stand up. In dinner dress, he waited in the shadows beyond the bright window, his head tilted back and one foot thrust forward. Immobile, he yet had about him a hurried and imperious air. At her first glance Daisy noticed only the dazzling white of his shirt front, for she was distracted not only by a fuller flooding of pain, but by Willy, who was bobbing about behind Max most ridiculously, trying to mouth something at Daisy over his shoulder.

She rose; masses of blue and green silk rustling away from her and falling at her feet. Stepping out of them and off the dais, she smiled. 'Why, Max dear!'

He nodded guardedly, but did not advance, so that it was she who had to go to him, which she did with delight and grace, her eyes never leaving his face, for if they did she knew they would inexorably slip to her folder of designs, which he carried, unwrapped, under one arm.

Resting one hand lightly on his shoulder, she looked beyond him into the despairing face of Willy. 'Your coffee, Willy. But don't be too long.'

She watched him go, then turned her smiling face to Max. 'You've been looking for me?'

'Yes. I rang your house an hour ago.' Max looked with interest about the shop, his glance alighting at last on her ruined window. 'David said you were here.'

'So David is home!' she could not help exclaiming.

'Yes, but apparently on his way out again.'

Daisy touched her face, then quickly dropped her hand. Max was searching for a place to set down the folder. She indicated a little table, then followed him to it. 'Some changes, Max?'

He laid down the folder and flexed his arm, as if its light weight had been irksome. The noise he made was neither affirmation nor denial.

'They must be very urgent.' She looked at his clothes. 'You've interrupted an engagement.'

'Helen and I are going back to Melbourne tomorrow. Only for the Cup, but we thought it best to settle this matter first.' He gave the folder a dogmatic slap and met her eyes for the first time. 'These won't do, Daisy.'

'Then we shall make them do,' she said calmly. She repressed an impulse to pound her cheek. 'I ought to have taken that pill,' she thought.

Max slapped the folder again. 'No, they won't do at all, not with a hundred changes. The whole basic scheme is terribly, terribly wrong. The fact is, Daisy, there's no integration from room to room.'

Daisy knew they were not as bad as that; she looked genuinely incredulous.

'No integration,' Max repeated. 'But the greatest disappointment of all is the drawing room. It's theatrical, Daisy. There's no other word for it.'

'On the contrary,' Daisy most pleasantly replied, 'there are a number of other words. 'Let me show you something, Max.'

She gave him no time for refusal, but drew him to her side and opened the folder. Holding him there with a flow of talk, she picked up and laid aside the sheets of paper, one by one, commenting on each with words that were intended to give them an extra dimension, to turn them into rooms. There they were (it was her intention to imply), casket after beautiful casket in which Max and Helen were to be lightly and suitably encased.

But doubt rose in her as she spoke. Max showed none of the answering glow to which she was accustomed. He had not caught fire. Standing with his hands clasped behind his back, inclining or cocking his head, he did not bother to hide either his patience or his boredom.

Daisy had fallen into the snare that awaits all professional charmers; she had fallen into glibness. Her charm had become a mannered imitation of itself. Her voice was as fluent as ever, but it was too fluent, and as she talked with increasing momentum into his elaborately patient face, it even took on a note of hysteria, which she heard with disgust but could not check.

'And as for your drawing room . . .'

She picked up the sketch, fumbled, and dropped it. Impassively, he retrieved it from the floor and gave it into her hands. 'It's no good, Daisy,' he said.

She became confused. 'You mean this?' And she indicated the drawing.

'No, not that. The whole thing. It's no good. You're wasting your time. I'm sorry.'

Nothing could have been crueller than the kindness in his voice. It was a great shock to Daisy to realise that he found her pathetic.

She stacked the designs, closed the folder. 'Very well, Max,' she said crisply.

His relief, his glance at his watch, were added insults. 'But of course,' he said, kindly still, 'I shall expect your account for the work you have already done.'

'Very well, Max.'

He turned to go.

'Max?'

'Yes, Daisy.'

He halted with some reluctance; Daisy observed it with disdain. With a forefinger, she lifted one strand of her beads. 'Who *is* to do your house, Max?'

He would not hedge. 'Hal,' he said.

Daisy threw back her head and let loose peal after peal of laughter. As clearly as if her eyes were not shut, she saw the haughty, enquiring expression that would now be on Max's face. And when she opened her eyes, there it was. She was pleased by this small triumph. She let her laughter die. 'You're in the hands of a gifted amateur,' she said scornfully.

'Gifted, yes. Most gifted,' he said promptly. 'And an amateur, I admit, and very, very young. Perhaps that accounts for his freshness, his originality, his throwing off of all the old, stale, tired formulae.'

She parried this with a laugh. 'You'll simply be living in a bigger gazebo.'

'You're mistaken. That boy's extraordinarily versatile.'

Daisy considered this with her head on one side, delicately raising and lowering her strand of beads, while behind her smiling mouth pain raged.

'Ah yes,' she drawled at last. '*I have* heard that he's versatile, in practically every way one can think of.'

Max's stance tautened; his mouth wordlessly snapped.

'And I guessed it would appeal to you,' continued Daisy with an ever-broadening smile, 'but I'm slightly surprised that his youth, freshness, and versatility should have the same kind of appeal for Helen.'

He could not quite believe her capable of so gross an insult. There was an uncertain, interrogative note in his voice as he said, 'Helen admires his talents enormously.'

But Daisy was determined to leave him in no doubt. While one part of her mind condemned as stagy and banal her game with her beads, she hoisted and dropped them for the last time. 'My congratulations, Max,' she said. 'I hope that you and Hal and Helen will be very, very happy.'

After that, she expected him to leave at once, but instead he clasped his hands and settled his feet. 'I'm deeply sorry you said that, Daisy, deeply sorry.'

'Max, I'm busy.' And she moved away from him, into the dimness near the door, lest he should see the tears of pain in her eyes and attribute them to loss of nerve.

Following and passing her, he stood with one hand on the door-knob. 'At heart, Daisy, you're a bully and a moralist. Helen has often said so. I'm sorry for your son, especially at present. No doubt you regard his little fling with Mrs. Purdy as the end of the world.'

Daisy went to the window, where she mounted the dais and began to collect her silks. 'His little fling,' she echoed, contemptuously stressing his choice of words. 'No, Max, if David is having a little fling, I can't see that as the end of the world.'

'I'm happy to hear that, Daisy. A man may be allowed some diversions, surely, even a man with David's high hopes. We're none of us so priggish as to condemn him.' Max gave an uninflected laugh. 'Most of us envy him, in fact.'

'Oh, you gay dogs,' drawled Daisy.

'But of course, though we're all very sorry for her, it would be regrettable if he married her.'

'How Edwardian you are tonight. It must be your waxed moustache.'

He fingered his moustache with a cold smile, watching her bent back, the rapid but ineffectual movements of her hands among the silks.

'David's little fling seems to be common knowledge,' she said absently.

'Oh, one hears these things, you know.'

And before he shut the door he said, 'That cooling unit of yours makes too much noise, Daisy. I'll get you a better one than that when I come back, at cost.'

She thought how like him it was to make such an offer now,

when their relations were certainly severed for ever. 'I got that one at cost, Max,' she said.

'Yes, I expect you did.'

'Goodbye, Max.'

His voice was unctuous with false regret. 'Goodbye, Daisy.'

She flung the silks from her as soon as he left. Half-blinded by pain, she walked carefully to her back room, where she took a pill, then sat down at her massive desk. But as soon as she sat down she began to shake violently. Her head nodded of its own accord, her teeth chattered, and her hands moved blindly among the litter on her desk until they encountered the telephone directory.

'Cairncross, Cairncross, Cairncross.' She muttered it like an invocation while she looked for his home number.

'Cairncross, Cairncross, Cairncross.' She dialled the number and waited, weeping and pounding with one fist on the desk.

But Cairncross was oddly obtuse. He did not seem to understand that she must have her teeth out that night. Speaking clearly and with maddening slowness, he reminded her that she was to go to hospital. 'That was your wish, Mrs. Byfield, not mine. And you wanted your denture in right away. It's not ready yet.'

'So you're using that as a stick to beat me with, Mr. Cairncross?'

'Mrs. . . .'

'I am in agony, agony. Is this your service, Mr. Cairncross?'

But all her shouting and goading could not move him. 'Tomorrow,' he kept repeating.

She gave in angrily. 'Very well. I have no alternative, and you know it.'

'Shall we say two o'clock?'

'My God! What do I care? Two will do.'

Willy, entering from the street and hearing her replace the receiver, sidled rather apprehensively towards the open door of her back room, but as he reached it she hurtled through it, colliding with him.

'So you sneaked back?' she shouted.

He took one step back, then stood still, his feet together and his fingers curled feebly against his chest. 'Daisy!' he pleaded.

'Don't Daisy me! You knew that Hal had the contract for the Dobies' house, didn't you?'

'I tried to tell you,' he wailed.

'Ha, but you *didn't*, you *didn't*. You let Max come in here and fling those designs in my face.' She pointed dramatically to the folder, neat and square on the small table. 'You subjected me to that humiliation. You made me lose my head and say things I would never have said if I'd had time to prepare myself. Is that your loyalty, Willy?'

'Oh,' said Willy, 'this is awful.'

'Yes, Willy, it is awful. You, Willy, to betray *me*! Me, who took you out of that novelty shop and taught you everything you know. All you did there was talk all day to those seedy little boys and those moronic girls with greasy hair. That rusty sink full of coffee grounds — remember? — behind the home-made screen. In those days you thought it cute to cover a screen with liqueur labels. And the Cruikshank and Phiz drawings — remember? — torn from library books and *tinted* by one of your clever little friends and stuck into gimcrack frames . . .'

'I was happy there,' interjected Willy, showing a little spirit.

'And broke,' she hoarsely accused him. 'You sold nothing.'

They began to bicker about what Willy had sold and what he had not sold, and on these petty details the momentum of her speech spent itself a little. She slowed; she faltered; and Willy took advantage of this to shout, 'Do stop this, Daisy. It simply isn't *you*.'

She glared. 'You fool, Willy. This *is* me.'

'Then I think you're horrid. You're positively common.'

'Is that what you think? Then leave me, leave me. Go and work with your nasty little friend.'

'No, I won't leave you, Daisy. But I shan't pretend Hal hasn't asked me to. He even offered me a partnership.'

'What kind of partnership?' she jeered.

Willy flushed. 'A business partnership.'

Daisy sat down abruptly in a broad-seated, gilded chair. 'Then take it, take it. I shan't care.'

'Oh, poor Daisy!' Bending his knees, half-squatting so that his eyes were on a level with hers, he cried again, 'Poor Daisy! No, it's no good. I couldn't leave you like this.'

Furious at having been found pathetic for the second time that night, she thrust her face close to his. 'I don't need you, you imbecile. You're not indispensable. Go, or I'll sack you.'

Willy stood up and gave a long wail. 'All right, Daisy, all right.'

'Now get me a taxi.'

'If you ask me nicely, Daisy.'

'Oh, *get* me a taxi.'

He looked at her for a long time, without animosity. 'All right, Daisy, I'll get you a taxi.'

. . . . .

Successes must accumulate. The first success condemns one to reach for the next, and the next, an endless striving. Daisy had always known and accepted this, but she had always believed, too, in its converse: that one failure breeds another, that the first failure undermines the will and relaxes the grasp. Thus, she felt her failure to dominate Max to be a natural sequel of her failure to dominate David.

The taxi-driver thought she was drunk. She half-lay in a corner, her head barely level with the top of the back seat. Pain so blurred her vision that in William Street neon signs were fused into sheets of light, curving around and above them in a ghastly tunnel through which the taxi was soundlessly propelled. Later, when buildings became dark and assumed unnatural perspectives, nausea made her shut her eyes.

When she heard the driver ask, 'Is this it?' she sat up and saw the dark bulk of her house, heard the familiar soughing of the harbour. 'Yes,' she said, 'this is it.'

She sensed the emptiness of the house as soon as she entered. She went straight to Possie's room and flung open the door. She saw the packed suitcases, the turned-down bed, and the note on the dressing table. 'A carrier will call for my things,' she read aloud from this note, and looked again at the suitcases. 'One of those cases is mine,' she said accusingly, to no one.

She did not give a thought to the new couple, coming next week. She knew they would not come.

Unable to sleep or even to rest, she ranged through the house, turning on lights as she went. Touching the furniture, pressing her hands on panelled doors, all she saw was age, and the overtaking dust.

Presently she went to the bathroom, where she knelt on the floor and retched into the toilet pan. When she stood up she made no effort to resist the self-pity that is almost inseparable from vomiting. 'I am sick, sick, sick, and nobody cares. Not even my own son, who is locked away with that great soft woman of his.'

'That murderess,' she added, without a fluttering of doubt.

For the first time in her life she had quite lost her other self, her guide, the cool little spectator in her head.

. . . . .

David stood at Isobel's darkened bedroom window, slightly to one side, his hand on the curtain, ignominiously peeping.

In the street below stood Theo Cass, teetering on his heels. Light from the street lamp, lying on his upturned face, showed him to be grinning. Behind him stood his car, a new Jaguar.

David, who knew that Theo could not see him, nevertheless felt that their eyes were meeting: his from darkness, Theo's from light.

Isobel, in the bed behind him, had been silent for a long time. David left the window and went to her very quietly, as if Theo could hear as well as see him. He sat on the edge of the bed, not touching her.

'Still there?' she whispered.

Angered by this mirror held to his own uneasiness, he said loudly, 'There's no need to whisper. Yes, he's still there.'

'It's late,' she said. 'The front door must be locked. Perhaps he's waiting for someone with a key.'

'Remarkably patient, your friend Cass.'

'David, I've done nothing to provoke him to this.'

'Did I say you had?'

'Your tone says it.'

'You watch for the slightest nuance, don't you?'

But he believed — and they both knew it — that she offered Theo Cass provocation enough simply by being what she was.

When he went to the window again Theo was still there, and still in the same attitude. Like a corpse, David thought, with his fixed grin and his strange teetering — a corpse under water, anchored by the feet, swayed by tides.

'Jesus!' he burst out. 'I hate that man.'

'Yes,' said Isobel. 'So do I.'

He was surprised to find her at his shoulder, so quietly she had come. He drew her back into the room. 'Are you trying to let him see you?'

'Oh, you're absurd. It's too dark.'

He flung away from her, walking about the room, speaking very quietly in spite of his injunction to her not to whisper. 'Look, I shan't come again until Saturday. No more of this sneaking and hiding. It's either got to be open or not at all.'

'But if it can be open on Saturday, why not now?'

'What? Like that?' He flung a hand towards the window. 'No,' he answered himself, 'not like that.'

Presently he said, 'I've never done this before. I've never skulked in my life before.'

Her voice came to him through the dimness, a little dry. 'Nor I. I scarcely knew that such situations existed, where all this skulking was necessary.'

He turned to her, wishing he could see her face, but she was visible only as a figure lying on the cane lounge near the window, an arm behind her head, a knee raised. 'I imagine it's quite a common situation,' he said. 'One lives in a society, after all, and one must keep the rules.'

'Or appear to keep them.'

'Quite so. Since appearance is all that's demanded, surely it's a small thing to ask.'

He sounded ready to argue, but was diverted by the slam of a car door, the soft, receding roar of an engine.

'He's gone,' said Isobel.

They became suddenly gay, laughing like successful conspirators, turning on the lights, talking loudly.

'It even looks a bit bare down there without him,' David remarked.

But when he was dressing, he said, 'All the same, it's ludicrous to be so much at his mercy.'

She was handing him his clothes, moving when he moved, keeping as near to him as possible. 'It's not for much longer,' she said. 'Only until Saturday, you say. And then, when we are married——'

'Why do you say it like that, as if you don't like the word?'

'David, it's not that I don't like it. It's simply that I can't believe it sometimes. Sometimes I feel we're children.' She smiled, taking his head in her two hands, and hiding her face in the crook of his neck. 'Children playing houses,' she said.

He put his arms about her and enfolded her as closely as was possible, and so that her raised arms should not impede him, she made a crouching movement, then thrust her arms through his armpits and clasped them at his back.

'But I do love you,' she said, as if in answer to some contention of his.

. . . . .

When David reached home he found all the lights on, and Daisy, her hair spiked like a cockatoo's crest, running round the house as if looking for some lost object.

She began to talk at once, without even greeting him, about her teeth, about Cairncross, Willy, Max Dobie, and Possie. But he could make little sense of her babbling, and was inclined to discount it; for he had lately seen her rally so often that he was wary of this show of helplessness, believing that she meant to snare him with it.

She would not go to bed, but flung away from his guiding hand like a petulant child. '*You* go to bed. *You* get some rest. You'll need it, you'll find, now that all this has come out.'

'All what?'

'All about you and your criminal woman.'

'You said something about Max.'

'Your little fling with Mrs. Purdy, that's what Max called it.'

'Well, it would have been known very soon in any case. It doesn't matter.'

She gave him a pursed, malicious smile. 'Yet you *look* as if it matters.'

'Oddly enough, you don't.'

'Why should it matter to me? Willy's gone. I shan't open the shop tomorrow. No one will care. And Max's house — Hal's doing that.'

'That's fortunate, as things have turned out.'

'Yes, a great piece of luck. Is that how you see it? Evidently all my work has meant to you is that it's kept you and fed you and educated you.' She looked him over as if trying to calculate the amount of money that had gone into each cubic inch of him. 'The sacrifices I've made for you!' she intoned at last.

'Indeed you have. And now, Mother, if Possie's really gone, we'll have to see about getting you someone for the next few days.'

'I can't afford anyone. I shall have to retrench. Do you think this house is cheap to maintain? And there'll be no money from you, now that you have that great fat woman to keep. I'll move,' said Daisy, with bitter pleasure. 'I'll move to a small flat.'

It suddenly occurred to David that she was rather enjoying all this, and since he knew nothing of the luxury of licence that follows the dropping of a role too long sustained, he suspected her once again of a last desperate effort to dominate him. All else having failed, he thought, she was falling back on pathos.

And pathetic she certainly appeared, wandering about her sitting-room, one hand clasped to her distorted face, the other searchingly and restlessly touching one or another of her possessions. 'I expect I shall have to sell all these,' she murmured, 'but it doesn't matter, it doesn't matter.'

As a performance, David thought it almost too good to be true, or would have, if he had not known how convincing a performer she could be. He watched her cautiously, waiting for her to betray herself.

She came to Hal's drawings, stacked on a chair. 'Here's something I shall certainly sell. Hal *gave* me these.' She looked at David as if expecting him to contradict her. 'I've already sold four of them to Myra, and I have her cheque, made out to me. So at least I've got some money out of the little spiv. But hard-earned, hard-earned,' she groaned lugubriously. 'Like every penny I've ever made.'

David had not expected her to so grossly overplay her hand. He went to the door, smiling to himself. 'I'll call for you at the dentist's tomorrow,' he said.

'I expected you to make the offer, to ease your conscience. But I neither want you nor need you.'

'I'll call in any case.'

As he was ascending the stairs she appeared in the hall below him. 'I suppose you think that only Max knows about you and that woman,' she shouted up at him. 'But if Max knows, everybody knows. Gordon Haggett knows. Everybody, everybody, think of that.'

'Hush, mother,' he said.

Chapter Fifteen

'Mr. Cass is lunching at the Federation Club,' Phillip Cass's secretary told David.

David, who knew that Phillip Cass usually ate from his desk, was unguarded enough to ask, 'Not the Federation Hotel?'

'No, Mr. Byfield, the club.'

'Is he lunching alone?'

'No, Mr. Byfield. With Sir Gordon Haggett.'

Replacing the receiver, David reflected that he had little hope of catching Phillip alone at the Federation Club. But he hungered for news of Theo, whose white grin and oscillating figure had appeared to him that morning so immediately on waking that it had seemed like the continuation of a dream. He thought he would get such news easily from Phillip, who disliked his uncle enough to be frank about him.

As for Gordon Haggett, a meeting with him was inevitable sooner or later, and David was in that state of tension where it is easier to rush to meet trouble than to sit waiting for it.

Before he left his chambers he carefully inspected his mirrored face, which had already set itself in a suitable expression. Grave, alert, and self-contained, it allowed little of his emotion to show. He felt it was a good face to outface with. Only the eyes, too much exposed by the tensely distended lids, were a little feverish in their very steadiness. He hooded them.

New lovers may be assailed at any time by a sudden and weakening memory of the beloved. Such a memory rose in David as he set foot on the first stair of the Federation Club.

Swiftly branching and flinging itself through him like a miraculous tree, it caused a spasm of blindness and a silent cry to his poor, poor, beautiful girl.

These words were all that stayed with him, and he mechanically repeated them to himself as he went through the door. 'My poor, poor, beautiful girl.'

When he looked into the dining-room he saw Phillip Cass and Gordon Haggett at a table on the far side. Neither of them looked up. Standing there in the doorway, he greeted several acquaintances, and was a little surprised to find that there was nothing ambiguous in the greetings he received in return.

He began to feel like a man keyed up to an operation, who, after having been scrubbed, shaved, swaddled, and stretched on a trolley, is left tense and uneasy in a cold ante-room, at the mercy of mysterious delays.

In the circumstances, he could not have met a better man than Horace Dangerfield, who came hurrying down the corridor from the lavatories, slightly drunk, his gait broad and swinging, his head down like a charging bull's.

He collided with David, righted them both, then said, 'Join us. He indicated the bar and reeled off several names. 'Love to have you meet them.'

'Sorry,' said David, 'I'm here to see a man.'

'About a dog,' said Horace, who did not scorn such jests. He waited until David had given a token laugh, then clapped a hand on his shoulder. 'Or a bitch, eh? Wish I was your age again. But listen. Seriously, now . . .' To suit the word, he made his face serious, even solemn. When drunk, his effects were of the broadest. 'Seriously, why don't you reconsider that proposition of mine? Coming with me to the States?'

'But I say!' laughed David. 'You've already been and come back since you made it.'

'But I say!' Horace mimicked his accent. 'But *I* say I'm going again, that's what *I* say. March, maybe April. Love to have you along. And bring her with you, if you're that caught up.' He raised a warning hand. 'Now get that look off your face. It doesn't cut any ice with me. I know all about it, and what's more, I know what it's like. Nobody will know her over there, think of that. Good for the girlie,' said Horace.

'Mrs. Purdy,' said David, without inflection.

Horace looked at him for a moment, very alertly. 'So she's to be called Mrs. Purdy, is she? Want to marry her, do you? No, don't tell me, don't tell me. Makes no difference to me. Only it'll finish you with that crowd of wowsers in there.'

He was indicating the dining-room with a jabbing thumb. 'To stay in with that mob,' he went on, 'you've got to play the game their way. But it's different in business. In business it's ability, ability, ability. That's what counts all the time, and to hell with the social stuff.'

Breaking off, he raised a hand in greeting to someone behind David, at the same time saying in a low voice, 'Here's Haggett.'

Gordon Haggett brushed by them with two nods, two quiet words. 'David. Dangerfield.'

They watched him disappear into the lavatories. 'One of the old school,' drawled Horace. 'It works, too, if you can put it over.'

'I read with him,' said David.

'So I've heard. Well, I don't suppose there's anything much wrong with the feller.'

David was watching the door through which Gordon Haggett had disappeared. 'Did you say you were leaving in March?' he asked.

'March or early April. Think it over. In the circs, you could do worse.'

'Thanks. I will think it over.'

'Good man. Good man.' Horace's voice was a little condescending.

David found Gordon Haggett washing his hands. 'I want to see Phillip Cass,' he said. 'Have I missed him?'

'No, he's still there. Do you want to see him alone?'

'Oh, I should hardly like . . .'

'That's all right, David. You may give him my farewells and apologies.' The older man was prolonging unnecessarily his hand-washing, bending seriously over the bowl and avoiding David's eyes.

'Thanks,' said David. 'Do you remember my telling you some time ago that Horace Dangerfield wanted me to go with him to the States?'

'I think so. Yes, I remember.'

'He's just repeated the offer. He even,' David said blandly, 'suggested that I bring my girl.'

'Is that true?'

'Well, that's what the man said.'

'No, I meant is it true that you have this girl, or woman, or whatever they call them these days? I believe "mistress" is dated.'

'Yes, it's true.'

Gordon Haggett had dried his hands and was now giving great attention to the insertion of his cuff-links. 'And it's Mrs. Purdy?'

'Yes, it's Mrs. Purdy.'

'One hears it, of course, up and down the street.'

'The discreet profession,' said David.

Gordon Haggett, flexing his arms to settle his cuffs, gave a fleeting, reluctant smile. 'Don't say anything more about it, David, not to me.'

'I don't think I intended to.'

'Yes, you did. You came in here for that purpose. But it's no good, David, I can't help you. I shan't censure, approve, nor advise you. Moreover — and this is important — I can't tell you one thing that you can't tell yourself.'

'I don't want censure, approval . . .'

'You wanted something. And I can't give it to you. I'm too damned old. I've forgotten what it's like, if I ever knew.' Smiling at the floor, he said wryly, 'Sometimes now I find myself speaking with my father's voice. The other day I found myself thinking that a client of mine ought to be horsewhipped. I have to guard against that. God help me if they ever put me on the bench.'

Footsteps ringing behind them on the terrazzo floor caused both of them to fall silent. David was at first annoyed by this intrusion, then realised that it did not matter; the conversation had already ended. He gave a strained laugh, which sank to a sigh of resignation. 'Well, I had better go and see Phillip.'

'Yes, good boy, good boy,' murmured Gordon Haggett.

Phillip Cass, eight years David's junior and dogged by ill-luck, had always treated David with deference. That he did not do so today, but greeted him with a kind of self-conscious bonhomie, David at once attributed to his own diminished prestige. In this he wronged him. Phillip had just become engaged to marry Gordon Haggett's daughter Pamela, and his changed manner was caused not by a fall in David's stock, but by a rise in his own. Because he now saw before him the possibility of success and of the proper use of his talents, his bitterness had slipped from him. His eyes glowed and smiled in his narrow face. He was confident, ebullient, and much more likeable.

He told David about Pamela. 'But I've beaten the gun a bit. It's not to be announced till Saturday.' And he added with a touch of his former sarcasm, 'We are a very formal family.'

David congratulated him. 'You must let me buy you a drink.'

In the lounge Phillip sat looking about him with the alertness and calculation of a prospective buyer viewing a house. 'Gordon's putting me up for membership here,' he said. 'And I'm leaving Theo. Setting up on my own.'

'You sound pleased,' said David.

'I'm pleased, all right. I've been Theo's dogsbody for six years.'

'How long has this present bout of his been going on?'

'Weeks. It's his longest yet. Betty blames the heat. Have you seen his new car? It's a Jag, a beauty.'

'I've seen it,' said David.

'He comes into the office and creeps around like a cat, talking to himself. Then he goes haring off after that woman Isobel Purdy. He's got some kind of obsession about her, the bloody fool.'

He spoke so naturally that David knew that no rumour had reached him. 'When did that start?' he asked.

'During the case. Didn't you notice?'

'Yes, but I thought it was only his usual attitude. He's always been like that.'

'Not quite like this. This is worse. In proportion to the woman, perhaps. To hear Theo tell it, she's something special. At first he used to say she was beautiful but grubby. Now he says she's beautifully grubby. He must have her, he tells me, and he's going to have her. "Okay," I say, "have her and get to hell out of here." But he can't get her. She's locked herself up in that flat. Odd, her going back there. Sometimes,' said Phillip reflectively, 'I feel sorry for that woman.'

'So do I,' said David.

'Theo talks a lot about her husband. It seems he read a letter — I think it was a letter — where Purdy describes how he first picked her up. According to that, she wasn't hard to make, but hell, it was years ago, and she could have changed. Theo quotes it quite a bit. He oughtn't to.'

'The discreet profession,' David said again.

Phillip laughed. 'Oh, we're not all like Theo.'

'Lately, I've begun to believe he's mad.'

'Mad and rich. That's why nobody takes him seriously. Professionally, I mean. He's lucky, in a way. He can do as he pleases, with Mrs. Purdy or with anybody else. Nothing will ruin Theo.'

David had been staring thoughtfully into his glass. Now he emptied it and set it down. 'I was wrong to let you run on about Mrs. Purdy,' he said. 'I'm going to marry her.'

He smiled at Phillip's astonishment. 'Oh come on, Phillip,' he said in a gentle, rallying tone. 'Nobody could be as amazed as you look.'

'God,' Phillip said weakly, 'I would never have said . . .'

'I know you wouldn't. That's why I'm telling you this. If you heard it later, you would have resented my allowing you to talk like that, and rightly so. You probably resent it now. I can only say I'm sorry.'

'Well, that's fair enough.' Phillip no longer looked astonished, but he looked and sounded perplexed. 'A lot of people aren't going to like it, you know,' he said slowly.

'One can't please everybody. And sometimes such things decide themselves.'

'Oh, I know, I know. You might say it's the luck of the draw. And hell . . .' Phillip stopped to give rather a perplexed laugh. 'Surely in this day and age a man can marry whom he pleases.'

'Surely,' David agreed.

There was a silence, both men staring at the table top. Then Phillip said diffidently, 'Look, how public is all this?'

Suddenly, David found himself unprepared for this question. 'Well, in the circumstances . . . What I mean is, no public announcement is intended.'

'You know you can count on my discretion.'

'I'm not asking for it, Phillip.'

'You have it in any case,' Phillip rather grandly declared. He half-rose from his chair in his eagerness to signal the drink waiter. 'You'll have another?'

'Not for me, thanks. I've to call for my mother at the dentist's.'

They left the lounge together, Phillip laying a friendly and insistent hand on David's shoulder to usher him first through the door. And on his shoulder this hand remained as they crossed the foyer and emerged into the street. David found its comradely pressure both comforting and humiliating.

Daisy was lying on a bed in Cairncross's anteroom, and when David entered she rose at once, clasping wads of lint to her mouth, and asked him something in a muffled voice.

Enquiringly, he offered his ear.

She lifted the lint a little, and her voice came in a thick

lisp. He thought she was asking him where the car was. 'Right outside at a meter,' he told her.

Cairncross put his head round the door of the adjacent surgery. Rimless spectacles glittered on his nose, and in his hand he held an instrument, also glittering. He looked over Daisy's head and spoke directly to David. 'It'll be a while before she can have her teeth in. Ridges will form there, hard ridges. She's to see me in a week.'

Daisy said something, clearly in protest, and they both turned to her, waiting politely for her to repeat it. Cairncross, who had suffered greatly, gave a frosty smile.

But she would not repeat it. Standing silently between the two tall men, turning her dull glare on each of them, she looked shrunken, savage, and trapped.

It was not until they were waiting for the lift that it occurred to David that she had been trying to say, '*I* am here, Mr. Cairncross.' She had resented being talked about as if she were absent, or an idiot.

When they reached home, after a completely silent journey, she went straight to her room and shut the door. David heard no key turn, but it gave the effect, all the same, of a locked door.

He had engaged a nurse, and as soon as she arrived he left to keep an appointment at his chambers. He was late, but he was becoming accustomed to time pressing hard at his back, appointments postponed or tardily attended, work in arrears, stays of proceedings applied for.

Late that afternoon, the nurse rang him to say that Mrs. Byfield had dismissed her by means of a note pushed under her door.

He did not go home, but worked at his desk until nine o'clock. Then he let himself out of the silent building and ate a steak at an empty café nearby. Behind him, two waitresses were talking of their husbands with a kind of rough, disparaging affection that he found oddly attractive. 'Working wives,' he mused, and remembered Charlie Hannaford saying, 'Work or kids. They've got to have one or the other, or they go bad.'

The atmosphere, the very smell, of that rainy day in Isobel's flat returned to him with great force. But it was the force of a dream, not of a remembered reality. The flat did not appear to him as he now knew it, but as quite a different place, just as the present Isobel seemed to have no connection with the woman he had tried and failed to conjure into life that day. And Theo, the casually despised friend of that time, was not the figure he had last seen swaying and staring, that he had felt to be dangerous, and worth enmity.

As for himself, the secure and complacent man of the past was one in which his present harassed, anxious, yet buoyant self could scarcely believe. Indeed, his effort to fuse the two selves left him only with the conviction that he had moved to another plane of existence since that rainy day. So strong was this sense of estrangement from his past that when, on leaving the café, he caught sight of himself in shop windows, he was even momentarily confused to find that his appearance had not altered.

No conscious intention took him on the detour past Isobel's flat; the turn was automatic.

A light was burning in her bedroom, but Theo's car was not outside. David cruised through the nearby streets, where he always parked his own inconspicuous Holden, but found no Jaguar there, and no Theo.

He parked in one of these streets and sat in the car for about ten minutes, while he allowed the image of Isobel, suspended high above the street in her illuminated box, to become clear and irresistible to him.

He rang from a public telephone box. 'My darling,' he said, as soon as she opened the door to him. Her hair was loose, and he inserted one hand beneath it and clasped the back of her neck. 'Have you any objection to marrying me next week?' he asked.

The door stood open behind them. She broke free and shut it. 'I thought you weren't coming until tomorrow,' she said.

'But here I am. And you haven't answered me. Will you?'

'Yes, I will.'

Her hair was damp and sweet-smelling. 'You've washed it,' he said.

'Yes, for tomorrow.'

As he entered the bedroom he turned off the light, then went at once to the window, where he stood looking down into the street. She came and stood at his shoulder. She did not speak, but he heard her sigh.

. . . . .

Daisy, after she had got rid of the nurse, got up and prowled through her shuttered rooms, ignoring the ringing of the telephone. She knew that people had been to the shop, had found it closed, and were now ringing to insult her with their false cries of alarm, their false condolences.

In a very few days, she told herself, they would give up. 'And in a month or two it will be as if I had never lived among them.'

It seemed to her now that her life among those people had been like the performance of a tight-rope dancer. She had amused and fascinated them, but they had regarded her as something of a freak. She had gained no hold on their affections.

Three words rang in her head. 'Nobody loves me.' And though she had recovered enough to be astonished that she, of all people, should be reduced to this banal cry, she had not recovered enough to suppress it.

When David came home she was in her room again, lying on her bed in the dark. To his solicitous but mechanical questions she gave no reply, until at last he laughed in exasperation.

'Can't you talk at all?' he asked.

Daisy could, but only in a thick and lisping voice she scorned to use. He was standing blocked against the illuminated corridor. She heard him laugh again, and saw him throw up his hands in defeat. Then he went away.

'Nobody loves me,' thought Daisy.

Chapter Sixteen

'SAIL-ING, sail-ing . . .' sang Myra.

'Over the water-y bl-hoo,' responded Hughie in a bold baritone. Then he dropped his voice and said briskly, 'But not today.'

'What? You mean you're not sailing today?'

'Not today,' Hughie said again.

'But it's Saturday.'

'I know. But Dud's got *Bikini Girl* up on the slips.'

'Oh. Up on the slips.'

'And we're going to clean her up a bit.'

'Then you are going out?'

'Not until three o'clock. You don't mind if I go?'

'No, Hughie, I don't mind.'

'What will you do?'

'I daren't tell you. It's too fascinating. It might make you stay home. Then Dud would be disappointed, and *Bikini Girl* would be dirty.'

'I'd rather like a day at home. The paper predicts rain.'

'Are you losing your enthusiasm for boats, Hughie?'

'God no,' said Hughie, who was, especially his enthusiasm for cleaning them.

'Then go,' said Myra. 'I have one hundred things to do. Do you realise that we'll be moving soon? And I must cook that corned beef.'

Hughie sighed. 'Sweetie, when do we get a change from corned beef?'

'Sweetie, as soon as we get a new housekeeper.'

It was a quarter past three before Hughie got the car out. 'Look here,' he said to Myra when he had kissed her goodbye, 'you'd better have a rest this afternoon. You're as jumpy as a cat.'

'Darling,' cried Myra, and kissed him warmly in return. 'Darling, I'm perfectly all right.'

'You seem all right now,' admitted Hughie, and patted her bottom.

It was a hot, high day, with no sign of the predicted rain, and Hughie took the road with pleasure. On the hill out of Rose Bay, Theo Cass's car whooshed past his with a soft parabola of sound, and he caught a glimpse of Theo at the wheel, slightly crouched, his face set in a rigid grin.

Appreciatively, Hughie followed the progress of the Jaguar until it disappeared over the brow of the hill. 'Say what you like,' mused Hughie, 'drunk or sober, there's no one can handle a car like that feller Cass.'

. . . . .

When Theo was drunk, he seemed to himself to be moving with a storm around him. Wherever he went, he bore about him this roaring cavern of sound, but where he stood, at the storm's calm centre, all was orderly. The lights shattering around him, the wild looming and dissolving of buildings, were of no concern to Theo except as a comic spectacle. He saw himself as dwarfed by the raging landscape, a little black figure, but very precise, very dextrous, and, above all, safe.

Owing perhaps to his great physical strength, he was able to maintain this beatific stage of drunkenness for much longer than most people. His eyesight became very acute at this stage, and on the faces floating up to his from the blurred edges of his storm he saw, with a kind of white clarity, every detail of hair and pore. Skin lost its human associations and became material, stuff. From staring eyeballs, light detached particles of glass. On a hand drawing near to light a cigarette, ridges in the nails showed like the grain in rough timber, while the hands themselves, those clumsy hooking devices with their jointed prongs, he saw as especially fascinating and ludicrous.

This detachment from human appearances made him feel lonely, unique, and immeasurably superior to all the animated shells about him. He found them very, very funny. Sometimes at the sight of them a great soaring whoop of laughter would be torn from him, but mostly the only outward sign of his mirth was the fixed grin that to the people who knew him was the special mark of his condition.

Only when he was drunk did Theo feel at harmony with himself, and this sense of harmony was most complete when he drove his car. Drunk or sober, he could see nothing ludicrous about a machine, and when he inserted himself behind the wheel his face would become serious and even dignified for a moment, and his hands still: a little pause for homage. Like himself, the machine was powerful, exact, and capable of withholding itself, and when enclosed in its curved metal casing he felt so much a part of it that he did not know if the machine was an extension of his body, or his body an extension of the machine. Flowing through them was a common current of power, the junction of which was the wheel, where his hands lay. Checking or meting out the power of the machine, it was his own power he commanded.

What made all this so wonderful to Theo was that this power *could* be let loose, that it *could* destroy, but that it was his whim to withhold it. So he drove fast and audaciously when drunk, but never recklessly, obeying lights and hand signals in the contemptuous manner of one so sure of his power that he has no need to flaunt it. Such checks were, indeed, challenges to his skill, as were the steep, twisting, harbourside streets he frequented at these times. Any fool can roar along an open road, expending energy, but Theo, drunk, stored his, hugging it to him, and his inner mirth was never more intense than when he saw but rejected an opportunity to astound by some piece of bravura.

When Hughie saw him, he was on his way once more to Isobel, although in his exultation in the journey he had almost forgotten that she was its object. He made a last, beautiful turn, swelling into her street like a conqueror, and would have gone on if the plane tree had not reminded him that this was his destination.

He drew to a stop beneath it. When the engine cut out there was a short period of complete silence, like deafness, to which Theo submitted with his hands on the wheel and his head bowed over them. It was not until he got out of the car that the roaring gathered about him again. He felt heat striking up from the pavement, down from the white sky, and the soaring and vertical lines of tall buildings like knife blades to his eyes.

Walking stiffly, he negotiated the two shallow steps and passed into the small lobby. Since the beginning of what he called 'Operation Purdy' he had often got as far as this, and the only reason he had got no further was that steep steps were a dreaded hazard, capable of mortifying him, of reducing him to an ordinary human condition.

Theo's famous drunken equilibrium was a trick. When standing, he held it by concentrating on his feet, by thinking of them as weighted, magnetically attracted to the earth. Thus secured, they would allow his body to oscillate slightly, but never dangerously. When he walked he imagined the pull still there, and established from the start a stiff, shuffling rhythm that was surprisingly easy to maintain. These exercises gave him much private amusement, and it was a point of honour with him to refrain from using his hands. Railings were not allowed, nor the support of walls.

But because stairs could only be climbed by lifting the feet clear of the ground, Theo had hitherto only stood and swayed and smiled, here in the lobby or out in the street. He had been waiting, without impatience, for his power to reach its peak.

Nevertheless, certain though he was that the day had arrived, his ascent was not easy. To sober eyes he would have looked like a badly manipulated puppet, with his slopes and jerks and too sudden unlockings of the joints, and even Theo himself was aware that his wonderful rhythm was in danger of failing him. On the last flight the labour of concentration was so intense that when he reached the top he could no longer remember why he had come.

He went quietly from door to door, seeking a clue. When he came to one marked 42, he knew at once that it was the right one, but could not recall who was behind it, or why it seemed of such importance that he should reach that person.

He did not see the bell. Clenching a fist, he rapped slowly, three times.

It was this knock, with its suggestion of a code, of an intimate directive, that made Isobel open the door. She had dressed too early, and waiting had made her tense and abstracted. She did not stop to calculate that David had rung only a few minutes before, and had not yet had time to make the journey, but ran to the door at once and opened it to its fullest extent.

Theo saw a woman in the doorway, standing perfectly still, and something in her attitude, slack yet resistant, immediately aroused in him feelings of frustration and contempt. It was by this response that he recognised her; he did not remember her name.

She did not move as he glided past her into the room, but he saw her head turn, following his movements, and he sensed rather than saw that she was afraid. He did not want her to be afraid, so he took off his hat and held it tightly against his chest with both hands. 'I'm very sick,' he said humbly.

She advanced tentatively into the room, like a shy visitor. 'But you can't stay here,' she said.

He heard these words, but they seemed quite without meaning. He walked slowly and carefully round her, in a wide circle, while she, at the centre of the circle, turned watchfully with him. He was pleased with this circling, which was a test of his balance, but he knew that he must not allow his triumph to show. He halted, feeling the weight in his feet, allowing himself to sway slightly. Then he took a step nearer to her, and as he did so he remembered her name.

'Isobel Purdy,' he said, and because he associated the name with beauty, he added dreamily, 'You're beautiful.'

But he did not see her as beautiful. Looking at her mouth, he saw it simply as a hole surrounded by two moving flaps; the upper flap sometimes lifting to disclose wet wedges of bone. He observed, too, the unsymmetrical nature of this upper flap, and how one side, livelier than the other, writhed and bucked, dragging the less mobile side with it. He saw the effort, the drag, and knew that she was talking, but he was too engrossed to attend to what she was saying.

'What do you want? You can't stay here. Please go.'

He observed that red grease had been applied to this flap, and had also coloured the tips of the minute hairs that grew about its rim. But he did not derive his usual enjoyment from his detached and magnified vision. He knew it was hampering him, defeating some intention. The effort he made to control it was just enough to make comprehensible her next words.

'Why do you stare like that? Oh, you're ridiculous.'

He smiled. 'So are you, dear heart, so are you.'

Her mouth was a mouth again, but near its downward dragging side there was some agitation, as if a minute bird fluttered there, struggling to free itself from the covering of skin. Theo slowly raised one hand and pointed to it. 'A little bird,' he said drowsily.

When she laughed, Theo felt it as a response to his own gathering mirth, but when he let loose one of his whoops she immediately covered her mouth with her hand, and he saw embedded, in the tip of each finger, a shining red beetle.

He looked unhappily down into the inverted crown of his hat. Laboriously, he told himself that this was Isobel Purdy, who was known to be beautiful, and that as soon as he touched her he would stop seeing her, and she would become beautiful again. The problem seemed to be to get close enough to touch her. Any sudden movement would upset his wonderful balance, so he must be very clever, and take her by surprise.

He tenderly stroked the brim of his hat, as if it were a little, furry animal. 'All you do is laugh at me,' he said.

He did not look at her, but heard her say, 'Look here, you must go. I'm expecting someone.'

He slowly put on his hat, forcing it down until it almost covered his eyebrows. Peering beneath the brim, drunkenly screwing up one eye, he mournfully agreed that he must go. 'Yes, poor Theo must go.'

This clearly disarmed her, and on his way to the open door he took advantage of her relief and her unfearing nearness to set both hands on her shoulders. He still looked harmless and clownish, with his mouth hanging open and his hatbrim obscuring his eyes, but when she stepped back a pace his grip on her shoulders tightened and he matched his step to hers.

Unable to dislodge his hands from her shoulders, and unwilling to descend to a struggle, she could only step backwards, laughing and begging him to go. And Theo heard the cries and words issuing from her bucking lips, but saw only the lips themselves, and felt both saddened and repelled. This was not what he had planned. He was too close to her; he still saw her too clearly. His vision had conquered all his other senses. Moving as if summoned from a dream, he worried about this while he followed her long, backward steps.

So round and round the room they went, like dancing partners essaying a new step, sometimes balking, sometimes executing a shuffle, and sometimes pausing, absurdly, for conversation.

'Your hair's coming down, dear heart.'

'Oh, stop this, stop this. Leave me alone.'

Forced at last to a halt by the wall at her back, she saw before her his set grin and his eyes glinting under the brim of his lunatic hat, and when she laughed again it was to ease the suspense of his pursuit, and at her own fear of turning her back on him. She was trembling violently.

He took her face between his two hands. 'Don't laugh too much,' he warned her.

But when she stopped laughing, the sudden silence in the room struck Theo like a blow. Alarm appeared in his eyes; he began to sag, and was saved from falling only by his painful, dragging grip on her face.

She in turn was supported by the wall. She compressed her lips; her face reddened; then the easeful laughter broke through again.

When David appeared in the doorway she caught one glimpse of his face, cool and unsurprised, before Theo plunged sideways and dragged her with him to the floor. Even as she fell, she found herself pondering on the meaning of that look, and on the fact that David did not come into the room, but maintained a spectator's stance in the doorway.

Theo lay inert. She rose quickly to her feet, with her eyes on David's. But he was looking not at her, but at Theo.

She swung her loose hair from her face, then let it drop again as she bent to pick up a hairpin. 'He must have been quite drunk,' she said, 'but he didn't seem to be, not at first.'

He did not reply to this, but came in, shut the door, then went to Theo and touched him with the toe of a shoe. 'Get up, Theo,' he said.

Theo rolled his eyes, but did not move, and Isobel said to David, 'I thought it was you.'

'Get up, Theo,' David said again.

'I mean when he knocked at the door,' said Isobel. 'I thought it was you. I think you'll have to help him up, David.'

David gave her a brief, blank look, then helped Theo to his feet. Theo leaned on him heavily, groaning, 'God, God, God,' while Isobel walked stupidly about the room, looking for hairpins, seeing them, but not picking them up.

'Can you stand?' said David. 'Here, better lean on me.'

'Let go. I can stand. Always stand.'

But as soon as David released him Theo made a headlong run, as if propelled by a push, until he reached the opposite wall. The music of his storm had quite faded, and his own stumbling footsteps were painfully audible to him. There was a look of disbelief in his eyes as he supported himself against the wall for a moment, then crumpled slowly, like a burnt-out tower, and collapsed.

There was a sharp little silence; then Isobel began to speak quickly, in a light, shaking voice, telling David what had happened. But he did not look at her, only at Theo, pensively, and when she had finished speaking he said, 'I suppose I'll have to get him a taxi.'

'I suppose so.' She looked down at her ruined dress. 'I shall have to change, won't I?'

But he seemed wholly preoccupied with the telephone, and did not answer her. She went to the bedroom and changed her dress, hearing all the time David's voice, first on the telephone, then speaking soothingly to Theo.

'Here, put an arm round my shoulders. Can you make it? Steady, steady. That's better.'

Theo was now querulous and sentimental by turns. Almost crying, he told David he didn't know he had moved in here. 'Wouldn't believe it. Wouldn't have come, you know I wouldn't . . .'

'Forget it,' said David.

'Nothing to me, nothing to me. Funny, it's nothing.'

'I've rung for a taxi. You had better go home.'

'Car's down there.'

'Yes, I saw it. But take the taxi, there's a good chap.'

'No, blast you. Think I can't drive. Always drive.'

'The taxi's waiting out front. Can you make the steps?'

'Funny bloody feller. Thinks I can't drive.'

'Theo, can you make the steps?'

'Steps, steps, steps. Give me a minute.'

Isobel went to the bathroom, where she filled the handbasin with cold water and sank her hands in it, up to the wrists. The nails she had painted with such care looked very pretty in the greenish water. She regarded them with appreciation and with a strange regret. Slowly curling her fingers, she observed how the white skin, resisting the water, was coated with tiny sparkling bubbles.

Watching these bubbles multiply and break away from the skin, she stood so still and vacant-eyed that she might have been mesmerized, except that no shift of her attention was needed to enable her to hear, from the other room, Theo's mutterings and David's clear overtones.

'Don't be a fool, Theo,' she heard him say. 'It's nothing, you ought to know that. How about getting downstairs now. I'll give you a hand.'

She turned her hands in the water, arching her wrists so that the branching blue veins were clearly visible. She heard Theo's dragging footsteps and David's tolerant laughter, and she plunged her hands violently to the bottom of the handbasin and shut her eyes.

As soon as she heard the door of the flat slam she began to splash handfuls of water on to her hot face. Her shaking hands sent the water jetting over her hair and down the neck of her dress, but she went on splashing for a long time, then pulled a towel from the rod and went to the bedroom gasping and drying her face.

It seemed unnaturally quiet in the bedroom. Then a laugh rose from the street, and a car door slammed. She sat down abruptly on the edge of the bed, hunching her shoulders and pressing her hands between her knees to stop them from shaking.

When David returned his first thought was that she looked almost ugly, with her mouth twisted and thinned and her wet, lankly-falling hair cutting off the rounded planes of her forehead and cheeks. He passed her, looking at her with light curiosity, then went to the window.

'That ass insisted on driving,' he said.

She replied that it was certainly foolish, and that she hoped he would get home safely. But for her shaking voice, they might have been some married couple fondly disparaging a departed guest, and as if to complete the illusion, he turned back into the room without looking at her, and picked up a magazine.

'I changed my dress,' she said.

'So I see.' He turned the magazine in his hands, as if wondering whether to read it or not.

'And now I must put my hair up.'

Riffling through the magazine, he nodded, and stepped aside to allow her to reach the dressing table.

'I've got this dress rather wet,' she said. 'Will it dry in time, do you think, or shall I change it?'

She was watching him in the mirror. He neither answered nor looked up. 'Shall I change it?' she asked again.

He said abruptly, 'You laughed.'

'Laughed?' she blankly repeated.

He flung the magazine on the bed. 'Yes. He was holding you, and you were laughing. Why?'

He did not sound angry, merely curious, but she looked at him fearfully. 'I don't know why I laughed,' she said. 'I hardly remember that I was laughing. But he put on his hat. He pulled it down. That was funny. I remember that.'

'Funny? I've never heard you laugh like that before.'

'No.'

'Funny. That's interesting, Isobel, very. You once told me that your husband was funny. That was at the jail, before it became impossible to mention his name.'

She swept one hand over the dressing table. 'I've no hairpins,' she said unhappily.

'They'll be out there on the floor. Theo shook them all out, I expect. You seem to have some kind of affinity with mad and violent men. They make you laugh.'

'He was not mad,' she said.

'Theo?'

Her lips moved, but she did not answer.

'Oh, you mean Richard?' said David. 'You mean your late husband?'

He waited, but again she did not answer. He put his hands in his pockets and settled his heels. 'I think they're two of a kind, your Theo and your Richard. It's clear that you'll always have men like that about you, passing you from one to the other. It's odd to think it was Richard, in a way, who passed you on to Theo. It was that notebook of his that put Theo on your trail.'

'What notebook?' she asked. Then she said quickly, 'No, really, I must get those hairpins.'

They went together to the living room. After he had helped her to pick up the hairpins she held them in her hand, staring at them. 'What notebook, David?' she said.

'We found it in that bureau.' David's voice was light and easy. 'We read it here. Theo and myself and a man named Charlie Hannaford.'

Isobel looked at the bureau. 'It is still there?'

'No. I destroyed it. I thought it may distress you.'

'Oh. Well, it doesn't matter. I found some, too. Loose bits of paper, mostly. I tore them up.'

'Without reading them?'

She did not answer, but turned and walked rapidly to the bedroom, sensing the doggedness of his following steps. She threw the hairpins on the dressing table and sat down on the low stool with her comb in her hand, but as soon as she raised her eyes to the mirror she saw that he was sitting on the edge of the bed, watching her reflected face. 'Without reading them?' he asked again.

'There was nothing in them,' she said. 'Nothing of importance.'

'Then you did read them. In that case perhaps I was wrong to destroy that book. I doubt now that it would have hurt you. He wrote that he had met you at some place called Bagshot, and that some old man had chucked you out,' David pleasantly explained. 'Those were almost his exact words. They may mean something to you. *Do* they?'

'No, not any more.' Although she still held the comb, she was making no attempt to comb her hair.

'Then it was you. He didn't name you, but I recognised you at once.' David knew as soon as he said this that it was the truth. It had always been Isobel sitting on her suitcase by the side of that road, and never any face but hers that he had seen assailed by those flying beats of light. 'Who was this old man?' he asked.

'It was more than ten years ago.'

'Were you living with him?'

'None of this matters.'

'Evidently not to you. But it did give Theo the idea that you would be easy, and one can hardly blame him. Your husband wrote that you were complete strangers, that you had never seen each other before, but that . . .'

But she broke in with a cry. 'None of this concerns you.'

He looked angry for the first time. 'It was pitch dark. He couldn't see that you were beautiful, but all the same, he knew it. He probably,' David said fastidiously, 'smelled it.'

Their eyes met in the mirror. She carefully laid down the comb. 'He did not say that,' she said flatly.

'I assure you, he did.'

'Where is this book?'

'I told you. I destroyed it.'

'He could not have known.'

'Perhaps it was a fancy of his. You told me yourself that he was a fanciful man. Fanciful, and funny.'

She was sitting quite still, hunched again. 'What else did he say?'

'Do you want me to quote it?'

'Yes, please.'

He did so, speaking pleasantly and carefully, finding no trouble in remembering the exact words. She nodded several times, as if affirming points, and when he had finished she said, 'Is that all?'

'Yes. It's all true, isn't it?'

She struck the dressing table with the flat of one hand. 'No, it is *not* all true. He could *not* have known.'

David had never seen her so assertive. He stared at her in amazement. 'Is that all you care about?' he asked.

She raised her face to the mirror and looked into his reflected eyes steadily and without supplication. 'What else is there to care about?' she said.

There was a long silence. Then he expelled a breath and said slowly, 'Isobel, your husband has corrupted you.'

But she turned about on the stool and almost shouted at him, 'No. It's *you* who would corrupt me.'

He saw her face so glowing with conviction as she thrust it towards his and shouted, 'You, you, you,' that he could only spread his hands, then drop them. 'Well . . .' He laughed angrily. 'Well, the whole thing's absurd, isn't it?'

She got to her feet, echoing him. 'Absurd, absurd. The whole thing's absurd. It's simply that you diverted me for a little while.'

'Yes, it's best to look at it like that. It was a diversion.'

'And it was my fault, all my fault. I wanted to be diverted. I am a coward.'

But the next moment the glow had left her face and a look of extreme terror appeared in her eyes. She flung out a beseeching hand and spoke confusedly. 'But it did seem possible, didn't it? It did, didn't it? David, David, listen. It did seem possible. It might be . . . Oh, can't it . . . ?'

'I don't think so,' he said in a kindly tone. 'Not now.'

She dropped her hand. 'No,' she agreed, but the look of fear did not leave her face.

David turned away. 'All the same, our diversion has cost you something, Isobel. I have a responsibility. What will you do now?'

'Do?' she repeated stupidly.

'Yes. It might be a good idea if you returned to England. Will you let me pay your fare?'

The little pulse was fluttering and bounding at the corner of her mouth. She raised a shaking hand to gently compress it with the tip of a finger. 'What I shall do,' she said, 'is to sit here for a while, sit here for a while . . .'

Seeing her familiar, withdrawn look, he experienced his usual response to it, that wish to bring her back to him, whatever the cost. It would have been not only easy, but natural, to reach out a hand to her and say, 'None of this matters, Isobel. It's all right, it's all right.' It was with a sense of outraging them both, and of warping something in himself, that he let her slip away from him for the last time. Speaking deliberately and distinctly, he said, 'I shall send the cheque in any case. You must use it as you think fit.'

'Yes,' she said vaguely.

Her eyes were very strange, he thought. Clouded and terrified, they looked at him as if asking, 'But who are you?'

'Goodbye, Isobel,' he said.

'Goodbye.'

He shut the door quietly behind him, without looking back, and ran lightly down the stairs, with a feeling of furtiveness that did not lift until he set his shoulder to the swing door and emerged into the street.

It was not until he got into his car, parked so bravely at the front door, that he remembered Myra, who would be waiting.

. . . . .

When the doorbell rang, Myra rushed to answer it, not realising until she reached the hall that she still held the kitchen fork in her hand. She hid it behind a bowl of Christmas bush and Agapanthus lilies, then composed her face in a friendly and expectant smile before she opened the door.

'David.' She grasped his wrist, at the same time frowning and peering behind him as if she suspected Isobel of being secreted there.

'She's not coming,' he said.

She drew him into the hall. 'Why not?'

But when he told her, she did not seem to understand. 'Look,' he said roughly, 'it's all over. It was a mistake, a diversion. That was her word, not mine. Diversion.'

'But this business of Theo Cass,' said Myra. 'Do you mean that she *asked* him to come?'

'She admitted him,' said David.

'My corned beef!' cried Myra.

He was surprised to see her take a cooking fork from behind a vase of flowers and rush away. 'The kitchen,' she flung at him over her shoulder.

The corned beef boiled over as she entered. Water surged from under the lid, ran hissing to the stove, and splashed from there on to the floor.

'Damn, blast, damn.' Myra turned off the gas and stood away from the stove, glaring. When David came in she transferred her glare to him and said, 'Well, I expect it's a great relief to you, after all.'

David was looking down at the gradually spreading pool of greasy water. 'I shouldn't have put it like that,' he said. 'I'm very upset.'

'Yes, I can see that. But you're relieved, too, aren't you?'

'So is Isobel. "You have diverted me." That's exactly what she said.'

'Diverted her from what?'

'Not *from* anything. She meant it was a diversion, a game.'

Myra looked at him oddly. 'Did she?'

'Yes, and she was right.'

'Well, if you're agreed . . .' Myra lifted the lid of the pot and looked sullenly at the corned beef. 'I can't even cook,' she said, dropping the lid back into place. Then she said with sudden vigour, 'But I still don't see what Theo had to do with it. What exactly did they *do*?'

'I told you.'

'But was that *all*? Heavens, we all have those wrestling matches.'

'She was laughing.'

'One does tend to laugh.'

'She could have put him out.'

'Isn't Theo rather large to shift around?'

'Then she could have called for help.'

'One does not call for help. That's a last resort.'

David looked at the floor, stepping back from the pool of water, which was, however, nowhere near his feet. 'I think this is something you don't quite understand,' he said.

'I think I understand it very well,' Myra replied. 'I understand that you've seized on this Theo Cass thing as an excuse to free yourself. You got yourself into something too big for you, and now you've very cleverly got yourself out again.'

'No, Myra, no. I wish I could tell you how I feel.'

'But you feel fine.' And Myra, laughing, prodded him in the stomach with her cooking fork. 'Saved for the Government!' she said.

David gave a strained smile. He felt this was no time for her foolery.

'Yes,' said Myra, 'you will be an important man one day. And when you die they will make a statue of you.'

She stood now with her feet apart, smilingly tossing the words at him as if this were a game they were playing, and she challenging him to play his part. 'One of those statues in parks. Pigeons will perch on your head, and boys and girls from offices will eat their lunches on the steps around your base.'

She walked slowly round him, as if the steps were already there. 'But they'll never look up, those boys and girls, not once. They won't have the least idea who you were. So what difference will it make, after all?'

He stood as still as the statue she was supposing him to be. He was aware of the bitterness beneath her raillery, and was deeply offended. This was a very different reception from the one he had expected. 'You're forgetting,' he said, 'that Isobel agreed. To her, it was a diversion.'

'How you cling to that word! You've told me that three times.'

'She was using me to escape. I was simply an escape. She implied as much.'

'An escape from what?'

David hesitated. 'From her husband.'

'Who is dead. So it must have been from her grief that she wished to escape. And you accepted that condition, gave her your support, then cruelly withdrew it. What do you suppose will become of her now?'

'She may return to England.'

'Oh no, she won't.' Myra threw the cooking fork on the

table and said with careless brutality, 'In fact, she's probably dead by now.'

But these words were hardly out before she raised a hand to her mouth and looked at David with shocked eyes. 'I didn't mean that,' she cried. 'I don't know why I said it. It just came out.'

David was looking as shocked as she. He said slowly, 'She said nothing to suggest . . .'

'Of course not. Of course she didn't.'

'Unless she meant that I had diverted her from . . .'

Myra grasped his arm and shook it. 'She didn't. She didn't. She couldn't have.' Then she cocked her head in a listening attitude, dropped her hand from his arm, and said tonelessly, 'Here is Hughie, I think.'

When Hughie came in, a little drunk, he found them standing about a yard apart, both stiff and silent. 'Hello, you two,' he greeted them. 'What spilled?'

All three of them looked at the pool of water on the floor, but neither Myra nor David answered, and Hughie looked from one to the other of them and said brightly, 'It's raining a bit outside.'

Again there was a silence. 'Well,' he said, 'what about mopping this up, someone?'

'Later,' Myra said absently.

'No, it's too bad, Myra. I can't slosh around in that. And I want to make some coffee.'

'I'm sure you don't have to slosh, Hughie.'

'Then what shall I do? Leap over it?'

And Hughie essayed a clumsy leap, barely clearing the pool of water. Pleased with this, he gave an abrupt shout of laughter, to which Myra and David responded with preoccupied little smiles, like busy mothers at the antics of a child.

Hughie looked deflated. 'I suppose I'll have to clean it up myself,' he said.

He went out, clicking his tongue, and David, without looking at Myra, said awkwardly, 'Look, I'm going now.'

She went with him to the door. 'You'll find her perfectly well,' she assured him.

'Of course.' But he still would not look at her, and seemed cold and hostile.

'David, I don't know why I said that.'

'No. Goodbye, Myra.'

She wandered back to the kitchen, where she found Hughie mopping up the pool of water. He gave her an oblique glance, full of curiosity. 'What was wrong with David?' he asked.

But she only shrugged wearily, and Hughie had to try again. 'It's all over town that he and Isobel Purdy are having an affair.'

'If they were, they're not now.'

'Oh, I *see*.'

'And if you're making coffee, I'll have some.'

She sat down at the kitchen table, her chin in her hands, watching him make the coffee. 'How's Dud?' she asked dully.

'Dud? Oh, Dud's fine.'

'You're a bit drunk, aren't you?'

'Yes, I *am* a bit drunk.'

'Well, that's nice,' said Myra politely.

He looked sideways at her, wondering at her abstraction. When he put her coffee before her, she did not drink it, but sat looking at it, her head in her hands.

'Come on, darling,' he said, 'drink up.'

Rousing herself with a sigh, she took the cup in both hands; her eyes, unfocused, looking at some point beyond Hughie's shoulder. Words formed in her head. 'Stale, flat, and unprofitable.' And she said them aloud, as if to herself. 'Stale, flat, and unprofitable.'

'What is?' asked Hughie.

'Everything. That's how I feel.'

'Why?'

'I don't quite know.'

Frowning, Hughie thought this over. He could see that she felt flat and stale, but jibbed at 'unprofitable', a word he

239

associated only with money. 'I don't know why you should feel unprofitable,' he said.

Myra dipped her head and took a sip of her coffee. 'Neither do I, but I do. I feel like death.'

From far away in the house they heard the ringing of the telephone. Myra went on drinking her coffee. 'Will you answer it, Hughie?'

He was gone about a minute. Almost dreamily, Myra finished drinking her coffee. She did not turn round when she heard his footsteps approaching the door.

'I say,' he said soberly, 'that was David.'

She nodded.

'He said to tell you she's dead. He didn't say who. He said you'd know.'

She nodded again.

'He said she threw herself out of her bedroom window and died as soon as she hit the street. I suppose he meant Isobel Purdy.'

'That's who he meant,' said Myra.

'Then why didn't he tell me so?' asked Hughie.

But Myra had pushed away the coffee cups and had sunk her head to her arms. She was sitting perfectly still and quiet, not crying, and could easily have answered Hughie's question, but she did not seem to hear it.

. . . . .

About two hours after Isobel Purdy had hurtled to her death, Daisy awoke from a sweating sleep, aware of footsteps outside her bedroom door. Muted by the carpet, they were sensed rather than heard. She raised herself on her elbows, staring into the darkness.

'David?' she called. It was the first word she had spoken for days.

A wail came, plaintive as a lost child's. 'Dai-sy. It's Willy. Oh, *where* are the switches?'

He appeared in the doorway as a thickening of shadow. 'Daisy?' he enquired doubtfully.

'Yeth, Willy.'

He gave a delighted laugh. 'Goodness, you lisp!'

'How did you get in?'

'The kitchen window was open. Daisy, *where* are the switches?'

'No light, pleath. You have a theek, Willy.'

'And what is a theek?' laughed Willy.

'Why have you come?'

He advanced into the room, saying accusingly, 'The shop's closed.'

'I know.'

'But don't you care? I was shocked. Thocked,' amended Willy, with a giggle.

Daisy set herself to speak slowly and with care. 'And what is shocking about it?'

'There! You can talk properly if you really try.'

He heard Daisy sigh, and guessed she had lowered herself back on the pillows. 'Poor Daisy,' he said lightly. 'Does it hurt?'

They were both silent while Willy felt for and found a chair. Lowering himself into it, he triumphantly announced that it was one of the chairs they had bought together at the Boden auction. 'I can feel the acanthus leaves on the arms. Wouldn't I make a good blind man? Oh, Daisy, please let me open the shop for you on Monday?'

'Why?'

'Because I want to. Please let me.'

'And Hal? Whath about . . . ?'

'I don't care. I've been feeling mean, and I do hate to feel mean. So it's only for my own sake I want to open it, to stop me feeling mean.'

'The thop . . .' she began.

'Oh no, not the *thop*!' cried Willy, slapping his knee. 'Oh, I love that!'

'The *shop*,' returned Daisy, with careful force, 'is better closed.' And she added, 'I don't care, any more.'

But Willy now found the one thing to say that would save

her pride. 'Of course, Daisy, if I come back, I must have a written agreement.'

Daisy, not deceived, met this proposal with gratitude and contempt. She felt that she herself could never return to the shop. Like a battered tight-rope dancer, she feared another fall. Her nerve had failed. And she had begun to worry, now, about money, for she regarded her many investments in land and industrial shares merely as a last, emergency fortification against poverty, while her outer line of defence was the regular income which had, so far, kept this inner fort unbroached.

'And a rise, too,' said Willy.

'You are taking advantage of my weakness,' said Daisy.

'I know. Aren't I awful? But you will let me, won't you, Daisy?'

On a tired sigh, Daisy assented.

'Oh, good. Now listen, Daisy, if your mouth's swollen, why not try hot foments? They're simply marvellous. Let me turn on the light, and I'll get some hot water and some cloths and things.'

Ten minutes later, Willy was sitting at her bedside, wringing out hot cloths. Over each of these, as he applied it to her mouth, he placed a woollen sock of David's. 'To keep the heat in,' he explained.

Distressed by her ravaged appearance, he tried not to look directly at her, and pity made him assume the tenderly scolding tone of a hospital nurse. 'Why you didn't do this for yourself, I simply can't imagine.'

Daisy longed to protest, to push his hand away and assert herself once more, yet could not bear to forgo the luxury of helplessness. 'I didn't think of it,' she said.

'That's the trouble with you, you don't think. The swelling's gone down a lot already. You'll be better in no time at all.'

'But not well enough to come back to the th . . . to the shop. Not yet.'

He was shocked by the fear in her voice. 'I'm almost

sorry your lovely lisp has gone, Daisy. And you know it doesn't matter about the shop. Leave that to me.'

She began to speak quickly. She had been thinking of giving up decorating, she told him. And as for the shop, she wondered if it would not be better to change their policy a little, to appeal to a wider public.

Willy said that in that case they could begin to sell all kinds of lovely *little* things. 'Some of that West German pottery, and lots of hoojahs and doodahs. Things people could give for presents.'

'In fact, almost a novelty shop,' he said to himself, with dismay and a little triumph.

'All cash sales,' said Daisy.

'And won't *that* be lovely?' carolled Willy.

From the kitchen he presently brought sweet biscuits and hot milk. 'A midnight feast in the dorm,' he said. And it was while they were drinking their milk that Daisy slyly remarked that it was too kind of Hal to give her all those drawings.

'But he didn't.'

'He gave them to me. He did.'

Willy did not argue further, though nothing gave him the measure of her lapse more than this feeble, stubborn, and doomed gesture of revenge. He merely shrugged and said, 'All right, Daisy. But Hal will sue you for sure, if only for the publicity. Hal's mad for publicity.'

But when he was leaving he went to her sitting room and took the drawings, telling himself that he would *not* allow her to make such a fool of herself.

In the hall, on his way out, he encountered David, of whom he had always been a little afraid.

'Oh hello, David. I've just got these drawings. I've just been . . . Oh dear, hasn't Daisy *changed*?'

David, brushing raindrops from his hat, murmured something about teeth. 'It's raining outside. Do you want a coat? There's a plastic one in that cupboard.'

Crying his thanks, Willy took the raincoat and wrapped it

round Hal's drawings. David was acting in the most peculiar way, he thought, still standing in the same place, and still going through the motions of brushing raindrops from his hat, which was hardly wet at all. When he received no answer to his goodbye, Willy even began to suspect him of being drunk.

But whether this was so or not, he suddenly found, to his amazement, that he was no longer afraid of him. Indeed, as he shut the door, he found the courage to say reprovingly, 'And I *could* wish that Daisy had a kinder son.'

Fortified by this victory over his cursed timidity, Willy stepped with confidence into the warm and sticky mist of rain. The only pedestrian in these streets, he passed through the limited light shed from lamp posts, hugging Hal's drawings to his chest and solemnly thinking that Daisy was done for.

But presently he began to experience the buoyant serenity that follows self-sacrifice. Seeking out puddles, he skipped over them, while the words, 'Daisy is done for,' ran through his head like a refrain.

'Daisy is done for, done for, done for.

Daisy is done for, done for, done for.'

. . . . .

Willy had not been gone for more than ten minutes before David's voice came to Daisy without warning through the darkness, telling her that Isobel was dead.

He spoke coolly, with a kind of perfunctory courtesy, as if telling her something of no great importance, but which he felt she had a right to know. Like Isobel at the prison, he was sending his body out to meet these externals of tragedy, and his body, schooled to propriety, was serving him well.

She did not speak for a long time, and when she did, her voice carried a plea. 'Perhaps she could not live with her conscience. Perhaps she found . . .'

Very coldly, he cut in. 'Mother, have you Possie's address?'

'What hath Pothie . . .?' She stopped abruptly, and he heard her draw a deep breath before she went on, slowly, in a voice as cold as his. 'What has Possie to do with this?'

'I want to find her. It had occurred to me that she must have the option of staying here if this new job doesn't suit her. I don't believe she was ever given that option. She may not want to come back, but we must at least give her that choice.'

'Oh, she'll come,' said Daisy. 'She'll come.'

'What is her address?'

'And you will go. I shall be left with Possie. And perhaps Willy. Possie, and Willy, and me.'

'I shan't go. Why should I? What is her address?'

'You will go in the end.' Daisy's voice rang for a moment with its former bell-like tones, but it was a slow and fateful bell. 'In the end it will be Possie, and Willy, and me.'

'Mother, her address.'

'Yes, I can give you that. There was a telephone call from a carrier who called for her things. I didn't answer the door, and he went away and rang. That nurse took it. It's on the telephone pad. Ring him. He'll have her address.'

David turned to go. 'Thank you, Mother,' he said, with the first touch of warmth in his voice.

'You're going out to get her now, tonight?'

'Yes, if she'll come.'

'She'll come,' Daisy said again.

Chapter Seventeen

LATER, looking back on that time, Hughie saw Myra always in the same attitude, sitting sometimes at the kitchen table, sometimes at her writing desk or dressing table, but always with her back bowed and her forehead resting on her folded arms. And although he knew that in reality she had not spent all those days like this, although he knew that she had eaten, and moved about the house sorting and packing, yet, on looking back, that is how he always saw her, in that attitude of quiet despair that was to be forever associated in Hughie's mind with the windless heat of that summer, with crates standing about in an echoing house, and with the death of Isobel Purdy.

Once before, when it had become clear that her first husband would not allow her more than occasional access to her sons, Hughie had seen her give way to grief, and he had considered this grief to be an understandable and proper response, though it had been rather unrestrained, expressing itself in bouts of weeping or in tired and cynical posturings. But this silent, numbed grief for a woman she hardly knew he could not understand at all, and was the more bewildered because he suspected it of being the deeper of the two.

He felt both miserable and embarrassed when he saw her like this, and would sometimes bend over her and put a hand on her stony shoulder. 'Look,' he would say, 'it was quick, after all. One second. Only a second.'

'Yes. I know,' she said.

But she believed that in that one second there must have been compressed the terror of a lifetime. 'One second,' she thought, 'of agony and disbelief.'

'But look,' said Hughie, 'you hardly knew her.'

'I know,' said Myra.

But her mourning was not only for Isobel. It was for herself, for love, and for all people in the world with their hungry spirits and their poor, breakable bodies; so that when Hughie became a little pontifical, and took a turn about the room, and coughed, and remarked that death is our common fate, there was an added emphasis in her reply. 'Yes, I know.'

Once she said, 'She was looking for something.'

Hughie was rather tired of it all by this time. In the supermarkets men had placed decorated conifers, and in houses and hotels the Christmas parties had already begun. But they were missing everything; Myra would go nowhere. 'Well,' he said, 'she may have found it. Who knows?'

'She didn't,' said Myra.

'Then perhaps,' he suggested, laughing, 'she looked in the wrong places.'

'Yes, I know. And so did I.'

'It seems you know everything, Myra.'

'I know nothing.'

'Who does?'

'But I *want* to know.'

'Well,' said Hughie, 'I can't help you.'

Myra's despair came to an end at last, as such things must. She felt, one day, a little hopefulness — like a light, it seemed to her, flickering at the end of an avenue of dark trees down which she had been endlessly running. But she had recovered enough, by this time, to wonder if she herself had not brought that light into being to answer her own need.

All the same, its promise stayed with her, and if there were times when it flickered out entirely, there were also times when its glow strengthened. But it was never, at any time, near enough.

Hughie often came home now to find her out, and while waiting for her he would wander through the house or stand with his hands in his pockets frowning down at the contents of open crates. Then she would come in, abstracted and dishevelled, and say she had been for a walk. She would grill a steak or prepare a salad, and after they had eaten she would continue with her sorting and packing. She refused to have the packers in, and since this was her only occupation, everything was packed far too early. The curtains and carpets that they had decided to keep had been sent to the cleaners, and some of the furniture to the restorers. The hearth of the house had disintegrated, and in its spaces their footsteps and voices rang and echoed. The stark windows exposed them to the outdoors. Through them they received the first radiance from the expansive morning sky, and later, the buzzing heat of noon. At night starlight and moonlight flowed into their bedroom, lying on Hughie's eyelids and striking into Myra's open eyes.

When the moon grew full, its light, disturbing but not waking Hughie, would make him turn on his side, and then Myra would turn with him, huddling into his back, fitting her body to his, but with her eyes still thoughtfully open.

'You're getting thinner than ever,' Hughie complained one day. 'It's all this walking.'

'Yes, it's silly,' said Myra, 'but I'm restless. I feel this house has already expelled me. It will be better when we move.'

· · · · ·

One Sunday night, at the very beginning of December, David saw Myra swinging down one of the steep hills into New South Head Road. Although she was dressed with some formality, and wore a hat, she was striding along as if she were on some country road, with her handbag crushed under one arm and her hands clasped behind her back.

She had a fierce, questing air about her, David thought. He had not seen her since Isobel's death, and it was with some apprehension that he drew into the kerb and opened the door of his car, waiting for her to round the corner.

But she was so preoccupied that she neither saw him nor

heard his hail, and he had to get out of the car and hurry after her.

Wheeling at his touch, she first looked dazed, then set her feet apart and her head on one side. 'Hello, David,' she said cautiously.

He could not help thinking that she looked rather eccentric, standing like a boy, with her flowered hat askew and her hands still clasped behind her back.

'Where is your car?' he asked.

'I didn't bring it.'

'Have you taken to walking?'

'I have, rather.'

He touched her arm. 'Get in. I'll drive you home.

'Been to church, have you?' he asked as he started the car. He could think of no other reason for that hat.

'Yes,' said Myra, in a snubbing voice.

'Was it a nice service?' he asked politely.

'You have described it exactly,' said Myra, who had left during the singing of a hymn, and, while walking up the aisle, had thrust her grandmother's prayer book deep into her handbag among the chequebooks and cosmetics. 'Clergymen have such shiny shoes,' she said. 'Why do I always see their shoes?'

After that, they did not speak at all until he drew into the kerb before her house, when they both sat for a moment looking at its façade, which was broken by oblongs of yellow light. All the rooms were lit, and the open door disclosed in the bright bare hall a haphazard tower of crates. Into this oblong of light came Hughie, to place on the top of the tower, carefully, a little wicker fishing creel.

'We move tomorrow,' said Myra.

'You must have been busy,' said David.

'Yes. And now there's nothing left to do but wait.'

David was watching Hughie, who was standing back looking at his fishing creel. Then he went away, and David said, 'Well . . .' and reached over to open the door for Myra.

249

'Is it true that you're to give evidence at her inquest?' she asked abruptly.

He withdrew his hand from the door. 'Yes, that's true.'

'Why? What difference can it make?'

'None. But I want to do the right thing.'

'Is that the right thing?'

'It's the right legal thing.'

'Is there any comfort in that?'

'Not much. But perhaps the right legal thing is all I'm capable of. I might do less harm by accepting my limitations.'

'And less good, too. Hughie says you needn't appear at all. He says the whole thing could have been hushed up.'

'There's not so much of this hushing up as people seem to believe,' he said mildly.

'Is it true that you actually offered to appear?'

'Yes, that's true.'

'You can't help but show up badly, much worse than you would have done before. I believe you're trying to punish yourself.'

'No, I don't imagine I'll get out of it as easily as that. I helped to kill her.'

'A number of people did. But in the end, it was she who killed herself.'

They both fell silent, thinking of Isobel, David with some desperation, for although he had resolved to fix her image, living yet static, in his mind, it was once again blurring, shifting, and changing shape. There were times when she was vivid to him, but at other times he felt that all he had left of her was her name, Isobel, with its falling cadences of regret.

He took Myra's hand in his, holding it lightly. 'I loved her,' he said.

But Myra had emerged at last from her cloying dreams. She withdrew her hand from his and with an almost matronly gesture straightened her hat.

'Surely,' she said sternly, 'there's something more to love than all this grasping and grabbing, all this using of people.'

He thought about this. 'Then perhaps you can tell me what it is,' he rather bleakly suggested.

But she only laughed. 'How the hell do *I* know?' she said.

'Well . . .' he said again. And this time she allowed him to open the door.

As she got out of the car, Hughie appeared in the brightly lit doorway of the house, facing them, his hands resting low on his hips. They watched him cross the porch. He wore shorts, and against the strong light his legs looked black, abnormally long, and knuckled with muscle. He descended the steps at a very slow run, light and prancing and slightly bandy, and advanced down the sloping path with an agility that suddenly seemed to Myra a little cautious and elderly. As he drew near them he waved both arms above his head. 'I *thought* it was you,' he said.

Then he bent and looked into the car. 'Oh,' he said doubtfully, 'David.'

'Hello,' said David. 'I'm just going.'

'Oh. You're just going.'

'Yes.'

'You won't come in for a drink,' said Hughie, 'or anything?'

'No, I won't, thanks, Hughie.'

'Well, if you won't,' said Hughie.

'Not tonight,' said David, who was ready to start the car, but could hardly do so while Hughie's hand still rested on the door.

'We move tomorrow,' said Hughie suddenly.

'Yes, so I believe.'

David wondered for how long Hughie would keep up this inane conversation. Hughie was a goat of a man, he decided, and must be a great mortification to Myra.

But Myra, in full but casual-seeming kindness, put a hand on her husband's arm. 'And now we must go,' she said.

'Yes,' said Hughie, suddenly releasing the door and standing straight as a soldier. 'Goodbye, old chap. Come to see us.'

'I'll do that. Goodnight, Myra.'

'Goodbye, David.'

He watched them walk away together. Myra's hand still rested on Hughie's arm, and as they went he saw her raise her face to the sky.

'*Look* at all those stars,' he heard her say.

Then he started the car and drove away, thinking how easy it was to strike an attitude, and how difficult to sustain it.